She longed to be with him

To spend time with him, to give their love a chance to blossom.

But she still didn't trust Griffin. Yes, Jill trusted him not to rush her into a physical relationship. She trusted him not to have a wife hidden away somewhere. She trusted his affection, his warmth, his humor. But when it came to the big story, her big break...her juices began to flow, her antennae shot up, her nose twitched in search of the scent—and her trust for Griffin disappeared. Her instincts warned her that no matter how badly he wanted Jill in his bed, nothing would stop Griffin from getting the story he was after— the story they were both after. Nothing was going to stop Jill, either.

ABOUT THE AUTHOR

Judith Arnold's fiction career began when she was a child composing her own bedtime stories. She still has a copy of the first short story she wrote—at age six. To date, she's been a playwright, a college teacher and now a full-time novelist. Composing songs and playing piano and guitar occupy her off-hours when she isn't mothering her two young, precocious sons. Judith and her family live in Branford, Connecticut.

Books by Judith Arnold

HARLEQUIN AMERICAN ROMANCE

One Whiff of Scandal
Judith Arnold

Harlequin Books

TORONTO • NEW YORK • LONDON
AMSTERDAM • PARIS • SYDNEY • HAMBURG
STOCKHOLM • ATHENS • TOKYO • MILAN

Published February 1989

First printing December 1988

ISBN 0-373-16281-2

Chapter One

The Granby Motor Lodge was a dive. A one-story structure, it was built in the shape of an L, with the shorter wing housing the registration office and a glass-walled coffee shop, and the longer wing a row of evenly spaced white doors set into a faded brick facade. Unlike the Ramada Inn in the heart of Granby, with its squeaky clean decor and its equally clean reputation, the Granby Motor Lodge didn't attract people visiting town on business or for social occasions. Rather, it was where people went for their illicit trysts. It was a motel where the registration book contained a statistically mind-boggling number of entries reading "Mr. and Mrs. John Smith," where cars could park directly in front of the room doors, where people could sneak in and out without being observed.

Despite its unsavory atmosphere, Jill Bergland went there every Sunday for brunch. The coffee shop lacked ambience, matching linen tablecloths and napkins, but it also lacked high prices. What Jill paid there for a three-egg cheese omelet with hash browns and whole wheat toast, a large orange juice and a bottomless cup of coffee would scarcely cover the cost of juice and coffee alone at one of the classier restaurants in town.

Since she was a regular, arriving each week at nine o'clock with the oversize Sunday *New York Times* beneath her arm, she was almost always seated at her favorite table, located by the glass wall at the farthest end of the room. Providing a view of the long wing and, beyond it, the dense forest that spread south into Lincoln State Park, the table was big enough for four, so Jill was able to spread out the newspaper sections and read while she ate.

She appreciated the ritual of her weekly brunch. Ever since she'd moved to Granby to join the staff of the *Record* more than a year and a half ago, her life had been nearly devoid of routine. Doug Mallory dreamed of transforming his modest semiweekly thirty-two-page gazette into a world-class newspaper, and he liked to push his reporters—all five of them—to the limit. They kept erratic hours, explored wildly divergent stories, collaborated and edited one another's work if necessary. When Jill entered the cluttered second-floor office space each weekday morning—and some weekend mornings, too—she never knew what assignment Doug might throw at her.

She didn't mind. She enjoyed the variety, and she didn't object to being asked to run down the street for doughnuts, as long as everyone—including her good friend, publisher and editor in chief Douglas Mallory himself—also had to take a turn. No chores or assignments at the *Record* were labeled strictly male or female. Jill got to write about sewer bonds as well as fashion shows, petty vandals as well as Junior Achievement award winners. She might be in charge of replenishing the doughnut supply one day and reviewing the monthly advertising budget the next. It was a far cry from her job at the *Chicago Tribune*—which was one of the main reasons she'd accepted Doug's offer of employment.

Autumn was prettier in Rhode Island than in Chicago, Jill acknowledged, shoving away her empty plate and pulling her recently refilled cup of coffee closer. She gazed out the window at the trees, the leaves of which were just beginning to turn color, and smiled. Even on a chilly, overcast Sunday morning, New England in October was a marvel.

The opening of one of the doors on the long wing of motel rooms caught her eye, and she abandoned the vista of the forest for the more titillating sight of the Granby Motor Lodge's customers. A couple emerged from their room, the woman large and blond, the man small and bald, with their arms twined possessively around each other's waists. They shut the door behind them, kissed passionately and then separated to climb into their respective cars.

Grinning, Jill reached for the magazine section. While she ate, she usually read the front page and the "Week in Review" section, but with her second and third cups of coffee she tackled the magazine's crossword puzzle. She flipped through the pages until she found the puzzle, rummaged in her purse for a pencil and studied the clues.

"Excuse me—could I have a look at your sports?" The voice behind her was soft, husky and definitely male.

Jill twisted in her chair to discover a man carrying a cup of coffee to the table next to hers. He was tall and lean, dressed in a gray crewneck, a plaid wool shirt-style jacket over it, blue jeans and sneakers. His hair was long and wavy, the color of mahogany, and his face, although not classically handsome, had an appealing

cragginess to it. His deep-set hazel eyes sloped down at
the outer corners, conveying an aura that seemed sad
and wise, as if he'd witnessed more in his life than he
would have liked. His nose was large and bony, his
cheeks hollow, and his jaw cut a sharp angle below his
thin lips. Jill couldn't guess from his appearance how old
he was; he might have been a thirty-year-old who'd lived
too hard and too fast or a forty-year-old whose looks
were just beginning to weather into an interesting reflection of worldly experience.

She had never seen him before, either here at the motel's coffee shop or anywhere else. But then, she hadn't
lived in Granby long enough to know everyone in town.

When she didn't speak, he rephrased his request.
"You're not reading the sports, are you?"

Tearing her eyes from him, she rummaged through the
folded sections until she found the one he'd asked for.
"Here," she said magnanimously.

"Thanks." The man took a seat at the next table. "It's
none of my business, of course, but you really ought to
read the Providence *Journal*."

Jill did read the Providence *Journal*, not only because its coverage included the entire state of Rhode
Island but also because she felt obliged to keep up with
the competition. Not that the Granby *Record* gave the
huge and prosperous *Journal* much competition.
"You're right," she said with a cool smile. "It's none of
your business."

"The Providence *Journal* has better editorials," the
man pointed out.

"The *New York Times* has better crossword puzzles," she countered, still smiling, although her cheeks
were beginning to ache from the strain. Thank good-

ness she really didn't care about the sports section. If she did, she'd ask this turkey to return it at once.

His answering smile seemed much less forced than hers. In fact, it was a smile warm enough to melt her resistance. He gave her a brief perusal, his green-gray eyes sparkling with humor, and then accepted her opinion with a friendly nod. Shoving his chair back, he stretched his legs out into the aisle between his table and hers and unfolded the sports section in front of himself, blocking her view of his face.

She let her gaze linger for a moment on his legs. The faded blue denim emphasized their length and their sleek musculature. His hips were narrow, his abdomen flat. She wondered who he was.

Forget it. she cautioned herself. In spite of the fact that her social life had gone from tolerably lackluster to virtually nonexistent when she'd moved to this sleepy, settled mill town on the Seekonk River, she wasn't interested in men who criticized her reading material while helping themselves to portions of it. Sighing, she took a sip of her coffee and resumed work on her crossword puzzle.

A few minutes passed in silence. Then the man suddenly said, "Anoa."

Jill flinched and spun around to face him.

He had lowered his section of the paper and was scrutinizing her puzzle. "Celebes ox," he read. "Sixteen down. The answer is anoa."

"I know," Jill said.

"Not *I-noa*. *Anoa*."

"I know," she said again, then chuckled at his pun. "I mean, I know what a Celebes ox is."

"Well, good for you," the man remarked. "I'll bet there aren't many people who can say that and really mean it."

"Only those of us who do crossword puzzles," she said. Her voice trailed off when she realized that the man was gazing past her out the window. She twisted around to see what he was staring at.

"The leaves look promising, don't they?" he said. "It's going to be a spectacular autumn."

Before turning back to him, she gave herself a moment to assess him. He lost points for finding fault with her choice of a Sunday newspaper, but he gained them for recognizing the splendor of the season, for appreciating the first flares of color in the forest foliage. He lost points for being a back seat driver while she solved the crossword puzzle, but he gained them for making jokes about Celebes oxen.

Forget it, she firmly repeated to herself. The man was after her newspaper, not her. When she finally risked glancing at him again, he only offered another genial smile and lifted the sports section.

She studied the puzzle for a minute, wrote "A-N-O-A" in the squares for sixteen down and decided she resented the man for butting in when she'd been having no trouble solving the puzzle. She was even more irritated with herself for allowing her thoughts to keep veering to him. With another sigh, she gazed out the window again.

A door to one of the motel rooms inched open and someone peeked out. Then the door opened slightly wider and a man stepped outside.

Not just any man, Jill noticed with a start. It was the mayor of Granby.

She bit her lip to keep from expressing her shock out loud. George Van Deen was immensely popular around

Granby. Last year he'd overwhelmingly won election to his second term as mayor. When he'd campaigned, he had portrayed himself as a fine upstanding family man. Sylvia Van Deen had spent most of the campaign at his side, gazing at him adoringly. The mayor had never introduced her as "my wife." He'd always introduced her as "my *lovely* wife, Sylvia."

He cut a dashing figure even as he emerged into the gloomy morning light from the shadows of the motel room. He was wearing a well-tailored navy blue suit, and his thick silver hair was groomed to perfection. He scanned the parking lot, darted to a car and climbed in. Within a minute, he was speeding out of the lot, his tires kicking up plumes of dust in their wake.

What a story: Mayor George Van Deen shacking up with someone at the Granby Motor Lodge! As a rule, Jill held gossip sheets and tabloids in contempt, but this wasn't just gossip—this was the mayor of Granby slinking out of the city's most notorious motel. Granby was a place where newsworthy events seldom occurred. If this scoop panned out, it would merit above-the-fold coverage in the *Record*.

No, of course not. The *Record* might be hurting for news, but that was no excuse for dragging a man's name through the mud—even if he happened to be the town's preeminent elected official. As juicy as the story was, Jill would have to sit on it. Maybe she would share it with Doug, they'd have a private laugh at the mayor's expense, and then they'd deep-six it. What Mayor Van Deen did between Saturday night and Sunday morning was a private matter, not grist for the media mill.

Even so, Jill couldn't contain her curiosity. She kept her eyes riveted to the door from which Mayor Van Deen had emerged, eager to see who would follow him out.

Another big blond woman she wondered, or someone slender and refined? Someone well-known around town, perhaps? His secretary, or Dolores Scharfe from the school board? The mayor was always meeting with the school board. Or...

A *man*? Jill's eyes popped wide, and she pressed her hand against her mouth to suppress a shriek as the door across the parking lot edged open again and a breathtakingly handsome young man stepped out. Like the mayor, he was dressed in an expensive-looking suit, but with his boyish blond good looks, he appeared equally well equipped to model swim wear.

"Oh, my God," Jill gasped under her breath. Mayor Van Deen and a *man*. No wonder they'd traveled all the way to the Granby Motor Lodge on the outskirts of town for their assignation. If Mr. Upstanding-Father-of-Three Mayor were seen in the company of this gorgeous blond lad, if anyone happened to see them coming out of a motel room together...

Someone had seen them. Jill had. Even as she cautioned herself yet again that the mayor's right to privacy ought to be respected, she couldn't keep her eyes from following his boyfriend as he ambled across the parking lot to a late-model silver Nissan Maxima and unlocked the driver's door. Her reporter's instincts compelled her to make note of the vanity license plate reading Buck. To make sure she didn't forget, she jotted "Buck" onto her crossword puzzle, filling the squares for seventy-three across.

"Elba," came a low voice by her ear.

Jill nearly jumped out of her chair. Glancing behind her, she found her uninvited assistant folding the sports section and eyeing the puzzle over her shoulder. "'Island in a palindrome,'" he read as he placed the section he'd borrowed on her table. "Seventy-three across. The answer is Elba. 'Able was I ere I saw Elba.'"

She felt her cheeks grow warm. She had done nothing wrong, other than to spy innocently on a public figure and his intriguing motel roommate, but still she felt embarrassed to have been caught at it.

The man beside her probably didn't realize why she'd written "Buck," so she wasn't truly caught. But she felt she had to say something. "Oh—of course, you're right," she mumbled, pretending ignorance. "I don't know what I was thinking of." She made a halfhearted show of erasing the letters, then stopped when she noticed that the man beside her was paying less attention to her than to the silver Maxima in the parking lot. Without shifting his eyes from the window, he rose to his feet, pulled his wallet out of his hip pocket and tossed a dollar bill onto his table. "Thanks for the newspaper," he said in a brisk farewell before jogging through the coffee shop and out the door.

The blond fellow remained seated behind the wheel for a couple of minutes, then started the engine and coasted slowly across the asphalt and away. From her side of the glass pane, Jill watched as the man who'd borrowed her newspaper raced to his own car, a Chevy of indeterminate vintage, scrambled into the driver's seat and tore out of the lot after the Maxima. She ought to have made a note of his license plate, as well, but she was too distracted by thoughts of the man himself, his long-limbed agility as he'd charged across the lot, his abrupt transformation from affable busybody to soldier on a mission. She was too distracted by a memory of his sparkling eyes, his easy smile...his downright attractiveness.

"Damn," she muttered aloud, slamming the magazine shut and gathering up the rest of her newspaper. She no longer wanted a refill of coffee. What she wanted was to find out the identity of the man with whom the mayor had spent the night in a prepaid room at the Granby Motor Lodge.

As for the other unidentified man who had disrupted her Sunday morning ritual—a man who, she understood in retrospect, had only been using her and her sports section as an excuse to keep tabs clandestinely on the mysterious blond fellow who'd caught Mayor Van Deen's fancy—well, he didn't really interest her all that much. If she'd found him good-looking, it was only because of the lengthy drought her social life had recently endured. Any stranger who approached her in an unthreatening, moderately friendly fashion was bound to pique her interest.

Particularly a stranger built like a marathon runner, with delectably shaggy hair and haunting hazel eyes.

Putting on her windbreaker, Jill admitted objectively that the blond guy in the Nissan Maxima, whatever his sexual orientation, was much more handsome than the man who'd borrowed her sports section. But she couldn't convince herself of it.

ONCE HE WAS on the interstate southbound with a safe margin of two cars and a pickup separating him from Wynan's car, Griffin Parker let his thoughts wander to the woman at the coffee shop.

Why had she written down Wynan's license plate? Random jottings, or was she after Wynan for some reason? What if she was one of his "girls"?

Griffin dismissed that possibility with a shake of his head. The woman hadn't even known who Wynan was.

If she had, she wouldn't have bothered to write down his license plate. *Buck,* Griffin thought with a wry laugh. The word could refer to Wynan's sexual prowess or his reverence for money. Griffin had a hunch it was the latter.

Maybe the woman was a private eye, recording every license plate in the motel's parking lot. If Griffin were a detective trying to catch a straying spouse, the Granby Motor Lodge was one of the first places he'd look.

She didn't seem like a private eye, though. She seemed like a pretty woman who could wolf down a macho breakfast and tank up on coffee, who enjoyed doing crossword puzzles—and who wasn't a snob. Snobs did crossword puzzles in ink; she'd been using a pencil. And she'd erased "Buck" from the puzzle, if that signified anything.

There was a name for the way she'd styled her hair, and Griffin struggled to remember it. A *something* braid. It wasn't like the sort of pigtail you'd find on a little girl but instead was a complicated business starting up at the top of her head and drawing more and more locks of hair into the weave as it wound down to the nape of her neck, at which point all her hair was joined into the braid as it dropped between her shoulder blades. It was a mature style, displaying the tawny spectrum of pale brown and blond hair, and it was subtly feminine and very seductive.

A French braid, was that it? He'd have to ask Ivy.

He should have found out who the woman was. But work was work. He'd gone to the Granby Motor Lodge for the sole purpose of keeping an eye on Alvin Wynan, Jr. Still, it was possible to keep his eyes focused on the Maxima while his mind lingered on the woman in the restaurant.

Her hair hadn't been her only outstanding asset. Griffin had been taken by her earnest brown eyes, her clear skin, the natural pout of her lips. Her nose had been a bit too long for the rest of her face, but, given his own twice-broken nose, he had no right to complain about prominent noses.

Whoever she was, she had exuded a strength, a purposefulness that fascinated him. He'd liked her bland attire—a turtleneck, a Columbia University sweatshirt, corduroy Levi's and cowboy boots—for the simple reason that it offered him the freedom to fantasize about what might exist under her shapeless apparel. Much like her hairstyle, her clothing had been sensible. Yet Griffin had detected something more beneath her sensible veneer, something dynamic and stubborn and sexy.

He should have asked her her name, at least.

The Maxima signaled to exit the highway. Hoping he wasn't conspicuous, Griffin followed it down the exit ramp and onto North Main Street, continuing south into the heart of Providence. Although it was late Sunday morning, the downtown traffic was fairly dense—which suited Griffin. The more cars on the road, the less likely Wynan was to notice that he was being tailed.

Wynan drove to the luxury apartment complex where he lived, not far from the *Journal*'s headquarters. Griffin cruised around the block, completing the circuit in time to see Wynan strolling from his parked car to the entry of the tower in which his apartment was located. Griffin pulled over to the curb and watched the building for ten minutes. Wynan didn't reappear.

Bored, Griffin decided to go home. It wasn't as if he were a policeman, waiting for the chance to cuff the dude and haul him to the nearest station for booking. Whatever crimes Wynan might have committed, Griffin hadn't caught him in the act—and, more than once, he found himself hoping he wouldn't. He had long ago had his fill of police-blotter cases. He'd covered that beat because he'd had to, because he'd needed to come to terms with the havoc and heartache that crimes inflicted on victims and their loved ones. But finally, a few years ago, the obsession had run its course and Griffin had moved on to other things.

He'd agreed to check into Wynan only as a favor to Ivy, and much to his great delight, his investigation was evolving from a shady two-bit crime item into a good solid corruption story. When a pimp met privately with the mayor of a midsize city in a dump like the Granby Motor Lodge, Griffin knew he was on to something hot. But that didn't mean he got his thrills from sitting around in his car staring at buildings.

Owing to the congested streets, it took him a half hour to reach his house in a modest neighborhood of old brick-and-shingle homes near the Pawtucket town line. He parked in the driveway that separated his house from Ivy's, locked the car, sprang up onto the back porch and let himself in through the kitchen door. After removing his jacket, he swiped the receiver from the wall phone and pushed the buttons for Jeanine's home number. He knew she wouldn't object to him calling her at home on Sunday.

She answered after a couple of rings, her voice typically raw from the countless cigarettes she smoked. "Hello?" she croaked.

"Jeanine, it's Griffin Parker. I just got back from Granby."

"Oh, yeah?"

"I got what I went for," he reported. "Wynan met with George Van Deen in a room at the Granby Motor Lodge, just as rumor had it he would."

"Uh-huh. You didn't by any chance get a picture of this meeting, did you?"

"There was nothing to take a picture of," Griffin told her. "These men aren't idiots. I saw them both come out of the same room but not at the same time."

"Right." Jeanine fell silent, ruminating. He could hear the click of her cigarette lighter and then the sound of her inhalation. "Look, Griff, I don't know what you've got here. Wynan's a dirty dog, and the mayor of Granby is supposed to be a good boy. But he's a man, and we all know how men can be. So he meets with a procurer. This is all swell, Griff, but what's the punch line?"

Griffin knew better than to take her slanderous view of men seriously. "I haven't figured out the punch line yet, but I'm working on it."

"Uñ-huh. Meantime, I need you covering city business. You're working for the Providence *Journal*, not the Granby *Review* or whatever the hell it's called."

"The Granby *Record*," Griffin corrected her. "There's a Providence connection in all this, Jeanine. Wynan's based in Providence. Besides, Granby's a suburb. We cover the state."

"The *Journal* does. You don't. You're assigned to metro, and that's where I need you. Tomorrow morning I want you covering the audit of the city budget."

"Sure. But I'm not dropping this other story."

"Did I say you had to drop it?" Jeanine rasped. "All I'm saying is, make something of it already."

"I will," Griffin swore. "Cut me some slack, Jeanine. We're talking Pulitzer territory here."

She issued a rattly laugh. "Yeah. You got a bridge you wanna sell me, too?"

Griffin joined her laughter before saying goodbye. He was used to his editor's sarcasm. She drove him hard, but she always gave him room to maneuver when he asked for it. She knew that his instincts were sharp, that he rarely came up empty.

His instincts this time told him that, while "Pulitzer territory" might be an exaggeration, he was definitely pursuing something important. When pimps met with mayors in fleabag motels on Sunday mornings, it wasn't to discuss donations to charity. Mayor Van Deen had a press conference scheduled for Thursday afternoon, and Griffin would be there, watching the mayor, looking for signs that the man was in trouble.

Someone banged on the back door. Griffin pushed himself away from the counter and crossed the kitchen to answer. Ivy's son, Jamie, was standing on the porch dressed in patched jeans, hightops and his ever-present Red Sox baseball cap with the visor turned rakishly to one side. He cradled a basketball in his arms. "Hey, Griff," he said. "Wanna go up to the playground and shoot some hoops?"

Jamie was nine years old. When he and Ivy had moved into the house next door a few years ago, Griffin had more or less adopted the boy. Ivy had just come through a divorce, and Jamie had been in desperate need of a pal, preferably a large male one.

For that matter, so had Ivy. She was a bright, lively woman, but she was tiny—maybe five-two on tiptoe. A week after she'd moved in, she had asked Griffin if he could hang curtain rods for her. Recognizing her difficulty, he'd also attached a new ceiling fixture for her in her dining room and stacked a few storage cartons on the top shelf of her closet. And while he was at it, he'd changed the oil in her car and installed a couple of smoke detectors and taught her how to insulate her hot water tank.

Ivy, in turn, took it upon herself to bring a touch of femininity to Griffin's bachelor existence. After the third time he asked her if he could borrow some milk and a couple of scoops of coffee, she developed the habit of stocking up on staples for him whenever she went to the supermarket. She explained that if he put his shirts on hangers as soon as the dryer shut off, they wouldn't be so wrinkled. She taught him a relatively easy way to defrost his freezer that didn't require the use of his hand-held hair dryer.

Griffin and Ivy became close friends. She told him about her divorce, which apparently had been exceedingly nasty, and he told her about his divorce, which had been reasonably pleasant, all things considered. She told him about her job as a social worker for the city, and he told her about his. She questioned him about Jamie's idiosyncrasies, and he reassured her that Jamie seemed like a pretty normal boy. Griffin was an only child, too, and he'd grown up in a single-parent household. He felt a special kinship with Jamie.

A year after Ivy had become Griffin's neighbor, he asked her out. "Get a baby-sitter," he suggested. "We'll go out for pizza, maybe take in a movie, come home and see what happens. How about it?"

Ivy considered his invitation solemnly before declining. "I love you, Griff, but you're too nice."

"I'm not so nice," he argued good-naturedly. "If you'd like, we can go dutch treat."

She laughed. "No, Griff—what I mean is, you're really too sweet. You're so mellow, and I'm so moody.

It would never work out. Besides, I like guys who look like Al Pacino. You look more like Peter Strauss. Don't get me wrong, Peter Strauss is a real hunk, but...Al Pacino turns me on.''

Griffin recalled seeing a couple of Al Pacino look-alikes calling on Ivy in the past year. He wasn't so sure he looked like Peter Strauss, but he took Ivy's rejection in stride. He had never expected to fall madly in love with her. He'd simply thought that since they were friends he would test the waters.

They remained friends. Griffin continued to coach Jamie in the finer points of basketball and to help Ivy with tasks that required someone over six feet tall—cleaning her rain gutters, replacing the light bulbs, sliding her skis across the rafters of her garage for summertime storage. And Ivy continued to keep his supplies of milk and bread and coffee from running out.

About a month ago she told him about Wynan. "I know this isn't your beat," she said, sharing a beer with him on his back porch one late-summer evening, "but I've been hearing some weird things from some of the girls about a pimp named Alvin Wynan, Jr. He's new in town, and he's strange."

By "girls," Griffin knew Ivy was referring to the prostitutes she counseled. Although he realized that Ivy occasionally needed to unload the tensions and frustrations of her job, he wasn't sure he wanted to spoil a beautiful September sunset by listening to sordid tales about some kinky pimp. "Okay, so he's strange," he said emotionlessly before taking a swig of the beer.

"I'm not telling you this for my health," Ivy retorted, bristling and pulling herself up to her full, if meager, height. "I'm telling you because there might be a story in it."

"I don't write that kind of story," he reminded her. "If you want, I'll pass the guy's name along to someone else."

"Listen to me!" Ivy roared. "The guy doesn't just rent out his girls—he sets his customers up to be blackmailed. He gets a john together with one of his girls in a room, hides in the closet, takes pictures and then blackmails the john. According to my clients, he expects to make big money doing this."

Griffin shrugged. It was sordid all right, but so what?

"Don't you see?" Ivy poked him in the side, causing him to wince and slap her hand away. "He's not going to make much money blackmailing some two-bit schlemiel. The only people he can make money on are big wheels, power people, rich men with a lot to lose. Am I right?"

Griffin conceded that she had a point. "Maybe. So what do you want me to do about it?"

"Investigate him. See what's going on. My girls don't like this thing. They don't like his style, and they don't feel safe about it. They want the bum off the streets."

"Fine." Griffin made a production of flexing his muscles. "I'll see what I can do to make Providence safe for streetwalkers who prefer sex to blackmail."

Ivy poked him in the side again. He threatened to bean her with the beer bottle, and then they both laughed.

Later, much later, he gave serious thought to what she'd told him. There probably wasn't much of a story in it, but what the hell. He could make some inquiries, check out Alvin Wynan, Jr., spend an hour or two on it and get Ivy off his back.

As things turned out, he wound up spending more than an hour or two on it. One of Ivy's prostitute-clients put him in touch with a woman who worked for Wynan, and she told Griffin that Wynan was trying, so far unsuccessfully, to ply his trade on Smith Street in the vicinity of the state capitol building. With that little tidbit, Griffin was able to confront his editor and say, "Cut me some slack, Jeanine. I'm about to enter Pulitzer territory."

He was excited about the story, but he was also patient. He wasn't going to blow the lid off anything until he was sure of what that lid was covering.

And in the meantime he supposed he could shoot some hoops at the school yard with Jamie, if the gray clouds looming overhead didn't open up and drench them.

He could shoot some hoops, and he could think about the woman doing the crossword puzzle in the coffee shop. He could think about her and wonder why she'd written in "Buck" instead of "Elba" for seventy-three across. If he hadn't been so concerned about what Wynan and Van Deen were up to at the Granby Motor Lodge, Griffin might have had the presence of mind to ask her whether she had an interest in Wynan, too.

He might have had the presence of mind to find out who she was. Any woman who knew a Celebes ox was an anoa was pretty damned special—particularly when that knowledge was combined with heartbreaking brown eyes and pouting pink lips and beautiful dark blond hair that was braided in an inexplicably erotic way.

Chapter Two

"Where were you yesterday?" were Jill's first words as she stormed into Doug's office the following morning. "I tried you all afternoon."

Doug leaned back in the leather swivel chair he'd treated himself to shortly after purchasing the *Record* with some money from one of his trust funds. As he'd explained to Jill, the previous owner of the newspaper, anticipating his retirement, hadn't wanted to sink any money into the enterprise during the final few years of his ownership. As soon as Doug had heard that his old hometown newspaper was up for sale, he'd bought it and invested a hefty sum to modernize the operation. He'd purchased word processors for the staff and redecorated the office space—which was located above a Laundromat and a sporting goods store on Main Street—with movable partitions to provide the reporters with more privacy, and he'd spend four hundred dollars on a very editorial-looking leather swivel chair for himself.

His was the only private office. His predecessor had had the good sense to wall the editor in chief's office in glass, so whoever held that exalted position could gaze out at his underlings and make sure they were all laboring away.

When Jill had arrived at work on Monday morning, she had stalked past the desk belonging to Miriam, the newspaper's receptionist/secretary/circulation manager, around the bend by Gary's desk and past her own desk, heading straight for the glassed-in cubicle. Doug had been seated in his magisterial leather chair, trying hard to make up his mind whether to select a jelly doughnut or a cinnamon cruller from the assortment in the pink-and-white box on his desk.

"I tried you every hour on the hour," Jill continued her tirade, "from three o'clock till *Sixty Minutes*—"

"I've always admired your persistence," he said, choosing a cruller and gazing placidly at Jill. "If you really want to know, I was at Karen's house. We had an awesome fight."

"All afternoon?" she asked, her impatience replaced by sympathy. Like Doug, his girlfriend was the product of one of Granby's most affluent families. They had started dating shortly after Doug had returned to run the *Record*.

"It was horrible," Doug related, looking not the least bit upset. "She wants to get married. I don't know what to do."

"You could try marrying her," Jill suggested.

Doug grinned and bit into his cruller. "Thanks for the advice." Jill wondered whether he would take it. She didn't care, except that she wanted him to be happy. "Hungry?" he asked, turning the box around.

She was briefly tempted by a honey-glazed chocolate doughnut, but she'd already eaten a bagel for breakfast. Lowering herself onto a humble vinyl chair, she shook her head. "Don't you even want to know why I tried to reach you yesterday?" she asked.

He shrugged. "Let me guess," he said, his blue eyes twinkling with amusement. "You wanted to hector me into doing right by Karen."

Jill grinned. She and Doug had always had this sort of relationship, playful and teasing. When they'd been classmates at the Columbia School of Journalism, he had regularly critiqued her taste in boyfriends, and she'd reciprocated. Although Doug was a handsome man and a stalwart friend, he and Jill had never attempted a romance themselves. The chemistry simply hadn't been right.

Jill liked Doug, even loved him in a platonic way. But he was too polished for her tastes, too privileged. His great-great-grandfather had owned one of the mills on the Seekonk River, and Doug had spent his life awash in money. He had known from the time he'd entered graduate school that he would someday return to Granby, ideally to take his position at the helm of the town's newspaper.

Jill, on the other hand, had grown up the third of five children of a high school math teacher and a homemaker in a small town an hour's drive from Indianapolis. Unlike Doug, she felt nothing pulling her back to her hometown, no sense of roots or tradition. The only times she ever went back were to visit her parents.

Doug had grown up and inherited his destiny. The only destiny Jill recognized for herself was to determine her own goals, aim high and try hard. Doug might have visions of glory for his newspaper because it would reflect well on his heritage. Whatever visions of glory Jill had were based on her desire to be the best damned reporter she could be.

They could never be lovers. But they could be colleagues and friends. And they could give each other unsolicited advice concerning their romantic entanglements.

"You're twenty-nine years old, Doug," she pointed out, eyeing the chocolate doughnut once more and then closing the lid. "Why not marry Karen? What are you waiting for?"

"I'm waiting to turn thirty. I keep thinking I'm going to undergo some enormous sea change on my thirtieth birthday."

"You won't."

"How do you know? You haven't turned thirty yet, either."

"Yeah, but if the right guy came along, I'd marry him tomorrow," she remarked. "Doug, listen—I wasn't trying to reach you to advise you on your nuptials. I wanted to tell you that yesterday morning I saw George Van Deen at the Granby Motor Lodge."

"What the hell were *you* doing there?" Doug asked, looking more than a little intrigued.

Doug's tone of voice reminded Jill that the people who spent time at the Granby Motor Lodge were usually engaged in some amorous activity. The thought of amorous activities brought to her mind a picture of the handsome stranger who'd borrowed her sports section.

She hastily shunted the image aside. "I was eating a very inexpensive omelet."

"I see. Was Van Deen eating an omelet, too?" Doug focused his gaze on the air in front of him as he visualized a headline. "'Mayor Caught with Egg on His Face.' I like it, Jill."

"He was caught..." She paused, prolonging the narration to build suspense. "He was caught coming out of a motel room."

"Oho!" Doug's eyes grew round. Jill knew she'd hooked him. "Who was the lucky lady?" he asked. "Certainly not his lovely wife, Sylvia."

"The lucky lady was a man."

Doug opened his mouth in shock. "A man?"

"A gorgeous blond man, if you want to know the truth."

Doug took a moment to digest Jill's revelation. He shook his head. "Uh-uh. Not George Van Deen. The guy's straight-arrow, Jill."

"I saw it with my very own eyes."

"They came out of the room together?"

"No," she said. "Same room, two-minute interval between departures. They obviously didn't want to be seen together."

"Did Van Deen have anything with him? Was he carrying anything?"

"An overnight bag, you mean? No. If he had a toothbrush, it was in his suit pocket."

"No briefcase?" Doug pressed her.

Jill frowned. "What are you getting at?"

"Sex isn't the only thing that goes on in motel rooms."

"We're talking about the Granby Motor Lodge!"

Obviously Doug felt she had a valid point. He meditated for a minute, licking the cinnamon from his fingers. "I know that joint is reputed to be the scene of many an extracurricular activity, Jill. But even so...Van Deen could have been there on business."

"What kind of business do people conduct in a seamy motel at ten o'clock on a Sunday morning?"

He shrugged again. His eyes met hers, and she knew exactly what he was thinking. "Illegal business," they declared simultaneously.

Doug sat up straight and shoved the doughnut box to the side of his desk. "Did you get anything on the gorgeous blond man?" he asked.

"He was driving a silver Nissan Maxima with a Rhode Island vanity plate reading Buck."

"Buck? I love it!" Doug smirked and reached for the telephone. "Let me call Mitch O'Day at the police department. He owes me a few."

Jill settled back in her chair and listened to Doug's end of the telephone conversation with the records clerk in the Granby police department. "Call me as soon as you've got something," he requested after providing Mitch with the license plate information.

"What kind of illegal business do you think Van Deen might be involved in?" Jill asked once he'd hung up. "You've known him a long time."

Doug smiled sheepishly. "Hell, we endorsed him in the election last year. Lord knows what he's gotten himself into."

"Would you prefer to have it turn out to be a homosexual affair?" she asked.

Doug grimaced. "On a personal level, I would prefer to have it turn out to be nothing. On a professional level..." His lips skewed upward into a devilish grin. "Either kind of scandal would sell a lot of newspapers."

The phone at his elbow rang, and he quickly lifted the receiver. "Yes?" His calm tone was belied by the eager glow in his eyes. "Thanks, Miriam. Put him through." Waiting for the call to be connected, he winked at Jill, then abruptly turned away. "Mitch? That was fast. What've you got?" He listened, scribbled on the memo pad in front of him, nodded and winked at Jill again.

"Super. I'll remember you in my prayers, Mitch." He hung up and grinned at Jill.

"Well?"

"Your boy's name is Alvin Wynan, Jr.," he announced.

"Alvin?" Jill wrinkled her nose. "He sure didn't look like an Alvin."

"What did he look like?" Doug asked.

"I don't know—a Todd maybe, or a Derek. Something blond."

"Junior," Doug reminded her. "He was named after his father." He glanced at his memo pad. "Downtown Providence address, registered the car in June, previous license and registration were Buffalo, New York." He tore the sheet of paper from the pad with a flourish and handed it to Jill. "Go to it, Bergland."

She snatched the paper, read it carefully and folded it in half. Then she stood. "I'm supposed to interview the girls' basketball coach at the high school over lunch today."

"I'll send Gary. You play with this for a while."

"Okay." She started for the door.

"By the way, Jill—" Doug called after her. She spun around, and he leaned back in his leather chair, regarding her intently. "The mayor's scheduled a press conference for Thursday afternoon."

"I heard. You put Hank on it, right?"

"I'm putting you on it, too."

"Yes, boss," Jill said, feigning servility. Doug couldn't help but guess that she was quite pleased by the assignment—pleased not only by the assignment itself but also by the fact that Doug was letting her follow through on what she'd begun. She'd been the one to see the mayor with Alvin Wynan, Jr., after all. She'd been the one to jot down the license plate number, the one to have her suspicions aroused. She'd been the one to come to her editor with the story—and she was going to be the one to pursue it, develop it and write it. It was hers, all hers.

Just as it should be.

HANK SEEMED more than a little miffed that Jill was going to attend the press conference. He was scowling when she asked him to wait for her as he was about to leave the office at a quarter past two.

The press conference was scheduled to begin at two-thirty. City Hall was a five-minute stroll up Main Street from the sporting goods shop and the Laundromat. "Let's walk over together, Hank," she shouted from her desk, yanking her blazer off the back of her chair and putting it on. She stuffed her notepad into her purse and raced through the obstacle course of partitions to catch up to him.

Hank was in his mid-forties, a generally dour man who'd been with the *Record* for ten years and who considered its new owner a spoiled rich kid. He had a portable cassette tape recorder with him, which reassured Jill. If Hank taped the session, she would be able to double-check her notes.

She stepped ahead of him and held the door open. Scowling, he exited into the hallway, moving toward the stairs. "How many reporters does it take to cover a small-time press conference?" he muttered, inflecting the question as if it were a tasteless ethnic joke.

"Two," Jill answered serenely. "One to operate the technology—" she patted his tape recorder, then tapped her forehead with her index finger "—and one to do the thinking."

"Ha ha. I don't know what you've got up your sleeve," Hank grumbled, "but the byline belongs to me. Are we clear on that?"

"I think that's Doug's decision, not yours."

"Yeah. The Ivy Leaguer." Stomping down the last few stairs, Hank snorted and groped in the breast pocket of his jacket for a cigarette.

Jill fell silent. What she had up her sleeve was an assortment of facts that were refusing to come together. Since learning the identity of Mayor Van Deen's blond acquaintance, she'd unearthed a smattering of data on him: he was twenty-five years old; he'd grown up in Ohio, attended Florida State University without graduating, lived for the past few years in Buffalo and moved to Providence the previous June; he was unemployed— or self-employed; and, for someone with no apparent source of income, he lived in a fairly luxurious apartment complex. He had no criminal or military record. He was single and without dependents. And—according to the one garrulous neighbor of his who had swallowed Jill's fib about investigating Wynan for a security clearance—he kept to himself, didn't run around with the ladies and seemed like a very nice young man. "And so handsome!" the neighbor had gratuitously added.

But what did it all signify? Why did this nice, quiet, so-handsome man feel the need to meet with the mayor of a midsize Rhode Island town in a tacky motel on a Sunday morning? And why, if what he and the mayor were doing was legitimate, had they felt obliged to leave their motel room separately? Jill had a lot more digging to do.

In the meantime, she'd see how the mayor behaved at the press conference. It was being held in the first-floor reception room at City Hall, a pompously pillared and domed structure that resembled a Roman temple. As Jill and Hank entered the room, she scanned the rows of folding chairs, looking for familiar faces. The young woman seated in the back row was an intern with the Boston *Globe*. Jill also recognized the news director from one of the local radio stations, a couple of third-string reporters and their cameramen from the Providence-based television stations and a rosy-cheeked pair of teenagers from the staff of the Granby High School newspaper. The regular reporters who covered suburban north for the Providence *Journal* were present, as well.

Hank moved to the left aisle in search of a seat, and Jill instinctively moved to the right, just as anxious as he was to put some space between them. She smiled impassively at a few of her colleagues, then hunted for a seat closer to the front. A man was seated alone in the second row, his tall body contorted in an effort to fit onto the narrow folding chair, his glossy brown hair long enough to cover the collar of his shirt. The chairs between him and the end of the row were all empty, and Jill strode to that row.

He looked up, and she gasped as her eyes met his. They were a riveting combination of green and gray, and they sloped down at the outer corners. They radiated wisdom, with a dash of cynicism mixed in, and she found them just as unnerving today as she had at the motel coffee shop last Sunday.

He seemed just as startled to see her. He leaped to his feet, a gesture of chivalry practically unheard-of among reporters at press conferences. Then his mouth spread in a slow, oddly mesmerizing smile. "How are your palindromes?" he asked.

At first she was too flustered to reply. She dragged her eyes from his and lowered them to discover that his outfit was not much different from what he'd worn the last time she saw him, except for a corduroy blazer in place of the plaid wool overshirt. Lifting her gaze again, she realized that he stood at least half a foot taller than she—and she was wearing inch-and-a-half heels.

"What are you doing here?" she questioned him, pleased that she sounded nowhere near as stunned as she felt.

He didn't answer immediately; he was busy giving her a leisurely inspection, studying the stylish lines of the peach-colored suit she'd worn to work that day in honor of the press conference, the modest V neck of her white silk blouse, the mid-knee hem of the skirt and the length of stockinged leg exposed below. "Nice outfit," he finally said.

"I asked you—"

"Same thing you're doing here, probably," he cut her off, allowing himself another appreciative glance at her slender calves and ankles.

So he was a reporter, too. A reporter on the trail of Alvin Wynan—just like Jill. A competitor. She wondered what he knew about Wynan that she didn't know. She was dying to ask, but all she said was "Whom do you work for?"

"The Providence *Journal*," he said, grinning. "Great editorials."

"Lousy crossword puzzles," she muttered, struggling against a combination of anger and uneasiness. She was angry because the man might be about to scoop her on the story she'd so recently taken on, and she was uneasy because she found him so damnably attractive—which, in turn, made her angrier. She didn't want to be attracted to a man who might be on the verge of stealing her story out from under her.

"Whom do you work for?" he returned the question, stressing the "whom" as if to mock her use of proper grammar.

She was annoyed that he was behaving cheerily toward her while she was seething with resentment toward him. It gave him an edge of superiority, at least in her mind. Bad enough that he worked for a much larger newspaper with much greater resources at his fingertips. He didn't have to be so insufferably charming, did he?

"I write for the Granby *Record*," she told him in a clipped voice. "This is my turf."

The subtle reproach in her statement provoked a tentative smile from him. He scrutinized her once more, apparently less interested this time in her legs than in her thoughts. "Look—I'm sorry about Sunday," he murmured.

His apology took Jill by surprise. She assumed he was referring to his having borrowed her newspaper for the sole purpose of spying on Wynan and the mayor, an act that took on an entirely new coloration now that he'd learned she was a fellow reporter. He didn't know that she hadn't also been spying on Wynan and the mayor at the time—and he didn't need to know. She liked having him apologize to her and having him think she was as far along in the story as he was.

She wasn't, though. She wondered whether there was some discreet way to find out what he knew. But before she could come up with a strategy, the mayor's press secretary swept into the reception room, set up a portable easel near the podium facing the rows of chairs, tested the cluster of microphones fastened to the podium and proclaimed the mayor's arrival.

Mayor Van Deen entered through a side door, accompanied by a small entourage. The mayor's lovely wife, Sylvia, wasn't present, but then she had no reason to be. The mayor himself looked as suave and self-confident as always, his silver hair Brylcreemed into submission and his suit tailored to his trim body. "Good afternoon, ladies and gentlemen," he addressed the assembled group, who had risen to their feet to welcome him. With a regal nod, he signaled them to resume their seats.

The man beside Jill waited for her to sit before he did. His etiquette again puzzled her, but only until she lowered herself onto one of the chairs and he took the chair next to hers. Evidently he'd wanted to see where she was sitting so he could sit beside her.

Her first reaction was that he was presumptuous. Her second was that he had a clean masculine scent, warm and spicy and vaguely reminiscent of tart apples. Her third was that even though he wasn't touching her, she was keenly aware of the muscular thigh just inches from her own and the broad bony shoulder that would surely collide with hers if she dared to shift in her chair. She was almost painfully conscious of the man beside her, of his rugged profile and his hair shimmering beneath the overhead lights and of his strong fingers bent around a felt-tipped pen as he prepared to take notes.

She ought to be concentrating on the mayor, not on the stranger at her side. Directing her attention to the podium, she listened as Mayor Van Deen announced, "I'd like to unveil our plans for the revitalization of downtown Granby, and then I'll entertain questions."

The man next to Jill drew a circle on his notepad.

The mayor, she chided herself, directing her gaze forward to the podium. One of the assistants was at the easel, setting up a large placard with an artist's rendering of a spruced-up Main Street.

The man next to Jill drew an arrow pointing toward the center of the circle.

Doing her best to ignore his cryptic doodles, she listened to the mayor as he described the city's plans for rehabilitating the downtown area. It was the usual stuff, not terribly informative, and Jill stifled her own urge to doodle.

Once he'd finished his prepared statement, the mayor opened the floor to questions. These, too, were the usual stuff—a query about how the renovation was going to be financed, another query about how much the mayor projected the downtown business to increase as a result of the renovation and another about his decision to limit the renovation to Main Street. He fielded the questions with aplomb.

Jill slumped in her chair, frustrated. What had she expected? Had she honestly thought George Van Deen had called a press conference to announce that he was coming out of the closet?

She shot a quick glance at the notepad of the man next to her. He had drawn a second arrow extending out of the first and then a third arrow, piercing the circle. The image struck her as sexual for some reason, and she swiftly looked away.

"Other questions?" the mayor asked, beaming unctuously at the assembled reporters. "Please feel free to ask about other city business, too."

Why not? Jill thought, rising to her feet. Reporters never got their stories by keeping their mouths shut. "Jill Bergland from the *Record*. Mr. Mayor, as a rule, do you conduct the majority of city business right here in City Hall?"

He appeared nonplussed by the question. So did all the other reporters in the room, who turned in unison to gape at her. No, not all of them. The man beside her wasn't gaping; he was peering up at her and smiling knowingly.

"Of course I conduct city business here," the mayor finally answered. "I've got a lovely office right upstairs, the use of which was granted to me by the fine citizens of this city in last year's election. And the door is open to my constituents, always."

"So you never feel the need to conduct business elsewhere?" Jill persisted.

The mayor sized her up with a hawkish look. "Ms. Bergland, if you're questioning my occasional decision to host a working dinner at one of the area's many fine restaurants or to organize a seminar in a conference room at the Ramada Inn—well, you're more than welcome to view our records on these special outside activities. Yes, I have taken business associates out for dinners during which city business has been discussed, and yes, I have an expense account to cover such outings. The books of this city are wide open, of course. You're all more than welcome to have a look at them. Just make an appointment with Jim Valenti, the city treasurer." The mayor deliberately looked away, seeking another question.

"Mr. Mayor," Jill persevered, dissatisfied with his answers but pleased that she seemed to have ruffled his usually well-preened feathers, "have you ever felt the need to conduct city business at a venue other than the Ramada Inn?"

He glowered at her. "I just told you, I have been known to go out for dinner at restaurants. If that's a crime, Ms. Bergland—"

"No, sir, it's not," she countered. "I just want to know where you conduct business."

"I think I've answered your question," he said, favoring her with a haughty scowl.

Jill reluctantly sat down. Maybe she'd shaken the mayor up, but she hadn't learned a damned thing.

The man beside her gave her shoulder a light squeeze. She flinched at his touch and twisted around to find him grinning. "Nice going, Jill Bergland from the *Record*," he whispered. "Are you always such a tiger during press conferences?"

She smiled faintly, aware that, coming from a fellow reporter, such a question contained an enormous compliment. Then she turned away, listening as one of the television reporters asked the mayor to predict the Granby High School football team's season record. The mayor extemporized at length about the strengths of the team, using the phrase "these marvelous young players" enough times to make Jill want to gag.

The press secretary pointed to his wristwatch, and the mayor acknowledged his cue with a smile of relief. "Well, we're running out of time, so if there are no further questions—"

"I've got a further question," Jill shouted, jumping to her feet again.

The mayor rolled his eyes heavenward. "Yes, Ms. Bergland?"

She knew her inquiry was pushing things, but she was determined not to leave the press conference empty-handed. "Mr. Mayor, can you tell us whether you've planned anything special to celebrate your wedding anniversary?''

Her question was greeted with boisterous laughter from the other reporters, who undoubtedly thought it was intended as a way of atoning for her earlier aggressiveness. It was the sort of home-and-hearth question politicians usually relished.

Mayor Van Deen clearly didn't relish it, however. Only one other person in the room besides the mayor wasn't laughing—the man next to Jill. A quick glimpse at his pad and Jill saw that he'd converted the circle into a bull's-eye target.

Maybe she was on the right track. Her companion seemed to think she was.

The mayor's expression transformed from chagrined to cautiously blank. "My anniversary is a month away, Ms. Bergland, and my lovely wife, Sylvia, generally makes the arrangements for our celebration. I think that'll be all," he concluded, addressing his press secretary more than the reporters. "Thank you very much." He and his aides swarmed out of the room amid a flurry of flashing bulbs from the cameras.

Deflated, Jill sank onto her chair and cursed beneath her breath. She'd jumped the gun with her last question. She'd alerted the mayor to the fact that people might have seen him doing something contrary to his image as the devoted husband of lovely Sylvia. Now he would be extra careful so as not to get caught.

"I'll buy you a cup of coffee," said the man next to her, breaking into her thoughts.

She turned to him, about to decline the invitation. But when his eyes captured hers and his mouth curved into a gentle smile of entreaty, she found herself unable to say no. "Who are you?" she said instead, giving voice to the question that had been nagging at her for days.

"Griffin Parker." He extended his hand, and she shook it, repeating his name in her head. She should have still been fretting over whether she'd endangered her investigation of the mayor with her questions, but all she could think of was that the stranger with the compelling hazel eyes had a name: Griffin Parker. And he had a wonderfully strong handshake.

"All right," she acquiesced. "A cup of coffee."

He stood, helped her out of her chair and cupped his fingers gently around her elbow, ushering her down the row to the aisle. She glimpsed Hank out of the corner of her eye and quickly looked away. She didn't want to give him a chance to reprimand her about her disrespectful questions to the mayor or about encroaching on his territory—or about leaving the press conference with a reporter from the *Journal*. Hank was a relative old-timer in these parts; he probably knew who Griffin was and whom he wrote for.

Acknowledging that sometimes cowardice was the best policy, Jill kept her gaze averted and let Griffin guide her out of the reception room, through City Hall's elegant mosaic-floored vestibule and outdoors. As soon as their eyes adjusted to the bright afternoon sunshine, Griffin let his hand drop from her arm. "Where should we go?" he asked.

"There's a sandwich shop across the street," she told him, starting down the broad concrete steps to the sidewalk. He fell into step beside her, his sneakers adding a slight spring to his gait. Once again she found herself imagining him running in a marathon. He was so lean and long limbed, so agile. She wondered whether his legs would look as good unclothed as his snug-fitting jeans implied they would...

What was it about this man that made her think such things? she wondered irately. Eight months without a date and a woman could become deranged.

Anyway, Griffin Parker was probably married or otherwise attached. His request that she have a cup of coffee with him was only a professional courtesy—and maybe an attempt to determine whether they were both pursuing the same story.

Still, even after they entered the sandwich shop, which was relatively empty in the midafternoon hiatus between lunchtime and dinnertime, she couldn't shake the suspicion that Griffin's curiosity about her went beyond the professional. Something in the way he gazed at her, in the way his eyes lingered on her hair, on her lips, on her legs...

If he was married or attached, then he was a two-timing creep. Because he was definitely checking her out.

They found an empty booth near the rear of the restaurant, and a waitress arrived to take their orders. They both requested coffee.

Once they were alone, Griffin rearranged his lanky body on the upholstered banquette and perused Jill across the Formica-topped table. "Do you know why I said I was sorry before?" he asked, angling his head toward the City Hall building across the street.

Anyone else might have been put off by his decision to skip the getting-to-know-you pleasantries. But Jill was a reporter used to raising difficult issues without beating around the bush, and she appreciated that kind of directness in others. Noticing the waitress approaching with their coffees, she waited until she and Griffin were served before answering. "I assume because you borrowed my sports section under false pretenses."

Grinning, he added a package of sugar to his coffee and stirred it. "That was part of the reason," he conceded before taking a sip. "The other part was, I'm sorry I didn't ask you who you were then. I can't believe how lucky I am to get a second chance. I've been thinking about you, Jill."

"Thinking about me?" she echoed, sounding braver than she felt. Candor was fine, but she was more than a little rusty when it came to man-woman interactions. She wished Griffin would slow down a bit.

"If I hadn't been so fixated on business last Sunday," he went on, apparently unaware of her nervousness, "I would have...I'm not sure, but by the time I left, I would have gotten your name. Your phone number, too. Maybe a commitment to have dinner with me."

"You're awfully forward," she mumbled.

He laughed, not at all rattled by her negative remark. "So are you, tiger. You really lashed into the old guy today. Are you out to nail him, for some reason?"

It took her a minute to realize that Griffin had shifted gears and another minute to shift gears herself. She ought to have been relieved that he was no longer talking about getting her telephone number, but she was disappointed.

"I'm not out to nail Mayor Van Deen," she said. "Just out to get the truth."

"How noble."

She watched him lift his coffee cup to his lips again. His hands were large, his fingers long and sensuous.

"You aren't on the *Journal*'s suburban north staff, are you?" she inquired, hoping she didn't sound too accusing.

"No. I work in metro. Sometimes a story doesn't respect the city boundaries, though."

"Do you think anyone besides us knows what happened at the Granby Motor Lodge last Sunday?" she asked him, figuring that now was as good a time as any to fish for information.

He took his time digesting her question, and when he smiled again, it was a reserved smile. "Do *we* know what happened?"

"We know that Mayor Van Deen came out of a room there."

"Yes, and given that fact, I've taken the liberty of assuming he must have gone into the room first. How about you? Do you think that's a safe assumption?"

Despite his deadpan expression, she knew Griffin was taunting her. But it would do her no good to get riled, not if she wanted to find out what he knew—and not if she wanted him to ask her out for dinner. "We know," she said slowly, "that someone else came out of the mayor's room. And sure, let's be reckless and assume that our friend Buck went into the room before he came out of it."

Griffin's glittering eyes narrowed on her, and his smile grew mischievous. "I don't mean to sound critical, Jill, but don't you think it's a bit wasteful, ordering a huge breakfast on a stakeout? A cup of coffee would have done the trick—maybe augmented by a section of the newspaper."

"I wasn't—" she began, then clamped her mouth shut. She didn't want Griffin to know that she hadn't been at the motel on purpose, shadowing the mayor and Wynan. It was bad policy to let a competitor find out how far behind one was in an investigation.

Too late. Griffin's eyebrows rose for a second. He took another sip of coffee. "What happened? You just stumbled into it?"

"Yes," she said. There was no point in lying; he'd already figured it out.

"Lucky break."

"I suppose." She tasted her coffee, stalling for time, wishing she knew what on earth it was she'd stumbled into. Now that she'd all but told Griffin she was essentially ignorant on the subject of Wynan's association with Van Deen, she doubted he would share any of his information with her.

To her surprise, however, he volunteered, "I kind of stumbled into it, too. A friend of mine asked me to look into something else, and it led me in a roundabout way to Granby. That's one of the things I love about this job—when you start out, you never know where a story's going to lead."

Jill's spirits brightened. Suddenly she no longer cared whether Griffin shared his knowledge of the Van Deen-Wynan connection. She was much too pleased to have found someone who felt the way she did about her work. "It's like doing a crossword puzzle," she concurred enthusiastically. "You're looking for the right solution, and you just keep plugging away at it, chewing over the clues and filling in the spaces until you've got it right. And along the way, you pick up all sorts of useful information."

"Yeah. Like the fact that a Celebes ox is an anoa."

"It's sad to think some folks live their entire lives without ever learning that," Jill joked.

Griffin smiled. She noticed the tiny laugh lines creasing the skin at the outer corners of his eyes and wondered, for the umpteenth time, why his eyes looked so worldly-wise to her, so bittersweet. Their colors shaped concentric rings around the pupils: a narrow inner ring of amber, a wider ring of green surrounding it and an outer ring of dark gray. Like the bull's-eye he'd drawn on his notepad.

"What do you think they were doing in there?" she asked.

"In the motel room?"

She nodded.

He continued to study her, sizing her up, obviously trying to decide whether he ought to confide in her. "I'm not sure," he said. "What's your guess?"

"A payoff, maybe," she proposed, figuring that if she came up with a theory first, Griffin might follow suit.

"Hmm?"

"Wynan was paying off the mayor at the motel," she said, then bit her lip when she realized she'd spoken Wynan's name. After a moment she relaxed, assuring herself that she couldn't have revealed anything Griffin didn't already know. And letting him know she knew it made her appear well-informed.

Griffin eyed her speculatively. "Why would Wynan be paying off the mayor?"

"I don't know. What's your guess?"

He gave her an enigmatic smile. "It's just as possible the mayor's paying off Wynan."

"Anything's possible," Jill said, praying for Griffin to toss her any scraps he could spare. When he didn't elaborate, she remarked, "Of course, it could always be the other thing."

"What other thing?"

"Oh, you know . . ." She traced a wavy line on the tabletop with her finger. "Two good-looking men in a motel room together . . ."

Griffin threw back his head and guffawed. "Do you really think that's what they were up to?"

"Anything's possible," she allowed, struggling to divine Griffin's opinion on the situation. "You're right, though—it was probably the mayor paying Wynan off."

"Are you asking me or telling me?" he shot back.

She molded her hands around her coffee cup, studying the man across from her as he studied her and reminding herself that he was her adversary. "Asking," she admitted.

He laughed again and brushed a shaggy lock of hair back from his brow. "Read the *Journal*—you'll find out."

She swore silently. Griffin might consider himself fortunate to have bumped into her at the press conference; he might wish to know her phone number and to secure her company for a dinner date. But he was first and foremost a reporter, and a shrewd one at that. He seemed to be going out of his way to make sure she learned nothing vital from him.

"How about..." She presented him with her most winning smile. "How about, I'll give you my phone number if you tell me whether a payoff went down last Sunday?"

"How about, now that I know your name I can think of plenty of better ways to get your phone number?" he parried with a complacent grin.

"How about, you can forget about ever having dinner with me in this lifetime?"

"How about, let's stop playing games." He drained his cup of coffee, and when he lowered the cup back to the saucer, his smile was gone. "I'm free tomorrow night if you are. I'd like to take you out. And—if it'll make it easier for you to say yes—I don't think a payoff went down last Sunday."

Once again Jill was surprised by his candor—surprised and grateful for it. More than that, she was touched by the comprehension that he wanted her to have dinner with him badly enough to reveal his thoughts on what might have transpired at the motel. Reporters vying with each other for a hot scoop didn't generally give voice to their theories, even when they worked for the same newspaper. Certainly not when they worked for competing newspapers.

He watched her, trying to make sense of the emotions flitting across her face. "How about it?" he asked gently. "Do I get your phone number, or do I get your company for dinner tomorrow night, or both?"

"Both." It was an impulsive response, but she knew at once that she'd made the right choice. Griffin had been more honest with her than she'd had any reason to expect. Regardless of whether he was her rival, he had earned her trust.

He pulled his notepad from an inner pocket of his jacket and opened it to a blank page. "Jill Bergland," he recited as he wrote down her name.

She supplied her number, then removed her notepad and pen from her purse. "Griffin Parker," she said as she printed it. She lifted her eyes questioningly. "I gave you mine—you give me yours."

Smiling, he told her his phone number. "You're one tough lady, aren't you," he remarked admiringly.

She returned his smile. "Read the *Record*—you'll find out."

Chapter Three

"Hey, Jill! Call on line two for you," Miriam hollered from her desk near the door.

It was Friday morning, a few minutes after nine o'clock, and Jill had just arrived at the office. She was chatting with Gary about his write-up on the interview with the high school girls' basketball coach when Miriam shouted to her about the incoming phone call. With a wave toward the receptionist, Jill darted around the partition separating Gary's desk from her own. She pressed the flashing button on the telephone console, dropped onto her chair and lifted the receiver. "Jill Bergland here," she said.

"Griffin Parker here."

A smile overtook her—a dopey smile, she could tell from the way her innards grew warm at the sound of his voice. She wanted to believe that her excitement about her impending dinner date with Griffin was merely a result of her having not gone out with anyone in close to an eternity. But she knew deep inside that what excited her wasn't the date; it was the man.

"Hi," she said, wondering if she sounded as pleased to hear from him as she felt.

"Hi," he said, drawing out the word in his low, husky voice.

"What's up? Are we still on for tonight?"

"I'm afraid not," Griffin said.

Jill felt her smile—and her spirits—sag. "Oh."

"I'm working on this budget audit story for Metro," he explained, "and my editor wants to run it in the Sunday edition—you know, with the lousy crossword puzzle."

Jill wasn't in the mood for jokes, but she kept her temper reined in. "The *Journal* must have strange lead time if you've got to get a story done two days in advance," she remarked.

"I could put this article off till tomorrow," Griffin allowed, "but if I don't finish it today, it's going to be hanging over my head all night, and I won't be able to give you my full attention. On the other hand, if I finish it tonight I'll be free all day tomorrow and we can see each other then. Unless, of course, you've already got other plans."

Jill meditated. Much as she'd been looking forward to seeing Griffin tonight, she knew exactly what he meant about having an assignment hanging over one's head, interfering with one's thoughts and gnawing at one's conscience. She had been in the same position plenty of times.

However, she didn't want Griffin to think that he could change plans on her at the last minute. "Tomorrow, huh," she mumbled, stalling.

"Morning, afternoon, evening, whenever," he said. "I really want to see you, Jill. But I want to come to you as a free man."

She laughed at his melodramatic plea. "I tell you what," she said. "Why don't we have lunch together?"

"If that's your best offer, I'll take it."

"It gets better actually," she assured him. "If it's a nice day, we could take a bike ride over to a park by the river and have a picnic."

"A bike ride?" He sounded doubtful.

"I'll borrow a bicycle for you," she offered. "You can drive to my house and we'll bike to the park from there. I like to ride every weekend."

"How wholesome and middle-American," he muttered. "All right. A bike ride. Promise you won't show me up by doing wheelies."

"Not only won't I do wheelies, Griffin, but I'll even make the sandwiches."

"No way. I was supposed to take you to dinner. The least you can do is let me supply the lunch. Is noon okay?"

"Noon is fine." She gave him her address and a few simple directions to help him find the house, then said goodbye.

Settling back into her chair, she felt a whisper of breath against her neck, too palpable for her to have imagined it. Swiveling her chair around, she found herself gazing into Doug's chilly blue eyes. "A minute of your time, please," he said gruffly.

Exhaling, she followed him into his private office. She suspected she was about to be chewed out for having failed to write an article about the previous day's press conference in time for the Friday afternoon edition of the *Record*. Not that the press conference would lack adequate coverage—Hank had put together a respectable piece about the downtown redevelopment project. Besides, Jill had attended the conference not to do a story on it but to gather information for a much more significant story down the road.

"Have a seat," Doug said with stiff cordiality.

Jill sat on the vinyl chair across the desk from Doug's leather throne.

He sat, too, and folded his hands on his blotter. "I don't want you to see him."

"I beg your pardon."

"I don't want you dating him, Jill."

"Dating whom?"

"Griffin Parker."

Astonished, she peered over her shoulder at her desk, which was visible through the glass wall. Had Doug been eavesdropping on her conversation with Griffin?

She spun back to him, infuriated. It was one thing for Doug to give her unsolicited advice on her social life—she'd certainly done as much for him and Karen—but it was quite another thing for him to monitor her telephone calls. "How dare you?" she raged. "Did you listen in on your extension or what?"

"Hank told me you left the press conference with Parker yesterday," Doug explained evenly. "And I happened to overhear a bit of your end of the phone call, when you asked him to have lunch with you. I didn't break any wiretapping laws, Jill."

"No, but you're about to break a few buttinsky laws," she snapped. "If you and Hank want to gossip about me, be my guests. But as far as telling me who I can and can't see on my own time—"

"Jill." Doug's tone was ameliorating, and he attempted to placate her by nudging a box of doughnuts across the desk to her. "Jill, ordinarily I wouldn't interfere—"

"Ha," she snorted, shoving the box away.

"But this is Griffin Parker," Doug went on, undeterred. "How well do you know the guy?"

For the first time since she'd entered his office, Jill regarded Doug with something other than anger. The truth was, she didn't know Griffin Parker very well at all. She knew that she was attracted to him; she knew that he appreciated crossword puzzles and autumn leaves and the thrill of unraveling a first-rate story as much as she did. And she knew that he'd shared one of his intuitions with her. That was certainly enough.

Or was it? "Do you know him?" she asked cautiously.

"Not personally. I know of him, though."

"And?" She waited, her anxiety increasing. "What, Doug? Is he married or something?"

Doug chuckled and shrugged his shoulders. "I don't know the first thing about his personal life, Jill. I only know what he's capable of professionally. He's an investigative reporter. His specialty is ferreting out corruption in high places. The man is very good at what he does, Jill. *Very* good."

"Well, fine," she said, subsiding in her chair. "I wouldn't want to date a mediocre journalist."

"Jill—wake up," Doug chided her. "Griffin Parker is working on the same story you're working on. Do I have to spell it out? You've got a conflict of interest."

"I do not," she argued, sounding less confident than she'd hoped. After all, she had been uneasy about Griffin at first, too, aware that they were competitors, worried that he might scoop her. But she trusted him now.

"Jill." Doug's voice took on a purring, almost offensively sweet quality. "You see the mayor at a motel in the company of a handsome young man of questionable virtue. Four days later, at a press conference, you barely mention the mayor's wedding anniversary and he gets all hot under the collar. We don't know what's cooking yet, but it sure smells good. It's got potential. Who knows? This could be the story to catapult the *Record* into the stratosphere. I don't want to lose it to a shark like Parker."

"He's not a shark," Jill protested.

"Jill, he's *good*. He'll do whatever it takes to get a story and to get it first."

She swallowed. "You're saying you think the only reason Griffin wants to spend time with me is to keep me from beating him to the punch on this story?"

"I'm saying it's a real possibility."

She was stung by Doug's insinuation. "You don't think it's a real possibility that he could be interested in me because I happen to be a reasonably pleasant human being?"

"You're more than reasonably pleasant. You're sharp and you're bright, and you've got great kazongers. You also happen to be working for his newspaper's chief competition in Granby."

"I don't have great kazongers," Jill muttered, just for the sake of disagreeing. "I'm not even sure what kazongers are—but I *am* sure you're in no position to evaluate mine."

"Come on, Jill," Doug said, his tone still mollifying. "Boil it down. Examine the evidence."

"When I first met Griffin, he didn't even know I was a reporter for the *Record*," she said in the man's defense, not bothering to add that he hadn't asked her for her number then. He hadn't taken an interest in her until the press conference.... Damn Doug for planting doubts inside her. "Anyway," she added, more to bolster herself than to convince her boss, "I'm not stupid. I'm not going to share my information with him—and

I'm not going to let him slow me down. I also happen to be very good at what I do, Doug. You know I am.''

"I just want to be sure you're aware of the risks here.'' He rotated the box to himself and ogled a jelly doughnut. "Understand, Jill," he said, pulling out the object of his desire and pinching it gingerly between his thumb and fingertips, "I've got high hopes for the *Record*. We may be a twice-a-week suburban rag right now, but we're going places—and I'm counting on this story to help us on our way.''

Jill nodded. "I promise you, Doug, I will not let Griffin Parker steal a Pulitzer from us.''

"Meaning, you're still planning to go out with him.''

"Meaning, have a little faith in me.'' Jill stood and walked to the door. But before she could leave, Doug called after her.

"Don't think I'm underestimating you, Jill," he said. "It has occurred to me that maybe *you* could steal the story from *him*.''

Jill didn't immediately turn back to Doug. The truth was, she had tried to wrest information from Griffin yesterday, and she wasn't necessarily above trying again, if the circumstances allowed. But as proud as she was of her ambition, she was also a little bit embarrassed that she would even consider such a grubby tactic. And she knew she wouldn't attempt to finagle anything out of Griffin if it meant imperiling their budding relationship.

If Doug wanted to believe she had ulterior motives in encouraging Griffin's interest, though, she saw no reason to correct him. "The thought's crossed my mind," she commented, presenting him with a cold smile.

"Bless your conniving little heart," Doug praised her before taking a bite of his doughnut. A smudge of confectioners' sugar wound up on the tip of his nose and a dark red blob of jelly leaked out the other end of the doughnut, landing with a splat on his blotter.

Perhaps there was justice in the world after all, Jill thought as she stalked out of the office.

"THE THING OF IT IS, she understood," Griffin said to Ivy. "I'm not used to that. It was amazing. She actually understood."

"I wouldn't have been so understanding," Ivy admitted. "You call her up eight hours before the date and break it? That's a lousy way to treat a woman, Griff. I wouldn't put up with that."

"Yeah, well you're not Jill," he said, as if that were all the explanation necessary.

They were seated on Ivy's back porch, drinking beer and watching the stars perforate the darkening night sky. Griffin hadn't gotten home from work until after eight o'clock, and he'd found Jamie loitering on his back porch at that hour, wearing his Red Sox cap and dribbling his basketball. The boy had begged Griffin to let him stay the night. "My mom's real mad at me," he'd said.

"How come?" Griffin had asked, swiping the basketball from Jamie in order to secure the boy's full attention.

"No reason." Griffin's piercing stare had forced Jamie to confess, "Just, I got in a little trouble at school."

"What kind of trouble?"

"Nothing much. A spitball fight in the cafeteria, and I didn't even start it, but Mrs. Lopes sent me and Mike Draper down to the principal's office and everything. I mean, really, Griff, it was no big deal. I just got yelled at and I had to bring a note home about it. And now Mom's being a real crab. So I figure maybe I ought to spend the night here with you."

Griffin wondered what would have happened if he'd gone out to dinner with Jill as planned, and if dinner had led to other things. Would Jamie have camped out all night on his back porch?

It didn't matter. He was going to be home tonight, alone. "Come on, hotshot," he said, giving the visor on Jamie's cap a playful yank. "Let's go talk to your mom."

As it turned out, Ivy, while mildly angry, was far from crabby when they arrived at her house. "No, I'm not upset," she swore, nudging Jamie toward the stairs. "And if you want me to stay that way, buster, you'd better get yourself into a pair of pj's and brush your teeth. It's late."

"It's Friday," Jamie protested.

"I'm getting upset," Ivy warned, giving her son another nudge. "You're on probation, Jamie. Now get going."

As soon as the boy had vanished upstairs, Ivy grinned and bounced back into the kitchen, where she'd been busy cleaning the dinner dishes. "What are you so cheerful about?" Griffin asked, glancing inside a pot on the stove and discovering some still-warm pot roast in it. He helped himself to a plateful.

"I just got a call from this guy I met at a workshop," she related, handing Griffin a napkin and shoving him toward the table. "His name's Bob Calabria and he's an assistant professor at Brown. He's asked me out for tomorrow night. I know it's short notice, Griff, but is there any chance you could baby-sit for Jamie?"

"I don't know," he admitted. If things went well on his picnic with Jill, lunch might extend to dinner.

"You've got a date?" Ivy asked, arranging the last of the dirty silverware in the dishwasher and shutting it. Abruptly she spun around and scowled at him. "You were supposed to have a date tonight with Jill, weren't you?"

"I'll tell you about it later," he promised, adding some salt to his meat. "Let me eat a little first. I'm starving."

Ivy pulled a couple of beers from the refrigerator, joined Griffin at the table and regaled him with a description of Bob Calabria. "He's short, dark haired, dark eyed, with kind of a big nose—"

"I can picture him," Griffin interjected. Given how excited Ivy was about the professor, Griffin felt safe in assuming the guy looked like Al Pacino.

"And he seems very smart."

"If he's teaching at Brown, he ought to be smart."

"Don't be so glib," Ivy scolded. "I'm ready to fall in love with this man, so show some respect."

"Yes, ma'am," Griffin complied, chuckling. "Be my guest—fall in love." He was feeling pretty romantic himself; he wouldn't tease her about her prospects.

Once he'd finished the pot roast, he and Ivy retired to the back porch to watch the sun set and sip what was left of their beers. "Okay," she said, bending her legs and wrapping her arms around her knees. "Now tell me why you aren't seeing Jill tonight."

"I had to finish an article," Griffin said. "But the thing of it was, I called her up just hours before we were supposed to go out, and I told her I was facing this deadline hassle, and she understood." He shook his head incredulously. "Wendy never understood."

"Let's back up a step here," Ivy requested, balancing her shoulders more comfortably against the porch railing and giving Griffin a quizzical look. "Why are you comparing her to your ex-wife?"

"I compare every woman I'm interested in to my ex-wife. They don't all come out on top, either."

"Only because your ex wasn't as bad as most."

"She was better than most. I can't think of anything bad to say about Wendy—except that she didn't understand certain things. She didn't understand that when you're really rolling on a story, it isn't easy to stop cold and come home and be a charming conversationalist at dinner. She didn't understand that newspaper work isn't nine to five. Jill understands that. She's a part of it— she's got to understand."

"Or so you assume," Ivy muttered.

It was more than an assumption. Griffin had never dated a fellow reporter, but as soon as he'd talked to Jill that morning, as soon as he'd explained the problem and she'd accepted his explanation without getting uppity about it, Griffin knew he'd found a soulmate. She was the sort of woman who understood the kind of life he lived, the excitement and the pressure of it.

How could she not understand? She lived the same kind of life.

His ex-wife *had* been better than most. During the three years they'd been married, Wendy and Griffin had had some terrific times. They'd cheered like maniacs at the Civic Center's Big East basketball games together, taken walks through Providence's "Little Italy" neighborhood and gone to second-rate rock concerts at the Palace. They'd loved each other. They'd been great in bed.

But Wendy had never understood certain things about Griffin. She couldn't understand why Griffin often worked strange hours, why he sometimes rolled out of bed in the middle of the night and rummaged through his notes, seized by an insight or a new angle on a story. She couldn't understand why he sometimes became uncommunicative, unable to shoot the breeze with her over dinner because he couldn't stop thinking about the gruesome murder he'd had to cover earlier that day or the assault victim he'd interviewed or the low-level clerk in the motor vehicle bureau who'd ruined his career for the sake of a hundred-dollar bribe. She couldn't understand why he kept pursuing crime stories with a near fanaticism, even when he'd tried to explain exactly what it was he was looking for in them: a way to come to terms with life's cruelties, a way to make sense of fate.

Wendy didn't understand, so she left. He didn't blame her. Her new husband was a proper gentleman, always attentive to her, always able to say exactly what she wanted to hear when she wanted to hear it, or so she reported the last time Griffin had heard from her, about a year ago. "The only thing is, he hates rock music," Wendy had complained. "But other than that, he's perfect."

Griffin was genuinely happy for her. He only wished that someday, he would find a woman as attuned to him as Wendy's new husband apparently was to her. Of course, Griffin's woman would have to like rock music, too.

He'd have to ask Jill about her musical tastes. She had so much going for her—her intelligence, her good looks, her willingness to forgive him for postponing their date, her sheer nerve in standing up at a press conference and grilling the mayor of Granby until he squirmed—that

Griffin realized he might actually be able to overlook an aversion to rock music on her part.

But he hoped he wouldn't have to.

JILL WAS in the driveway, examining the bicycle she'd borrowed from her landlord's grandson, when Griffin arrived. Zack's bike was rusty and too small for Griffin, but it seemed to be functioning. Jill had originally hoped to talk Doug into lending her his fancy ten-speed, but given his disapproval of her decision to socialize with Griffin, she'd thought it best not to ask him.

The day had brought perfect weather for a picnic: by late morning the temperature had reached sixty degrees, and the autumn sky stretched cloudless above Granby, a clear crisp shade of blue that Jill suspected didn't exist anywhere other than in New England. In deference to the occasional breezes that hinted of the cooler season approaching, she had donned a Fair Isle sweater, corduroy jeans and her comfortably broken-in boots, and she'd braided her hair so it wouldn't blow into her face while she rode.

Griffin climbed out of his aging Chevy and, toting a shopping bag, came up the driveway. "Lunch," he said, lifting the bag. "I hope you like roast beef subs and Coke."

It wasn't chateaubriand and Bordeaux—but Jill didn't mind. "Sounds delicious," she called over her shoulder as she went to get her bike from the garage.

By the time she returned, Griffin had climbed onto Zack's bike and wedged the shopping bag inside the chrome basket bolted to the rear fender. He had to bend his knees outward to get his feet onto the pedals.

"My bike's newer, if you'd rather ride it," she offered.

Griffin eyed her bicycle. "That's a girl's bike," he said with a contemptuous sniff. "I wouldn't be caught dead riding a girl's bike." Then he broke into a laugh.

Jill laughed, too. She straddled her bike and coasted down the driveway to the street. Griffin gave a couple of strong pumps on the pedals of Zack's bike and easily passed her. When he braked to slow down, the front wheel started to wobble.

"Do you want me to carry the lunch?" Jill asked, watching him with mild concern as he struggled to regain his balance.

"I'm not going to fall," he promised. "Just give me a minute to get the feel of this thing. I haven't been on a bike in ages."

"Really? I ride all the time," Jill told him. "What do you do, jog?"

He laughed again. "If I had enough spare time to jog, I sure as hell wouldn't waste it jogging. I can't think of anything more boring than running slowly on purpose."

Jill scrutinized his lanky physique. "You're built like an athlete," she remarked. "What's your sport?"

Once again his strong strokes on the pedals propelled his bike ahead of hers. He slowed down and waited for her to catch up. "Basketball," he told her.

Given his height, she wasn't surprised. "Do you play on a team?"

"Nothing formal. A bunch of guys from the *Journal* get together every Wednesday night at the Y. And I'm coaching my neighbor's kid, although I don't get much of a workout with him. Where are we going, anyway?" he asked when Jill signaled to turn the corner.

"To my favorite park, on the shore of the Seekonk. Is that all right with you?"

"Sure," he said, following her. "The real question is, is it all right with you that we're eating lunch in a park instead of dinner in a restaurant?"

"Of course it is," she said, surprised that he felt it necessary to ask. She'd told him yesterday that she wasn't annoyed about the change in plans.

He gazed at her for so long he nearly coasted into a parked car. "Okay, Jill," he said, smiling slightly once he'd veered back toward the center of the street. "I've got one more question for you—do you like rock music?"

"Love it."

His smile widened. "Who are your favorite performers?"

She wanted to look at him forever, to absorb his grin, to let the sparkling light in his eyes penetrate her soul. "It depends on my mood," she said. "If I'm feeling mellow, I'll listen to the oldies—the Beatles and that kind of stuff. If I want to get down and dance, I'll put on some Eric Clapton or Bruce Springsteen."

Griffin's smile grew even wider. "Yeah," he concurred. "Clapton's good. So's Springsteen."

"Of course, if I'm in a very special mood, I'll listen to the Slugs."

"Who?"

"The Slugs. That's my brother Nicky's band."

"Your brother's in a rock band?"

"One of my brothers," Jill told him. "He's got blue hair and a pierced ear. This is his third band, and they're wretched. But who knows? Maybe they'll catch on."

"No kidding." Griffin shook his head, amazed. "I'm almost afraid to ask what your other brother does."

"Brothers," she corrected him. "Craig's the oldest— he's an accountant in St. Louis. My baby brother, Eli, just got certified this past summer to teach Outward Bound courses in Colorado. And between Eli and me is my sister, Cindy, who's working on her Ph.D. in microbiology."

Griffin seemed temporarily at a loss. "Five?" he finally said. "There were five kids in your family?"

"Five kids, two bathrooms. Life was tough," she summed up with a grin. "There's the park."

Griffin didn't say anything until they'd crossed the final intersection and dismounted at the entry to the pretty municipal park overlooking the river.

Jill often rode to this park. She liked its winding paths, its trees and manicured flower beds and its view of the river. Across the river and neighboring the park to the north were century-old mills. Both still functioned, providing a tangible link between Granby's past and its present.

For some reason Jill thought the park looked more beautiful than usual. Perhaps it was because the flower beds were ablaze with yellow and orange marigolds and rust-colored mums, or because the leaves of the trees were currently arrayed in the same vivid fall colors, or because the river reflected the magnificent blue sky above it. Or perhaps it was because she was with Griffin.

A few other people were also enjoying the glorious weather in the park, but Jill found a fairly secluded picnic table beyond a small cluster of birch trees on a rise overlooking the river. She leaned her bike against one end of the table, and Griffin parked Zack's bike against the other. Then he unpacked their sandwiches and popped open the tops of two chilled cans of cola.

"Okay, tell me this," he demanded, sitting beside her on one of the benches and unwrapping his sandwich.

"How does a woman who's got a blue-haired brother and a rock-climbing brother and an accountant brother—to say nothing of a brainy scientist sister—wind up in the news business?"

Jill shrugged. "I've wanted to be a newspaper reporter for as long as I can remember," she said. "I bought my first bicycle so I could get a job as a newspaper carrier when I was twelve. I edited the school newspaper in high school, studied journalism in college and grad school, read *All the President's Men* five hundred times...." She took a sip of soda. "How about you?"

"I came to it at a young age, too."

"Were you a newspaper boy?"

He shook his head. "Younger than that. I caught the bug when I was seven."

"Seven?" She grinned. "Let me guess—your parents bought you one of those toy presses and you printed up a neighborhood newspaper."

"No." Griffin appeared unexpectedly pensive. He took a bite of his sandwich, chewed, stared out at the river for a long minute. Once he'd swallowed, he turned back to Jill. "My father was a newspaper columnist up in Worcester, Mass. He did local commentary, and he was good at it. In fact, he still is good at it, only now he's kind of reached emeritus status."

"And he inspired you to follow in his footsteps?"

Griffin shook his head. "He didn't push me in any particular direction. He was always straight with me about the pros and cons of journalism. I think he would have been just as happy if I'd done something else with my life."

She still sensed a wistfulness in Griffin. The way he spoke conveyed a near reverence for his father. Perhaps

Griffin had become a reporter out of admiration for his dad.

He took another bite of his sandwich. Jill ate, too, waiting until he was ready to finish his story—she knew he had more to tell her. He swallowed, put down his sandwich and cupped his hands around his can of soda. "When I was seven," he said, his gaze again on the river, "my mother died."

That wasn't what Jill had expected him to say, and she took a moment to recover. As the horror of it dawned on her, she touched his arm. "Oh, Griffin—how awful."

He shot her a quick smile. "It wasn't exactly a barrel of laughs," he granted. "Anyway, my father didn't want me to have to go home to an empty house after school, and he didn't want to impose on the neighbors. So most afternoons I used to hang out at his office instead. I'd do my homework there, and then I'd run errands and teach myself how to type and get in everyone's way... and I guess I got hooked."

She studied him as he studied the water. His nose in profile cut a proud strong line below his smooth high brow, and the one eye she could see glittered with flecks of silver and green. "It sounds as if you made the best of a dreadful situation," she said. "What a terrible thing for a small child—"

"Hey, no tears," he said, managing a crooked grin. "It was special, growing up with my dad the way I did. We're close, Jill—to this day my dad and I are incredibly close. We've been through a lot together, and we're really tight." At last Griffin turned back to her. His mouth shaped a heartfelt smile.

"Does your father still live in Worcester?" Jill asked. "Do you get to see him often?"

Griffin shrugged. "We phone each other a lot, and I'll get up there to visit him maybe once a month. He got remarried fifteen years ago, and his wife had a couple of little girls from her first marriage. So until recently he hasn't had much free time."

"How come you didn't stay in Worcester?" Jill asked. "It sounds as if you wouldn't have had any difficulty working with your father—especially since you were already running the newspaper there when you were seven years old."

Griffin grinned. "I wanted to go somewhere new and make my own name. How about you? Granby isn't your hometown, is it?"

"No. I grew up in Ellington, Indiana, where the only newspaper in town is the one the high school publishes—which I'd already spent four years writing for and editing. If I'd wanted to live there and do serious journalism, I would have had to commute to Indianapolis." She took a bite of her sandwich. "My boss is a Granby native, though. He grew up here, and he always knew he'd come back and run the *Record* someday."

"Douglas Mallory."

"Do you know him?"

"He's been pointed out to me at a few gatherings," Griffin told her. "Preppy-looking guy with reddish-brown hair and a swelled head, right?"

"Two-thirds right. Who told you his head was swelled?"

"My instincts told me," he answered. "He's got that look about him."

Jill smiled and shook her head. "He's pretty self-confident, but he isn't conceited. He's got high aspirations—but don't we all?"

Griffin twisted on the bench to face her. He gave her a leisurely appraisal, lowering his eyelids against the bright sunlight. Then he grinned. "Maybe," he conceded. "You and I do, anyway."

Jill experienced a twinge of undefinable emotion in the wake of his statement. It was partly satisfaction that he recognized her ambition and didn't hold it against her and partly apprehension that they were still first and foremost competitors vying for a story. But mostly it was something else—an affinity, perhaps, a comprehension that she and Griffin were two of a kind. It occurred to her that allowing herself to become involved with another reporter might turn out to be a complicated matter. It might turn out to be easier, because they understood certain fundamental things about each other. Then again, it might turn out to be harder, because, perhaps, they understood each other too well.

It was much too soon for Jill to be contemplating the possibility of becoming involved with Griffin. Yet she couldn't help it. Ever since the first time she'd seen him, she'd been thinking about him, dreaming about him. Merely sitting with him outdoors in a safe sunlit park, she was aware of his nearness in a deep, anxious way.

As far as she was concerned, they were already involved.

She steered away from that disconcerting thought by asking, "Does your editor have a swelled head?"

Griffin seemed reluctant to allow the conversation to veer in a less personal direction, but he diplomatically followed Jill's lead. "My editor is too hardheaded to be swelled-headed."

"Oh? Is he a real slave driver?"

Griffin smiled. "My editor's a woman—or, more accurately, she's what's usually referred to as a tough broad. She chain-smokes, and she thrives on a diet of caffeine and Raisinets, and her favorite expression—at least the only one I can repeat in public—is 'Get to the punch line.'"

"She sounds like something out of central casting," Jill noted, grinning.

"She's a character, all right," Griffin admitted.

"Is she angry that you're seeing me today?"

Griffin seemed baffled by Jill's question. "I don't generally submit my private plans to her for approval," he said. "Why do you ask?"

Jill wondered how far she should trust Griffin. Her brain warned her to play it safe; her heart, however, told her that she wanted to trust him completely. Her heart won. "When Doug found out we were going to see each other, he was angry about it."

Griffin took his time digesting her statement. His expression was inscrutable as he scanned the river, as he lifted his can of soda and emptied it in a long swig, as he set the can down. "You *do* submit your private plans to him for approval?"

"Not exactly," she explained. "Doug and I have been friends for years. We went to graduate school together, and we've always meddled in each other's social lives. But no, I don't care whether or not he approves. If I did care, I wouldn't be here with you now."

She detected a softening in Griffin, a slow release of tension. He smiled and arched his arm around her shoulders, pulling her closer to himself on the bench. Not close enough for her to melt into him—or to resent his presumptuousness—but close enough for her to understand that he was pleased by her answer, pleased by her independence and very pleased by the fact that she was, indeed, with him right now.

She closed the distance between them, sliding along the bench until their legs and hips were touching. Encouraged, Griffin lifted his hand beneath her braid to stroke the skin at the nape of her neck. His caress was gentle and surprisingly erotic. Jill's body reacted not only where he was touching her but lower, in her breasts and hips and belly, in her heart as it began to beat more rapidly, in her cheeks as they began to grow warm. Her eyes met his, and then she lowered her gaze to his lips, expecting a kiss. Wanting one.

He spoke instead. "Why was Mallory angry? Is he jealous? Are you and he...?" He left the question dangling.

"Lovers?" Jill completed. "No."

Griffin's fingers slid over the braided strands of her hair and his eyes searched hers. He again seemed on the verge of kissing her. She nodded slightly, assuring him that she welcomed his advance.

Instead, he asked, "Why was he angry?"

Even as he questioned her, he continued to explore the sensitive skin above the neckline of her sweater, twirling his fingers through the few stray tendrils that had unraveled from her braid. The delicate stroking sent a hot shiver of sensation down her spine and forward through her hips, filling her body with an undefined but potent longing.

She could initiate the kiss, she supposed. If he didn't kiss her soon, she could tilt her face up and pull his lips to hers. The anticipation was beginning to drive her crazy.

"Doug was angry," she said, hoping Griffin couldn't detect the breathlessness in her voice, "because you and I are working on the same story."

"So?"

"So, he thinks you might intend to sabotage me or slow me down, or—I don't know—you might try to get information from me."

"Me? Try to get information from you?" Griffin tossed back his head and laughed. "Jill, I'm about three light-years ahead of you on this story. Why the hell would I be trying to get information from you?"

She recoiled from him, her desire for a kiss evaporating in a sudden flare of indignation. "Three light-years?" she snapped. "Talk about swelled heads, Griffin! What makes you think you're so far ahead of me?"

"Oh, come on," he goaded her. "You told me yourself you stumbled onto the story."

"And you told me you did, too."

"Yeah, but I stumbled onto it long before you did. And I know a hell of a lot more about it than you do."

"You sound pretty damn sure of yourself, Griffin. Maybe too sure of yourself."

Griffin shook his head, still chuckling in spite of her obvious outrage. "I read yesterday's *Record*," he told her. "If you'd had anything close to what I've got, you would have gone ahead and printed what you had."

"Oh? I read the *Journal* yesterday and this morning, and I didn't see anything about the mayor of Granby under your byline."

"It's not a Providence story," he pointed out. "And anyway, I haven't had time to write up what I've got. I spent all day yesterday finishing that report I told you about on the city's budget audit."

"Or so you want me to believe," she said with a skeptical sniff.

He frowned, clearly annoyed by her failure to believe him. "You told me you were out to get the truth," he taunted her. "Looks to me like you don't know the truth when it's tossed in to your lap."

"What I know is, the truth is a slippery thing. I like to have proof."

"You want proof that I spent yesterday writing about the budget audit? Check tomorrow's edition of the *Journal*."

"I will," she vowed, her irritation bubbling over into full-fledged anger. "I'll read the whole newspaper from cover to cover, looking for your byline. And maybe I'll also find something else under your name, some little item about how you saw Granby's mayor in the company of a gorgeous blond hunk named Alvin Wynan, Jr., at the Granby Motor Lodge. I mean, let's face it, Griffin—as soon as you got me to agree to cancel our dinner date, you could have spent all day yesterday working on anything. Even the story you're light-years ahead of me on—especially that story."

Griffin's arm fell from Jill's shoulders and he presented her with a look of thinly veiled disgust. "Yeah," he said in a low, taut voice. "I broke our dinner date so I could beat you to the punch on some sleaze-ball feature about your mayor. And then, because I had so much extra time on my hands, I wrote another piece on how inept Jill Bergland of the *Record* is. And then I put together a sidebar on how, as a newspaper, the *Record* isn't fit to house-train dogs on. And then in the evening, when I was supposed to be wining and dining you, I killed a couple of hours designing a crossword puzzle for the Sunday paper in which half the answers are misspelled, just to drive you up the wall."

His anger seemed way out of proportion to what she'd implied—but then, perhaps her anger had been way out of proportion, too. All he'd said was that he was ahead of her on the story.

No, he'd said he was "three light-years" ahead of her, which was a patent insult.

Even so, she thought she ought to try to salvage the afternoon. If they both calmed down, if they both discussed the situation rationally, if he confessed to her that, until their competitiveness had reared up, he had wanted to kiss her as much as she'd wanted to kiss him... "Griffin—"

"Forget it, Jill," he cut her off, gathering the trash from their picnic table and stuffing it into the empty shopping bag. "I'm not going to sit here and defend my actions as a journalist to you. If you want to think of us as two reporters chasing the same story and nothing more, swell. I'll defer to your judgment." Without giving her a chance to respond, he stood and carried the bag to a trash can a few yards away.

Jill considered running after him, then thought better of it. He was behaving much too touchily—like someone with a guilty conscience, she acknowledged. Maybe her accusation had cut too close to the truth. Maybe he *had* been working on the Alvin Wynan story yesterday.

Maybe, now that Jill had figured out what he was up to, he would rather take flight than admit that he had done exactly what Doug had suspected him of doing.

In which case, she concluded, her indignation transforming into a painful feeling of loss, two reporters pursuing the same story was all she and Griffin would ever be, all she would ever allow them to be.

Chapter Four

For the first time in ages, Jill didn't have Sunday brunch at the Granby Motor Lodge. She stayed home, sipping a vile-tasting cup of instant coffee and leafing through the Providence *Journal*, one section at a time. She scanned each and every page, devoting as much attention to the real estate and travel sections as to the news and commentary. She even perused the sports section, skimming over box scores and NFL hype, Big East predictions and high school lacrosse results, searching for George Van Deen's name. The mayor was mentioned briefly in an item about the Granby High School football team. Not surprisingly, he was quoted as describing the team as "these marvelous young players."

In the entire newspaper she found only one article bearing Griffin's byline—an in-depth analysis of the Providence city budget's recent audit. It was a good piece, clearly written and well organized, and although Jill didn't give a hoot about the status of Providence's municipal budget, she found it informative and interesting.

There were no other articles by Griffin in the paper. Nor was there a single article by anyone at all about Alvin Wynan. Jill checked the leisure section, the business pages, the filler on the last page of the classified ads. If anything had been published about Wynan and his mysterious association with the mayor of Granby, she would have found it.

Griffin had been telling the truth yesterday. Jill's accusations had been totally groundless. He hadn't broken his dinner date with her in order to beat her to the presses with what was for both of them still a half-baked story.

If she wanted to, she could blame Doug for having fed her all his suspicions about Griffin. But it was her own fault for having swallowed what Doug had fed her, for having accepted his innuendo as fact. Skepticism was essential in a reporter, but Jill could have given Griffin the benefit of the doubt. Her failure to trust him may well have destroyed any chance of forging a friendship with him.

Just as skepticism was essential for a reporter, pride was something a reporter was better off without. A good journalist had to be willing to stick her neck out, to ask impertinent questions, to be pushy and obnoxious and oblivious of whether she was making a fool of herself. The same lack of pride that enabled Jill to patronize the cheap restaurants at the Granby Motor Lodge and drag Mayor Van Deen over the coals at a press conference also enabled her to call Griffin up, apologize and beg him to give her another chance.

She found his number in her notepad and dialed it on her bedside phone. After twelve rings, she cursed and hung up.

Griffin could be anywhere at ten o'clock Sunday morning—tailing Wynan to another motel, mooching a section of a newspaper from some other unsuspecting woman in some other coffee shop... waking up in another woman's bed and reaching sleepily for the warm, soft body beside him.

No. Jill refused to consider that possibility.

She tried his number again, hung up after only five rings and knelt in front of the shelf of her night table, where she stored all the out-of-date phone books she'd liberated from the *Record* office when the most recent ones were delivered. Numerous Parkers were listed but only one "Parker, Griffin," and the phone number beside the name matched the number he'd given her. She jotted down the address, then went back to the living room to look up his street on her Providence map.

Twenty minutes later she cruised her car to a halt at the curb in front of his house. It was a cozy-looking place, two gray-shingled stories beneath a peaked roof, with a brick chimney abutting one side of the house and a driveway on the other, separating his property from the yard next door and leading to a garage behind the house. Griffin's old Chevy was parked in front of the garage.

Jill might not boast an overabundance of pride, but she was just as susceptible to jitters as anyone else. She'd been so anxious to track Griffin down and apologize to him, she hadn't bothered to change from her worn corduroys and baggy wool sweater to something more attractive or to rebraid her hair more neatly. Leaning across the front seat of her car, she groped in the glove compartment for the roll of breath mints she kept there for just such occasions.

"Courage," she murmured to herself, intoning the word as her fellow journalist Dan Rather had when he'd made the word his sign-off a few years ago. Then she threw back her shoulders, climbed out of the car and stalked up the front walk.

Her boots made a scuffing noise against the concrete steps as she climbed to the small porch. She pressed the doorbell, inhaled a steady breath and practiced her bravest smile.

The door opened, and Jill felt her smile dissolve into a wince. Standing on the opposite side of the threshold was a very pretty woman in a pink sweat suit. The woman was short and slim, and the combination of her petite build, her naturally bobbed nose and her short black hair put Jill in mind of a pixie.

"Yes?" the woman asked.

Jill swallowed and silently ordered her facial muscles to relax. "Is this Griffin Parker's house?" she asked in as level a voice as she could manage.

"Yes, but he isn't home right now," the woman told Jill.

All right. Griffin was married. That he'd made one date with Jill, broken it and made a second date with her without once mentioning that he happened to be married qualified him as a louse, but not a particularly exceptional one. Married men cheated on their wives all the time.

No real harm done, Jill consoled herself. It wasn't as if they'd had an affair or anything. He hadn't even kissed her. She'd ached for him to kiss her, but he hadn't.

So why did the truth hurt so badly? Why did she feel like bursting into tears?

The woman seemed to be waiting for Jill to speak. "Will he be back soon?" she asked. Stupid question, she reproached herself. She certainly didn't want to stay here, shooting the breeze with his wife until he got home.

"Probably. He took my boy, Jamie, down to the playground to play basketball. They left nearly an hour ago—they should be back any minute. Why don't you come on in and wait?"

"I don't know," Jill mumbled. Her mind registered that the woman had referred to *her* boy, not *their* boy. Apparently she had a son from a previous marriage. Whether Griffin was a father or a stepfather was irrelevant, though. Either way he was still a louse.

"Really—they'll be back any minute," the woman insisted, holding the door open and beckoning Jill inside. "Who are you?"

"My name is Jill Bergland."

The woman's eyebrows rose as she appraised Jill. "Oh, so you're Jill. Come on in. Griff's told me all about you."

Jill swallowed again, not to steady her voice this time but rather to keep her coffee from returning on her. Why on earth had Griffin told his wife all about Jill? Did they have an open marriage? Were they swingers? Doug's voice echoed in the back of her mind: *How well do you know this guy?*

The woman in the pink sweat suit bounced through an entry foyer, past a stairway and down a hall to a large sunlit kitchen in the rear of the house. A couple of grocery bags stood on the kitchen table waiting to be unpacked. Jill's queasiness increased.

The woman seemed not at all fazed by Jill's presence. "I'm Ivy, by the way," she said. "Have a seat while I finish putting these things away. I hate shopping on Sunday mornings, but when you work a full-time job, what are you going to do?" She seemed much too energetic as she pulled a half gallon carton of milk and a box of shredded wheat from one of the bags. "So you're Jill," she repeated, pausing by the refrigerator and giving Jill one more assessing glance. "That's a French braid, all right."

Jill nervously touched her hair. "I beg your pardon?"

"Griff described your hairstyle to me, and I told him it sounded like a French braid. I wish I could keep my hair long, but it's too much work. This—" she patted her short cap of hair "—I just wash it and let it dry any which way."

Jill smiled weakly and turned from Ivy to study the room. It was fairly nondescript: white cabinets, middle-aged appliances and green-and-white-striped café curtains framing the window above the sink. She saw nothing to indicate that a child might live there—no crude crayon drawings, no school calendar or lunch box.

"What else did Griffin tell you about me?" Jill asked, far from certain that she wanted to hear the answer.

Ivy placed the milk in the refrigerator, shut the door and leaned against the counter, grinning. "You want the truth? He told me that you're very understanding."

Not understanding enough to indulge in a fling with a married man, she almost blurted out. She tried futilely to fight off the heavy sense of gloom that crowded in on her at the thought that Griffin could be a two-timing rat, married to a woman who evidently condoned his adulterous behavior. She wished she could convince herself that she had no cause for despair. After all, she and Griffin were hardly lovers; they'd shared one picnic lunch that had ended dismally. Jill hadn't lost anything—there was nothing between her and Griffin to lose.

And yet she did feel a loss, keen and painful, a loss of immeasurable proportions. "I'd better leave," she resolved, pushing herself to her feet. "I really think—"

She was interrupted by the thump of footsteps on the back porch, the sound of a young boy's laughter and then of Griffin humming the theme song of the Harlem Globetrotters. He flung the back door open and bounded into the kitchen, spinning a basketball on the tip of his index finger. He had on a short-sleeved sweat-shirt with UMass emblazoned across the front, a pair of jeans so old the whitish-blue fabric had split at one knee, and high-top sneakers. The boy with him appeared to be around nine or ten years old. They were both perspiring, and they were both beaming. "Did we beat 'em or what, Griff?" the boy hollered as he pranced around the room. "Did we beat the pants off 'em or what?"

Griffin saw Jill and his grin vanished. He stopped humming; he let the basketball roll off his finger and bounce aimlessly across the floor. His eyes were riveted to her, his expression quizzical. She couldn't tell whether he was happy or appalled to see her.

"Hi," she said in a tiny voice. "I was just about to leave."

"No, don't leave." He ran his hand over his sweat-damp brow, shoving back his hair. Then he shot a quick glance at Ivy.

"I just finished putting away your groceries," she said. "I figured you wouldn't mind if I let Jill wait for you inside."

"You've met?" he asked, turning back to Jill.

"Sort of," she mumbled, wondering if he could detect the condemnation in her tone.

His gaze latched onto hers, seeking an explanation for her presence in his house. But before he could question her, the boy spoke. "Mom, it was great," he said in a booming voice as he crawled under the table to retrieve the ball. "Griff and me were practicing, and then these big guys came over. They musta been junior high kids at least, and there was three of 'em, and they challenged us to a game. And guess what?''

''You won,'' Ivy concluded—an easy guess to make, given the boy's exuberance.

''We licked 'em but good,'' the boy gloated. ''Didn't we, Griff?''

Griffin didn't respond; he appeared not to have heard the boy's question. His eyes lingered on Jill, registering a mixture of bewilderment and pleasure. The gulf between him and Jill seemed much too wide—especially with a rowdy boy ricocheting between them—but Jill didn't dare to try to close the distance. Neither did Griffin. He only stared at her, inquisitive, the merest hint of a smile on his lips.

''Hey, Griff,'' the boy shouted, moving directly in front of Griffin to snare his attention. ''I said, didn't we lick 'em?''

''Yeah, we did,'' Griffin confirmed, his gaze flickering toward Ivy for an instant and then back to Jill. He opened his mouth to say something to her, but the boy continued speaking before Griffin had a chance.

''We whipped their butts,'' the boy boasted, dribbling the ball across the kitchen to the back door. ''I was Magic Johnson, and Griff was Kareem Abdul-Jabbar.''

''Watch out, Lakers,'' Griff muttered sarcastically, although his eyes sparkled with humor. When Jill offered a begrudging smile, his entire face brightened.

''We were a team,'' the boy elaborated. ''I did all the inbounding, and Griff did all the shooting. We were great. Weren't we great, Griff?''

''We certainly were, Jamie,'' he agreed, turning from Jill and affectionately tugging on the visor of the boy's baseball cap. Then he looked back at Jill, searching her face for a sign that she shared his delight at this victory. She didn't, though—she was still too edgy and confused to care whether he won a school-yard basketball game. Clearly he didn't find what he was seeking, and his grin faded.

Ivy glanced from Griffin to Jill. "Well," she said tactfully, "we'll be on our way."

He broke his gaze from Jill again, spinning around to Ivy and pulling his wallet from his hip pocket. "How much do I owe you?"

"Forget it," she said, shooing his money away with her hand.

"Come on, Ivy—"

"Don't be silly," she argued. "How much do *I* owe *you*? Let's not get into dollars and cents here. Come on, Magic," she called to her son. "Time to do a full-court press home. Nice meeting you, Jill."

Jill missed none of the exchange: Griffin had wanted to reimburse Ivy for the groceries she'd bought, and now she and her son were leaving, going to their own home. Ivy wasn't his wife.

His girlfriend, Jill decided, amending her original theory. Ivy was his exceedingly open-minded girlfriend.

"Thanks again," Griffin said, ushering Ivy and her son to the back door and waving them off.

He closed the door, pivoted around and faced Jill across the sunlit room. For a long moment he just stared at her, his expression unreadable, as they accustomed themselves to the silence and the fact that they were alone. Then he strode to the sink, twisted on the faucet and splashed a few handfuls of cold water onto his face.

Not knowing what else to do, Jill watched him, trying not to dwell on the lean strength of his forearms, the faint tracing of hair over the sun-burnished skin, the boniness of his wrists, the graceful length of his fingers. She tried to be impervious to the powerful arch of his back as he bowed over the sink basin, the trimness of his hips, the stance of his legs.

Two-timing rat, she reminded herself.

He stood up, shook the excess water from his hands and pulled a square of paper towel from the roll fastened to the wall near the sink. Turning and leaning against the counter, he methodically dried his hands and face. His hair remained damp, though, a dark dense sweep across the crown of his head. "You didn't happen to notice what brand cereal Ivy bought for me, did you?" he asked.

For a man who had a great deal of explaining to do, Griffin's question struck Jill as inane. "Shredded wheat," she replied tersely, deciding that maybe they were better off avoiding the riskier subjects.

Griffin grimaced, then permitted himself a grudging smile. "Ivy thinks she's going to prolong my life by weaning me from sugary breakfast cereal. Little does she know, but I wind up dumping two teaspoons of sugar onto the shredded wheat before I add the milk."

Why was he telling Jill this? To prove to her that he and Ivy didn't eat breakfast together on a regular basis?

"I'm glad you came," he went on when Jill remained silent. "We kind of screwed things up yesterday, didn't we?"

This was stupid. Jill had a few vital issues to clarify with the man before she could begin to dissect what they'd screwed up yesterday. And instead of demanding the clarification she needed, she was standing in the doorway to his kitchen, tongue-tied. She was a reporter; she knew how to ask questions. "Is Ivy your wife?'' she inquired, doing her best to disguise the quiver in her voice.

Evidently Griffin believed the question was valid. He didn't smile, didn't laugh, didn't erupt in anger. ''No,'' he answered, lofting the used paper towel into the trash can near the back door.

He remained near the sink, refusing to crowd Jill. She appreciated his sensitivity—but not enough to let him off the hook. ''Is she your lover?''

''No,'' he said again. ''She's my neighbor. And a good friend. We run errands for each other sometimes, and we have keys to each other's houses. But no, we've never been lovers.''

His answer was forthright—and so was his gaze. Jill detected nothing false in his attitude. She'd been wrong to distrust him yesterday, and she knew from his tone of voice and from the steady light in his eyes that she would be wrong to distrust him again today.

She leaned against the wall by the doorway, preserving her strength for their conversation. ''I probably shouldn't have dropped in on you like this,'' she conceded. ''I tried to telephone you, but nobody answered.''

Griffin nodded. ''I took Jamie over to the playground about an hour ago while Ivy went to the supermarket.'' A heavy lock of hair slipped down his forehead, and he pushed it back. ''Why did you try to telephone me?''

''I wanted to apologize,'' Jill said, lowering her gaze. Even with Dan Rather's exhortation ringing in her ears, there was a limit to how courageous she could be. She could make her apology, but not while she was looking into Griffin's spellbinding hazel eyes. ''I went through this morning's *Journal* and I found your article about the budget audit—and nothing else. I was wrong to think you would break our date just to scoop me on the Wynan story."

Griffin mulled over her statement. "Maybe you weren't so wrong."

Jill jerked her head up and gaped at him.

He shrugged. "I'll admit I'm not above such tactics, if the story warrants it. But..." He sighed. "The only reason I'd ever break a date with you, Jill, would be if I thought it would make things better for us. Which was exactly why I broke our date Friday—I thought Saturday would be better. I didn't want to be under any pressure when I saw you. I didn't want anything to distract me. I wanted everything to be perfect." He smiled grimly.

"Funny how things turn out sometimes," she muttered.

"Look, maybe I was wrong, too," he offered. "Maybe I goaded you a little too much. And then we both blew our cool. I'm usually pretty even tempered, Jill. It kind of surprised me that I went over the edge. And...I'm sorry, too. Okay?"

Jill wanted to rush across the room, to hug him and assure him that all was forgiven. But she held back, still wary. "There's so much I don't know about you, Griffin," she said, flattening her palms behind her as if by clinging to the wall she could keep herself from running to him.

He contemplated her charge, then shrugged. "What do you want to know?"

She weighed several possible questions before deciding to start simply. "Ivy called you Griff," she pointed out. "So did her son. Is that what you prefer to be called?"

"If it's someone I feel comfortable with, sure," he said. "I'd like to think you fall into that category."

"Ivy mentioned," Jill continued, feeling a little bolder, "that you've told her a lot about me."

Griffin shrugged again. "I'm not sure what constitutes 'a lot,' but yes, I've talked to her about you."

"You told her about my hair," Jill said, resisting the urge to grin.

"Among other things."

Jill reflected on her brief dialogue with Ivy. According to Ivy, one of the things Griffin had told her was that Jill was understanding. "What else did you tell her?" she asked, wondering if he'd utter such a compliment to her face.

"I told her it was your idea to go biking and have a picnic lunch," he reported, shoving his floppy hair back from his face once more. "We disagreed over whether that made you middle-American or all-American."

"Middle-American, I think," said Jill. She knew she was stalling, avoiding the more important questions. But it felt good to be talking this way; it soothed her bristling nerves. "I'm from Indiana. How middle-American can you get?"

"Wasn't that movie about the bike racers set in Indiana?"

"Breaking Away."

"That's the one." Griffin regarded her from across the room, his expression still inscrutable. "What else do you want to know about me, Jill?"

"Other than the fact that you're capable of some pretty low-down tactics to get a story?" she shot back, sensing the need to shore up her defenses against him. She didn't want to get too close to him, too friendly.

Her accusation didn't rattle him. "Other than that I'm as greedy as you are when it comes to getting a good story, what else would you like to know?"

She let his dig pass unanswered. Gazing around the room again, she took note of the four chairs placed around the table and recalled how at home Ivy and her son had seemed in Griffin's house. She also recalled Doug's warning that she didn't know Griffin very well. "You aren't married?" she asked.

He shoved away from the counter and started across the room to the doorway where she stood. "Not anymore," he said. "I may be capable of a few low-down tactics, Jill, but not cheating on a wife."

"You're divorced," she concluded unnecessarily.

"Three years now."

"Did you leave her?"

It was much too personal a question, and Griffin didn't owe Jill an answer. That he was willing to give her one touched her. "She left me," he said. "She seemed to think I was more involved with my work than with her. I didn't cheat on her, but sometimes my concentration strayed, and my wife couldn't live with that. So she walked out. She's remarried, and there are no hard feelings on either side."

No wonder Griffin thought Jill was understanding. He'd already had a bad experience with a woman who didn't understand what newspaper work was about. But Jill understood what he meant by his concentration straying. She understood that, saddled with an unfinished story and an encroaching deadline, he preferred to postpone a date instead of keeping it and, in all likelihood, spoiling it.

"Any other questions?" He halted several inches in front of her and gazed down into her face. "Anything else you want to know?"

She peered up at him, at his piercing eyes and his hawklike nose, his disheveled mane of hair and his thin, sensuous mouth. She recalled the way she'd felt yesterday, sitting beside him on the park bench in the shade of the birch trees, and the way his hand had felt at the nape of her neck, and the way his lips had neared hers.... "If we hadn't gotten into a fight yesterday," she asked, her voice low but certain, brimming with every ounce of courage she had inside her, "were you going to kiss me?"

He reflected no surprise at her question. It was clear that he considered it no less valid than any of the others she'd asked, no less worthy of serious contemplation. He lifted one hand to the wall beside Jill's head. "Yes," he replied, planting his other hand on the other side of her head, trapping her between his body and the wall. "That's exactly what I was going to do."

He bent his head, touching his lips to hers. They were warm, strong, as sensuous as they looked. But before Jill could respond, he pulled back.

Her eyes met his and she tried in vain to make sense of their intense silvery radiance. "Like that?" she asked in a near whisper.

"Actually, no. More like this," he said, shifting his hands from the wall to her cheeks and tilting her head up. Pulling her toward him, he covered her mouth with his again, the restraint of the previous kiss no longer in evidence. His lips took hers, pressed into hers, teased and coaxed them until they were moving in tandem with his, inseparable from his. When he opened his mouth she opened hers; when his tongue ventured past her teeth she welcomed it with a soft moan.

Without the wall to bolster her, she had no choice but to lean on Griffin. She circled her arms around him and dug her fingertips into the supple muscles of his upper back, savoring the smooth shape of it through the soft fabric of his sweat shirt.

He sighed, sliding his fingers forward to her chin, stroking his thumbs across the silky underside of her jaw. His tongue probed deeper, surging against hers, bathing every surface of her mouth with erotic heat. Then he lowered one hand to her waist, lifting her slightly to accommodate his height and aligning her hips with his.

She felt his building arousal, the sudden glorious hardness of him against her thighs. She felt her own arousal even more acutely, rippling through her body in feverish pulses, making her want him, want him in a crazy, unreasoning way.

Without conscious volition, she tensed her thighs against him, urging her hips forward. He shuddered and let his hand move lower, cupping her bottom, holding her to him for a breathless, timeless instant. Then he slowly, reluctantly released her.

"Yeah," he murmured hoarsely, loosening his grip on her, allowing his glazed eyes to refocus on her upturned face. "Something like that. Any other questions?"

Unsure whether her voice would function, she ran her tongue over her lips, recapturing the salty taste of him. Although their bodies were no longer in such intimate proximity, her nerves continued to bear his imprint; her flesh remained submerged in the feverish sensations he'd set free inside her. Aware that he was waiting for her to say something, she shook her head. No, she had no other questions, no other questions at all. One potent kiss from Griffin seemed to answer everything.

His thumb continued to move against the skin of her throat, refusing to let her shift her head and break the silent bond of their gazes. She comprehended the intense glow in his eyes now; it was a glow of desire, hunger, longing. She was sure her eyes were glowing just as brightly, communicating the same passionate message.

"I've been shooting hoops all morning," he said, his voice gradually regaining its familiar texture. "I should take a shower."

In the aftermath of that spectacular kiss, Jill felt more than a little overheated, too. She nodded, wondering what he had in mind for after his shower.

He didn't leave her in suspense for long. "Come upstairs with me, Jill," he murmured, tracing the curve of her earlobe with his finger. "Come upstairs. I won't be long, and when I'm done..." He bowed and brushed his lips lightly over hers again, a promise of greater things to come.

As dazed as his kiss had left her, she was still rational enough to figure out that, in addition to a bathroom with a shower, the upstairs of his house had to contain his bedroom. His bedroom and his bed and Griffin himself, emerging clean from his shower, refreshed and rejuvenated...and naked. "Griff." The nickname fell from her lips naturally, and she and he shared a gentle smile at the sound of it. "Griff, I think maybe...maybe it would be better if I stayed down here."

His smile faded, but he didn't back away. He looked not angry but curious. And disappointed. "Why?"

Her thoughts took shape as she verbalized them. "Well—it's kind of too soon for me. I'm not real quick about these things. I like to take my time."

He studied her intently. "And you're still not sure you trust me completely."

"It isn't that," she protested, then bit her lip. Maybe Griffin's quiet accusation held a grain of truth. "It's not that I don't trust you," she said, still sorting through her thoughts. "But I don't want things to fall apart the way they did yesterday. We're competitors on a story. We've got to be sure we can keep the professional and the personal separate. Don't you agree?" She glanced up at him hopefully, praying that he would prove to be as understanding as she was alleged to be.

He took his time digesting her statement. "We're a lot of things, Jill," he noted. "We're competitors on a story, and we're also adults. I think we can handle this."

"We couldn't handle it yesterday."

He smiled wryly. "It must have been that bike I was riding," he contended. "Put me on a little kid's bike and I wind up acting like a little kid. What's your excuse?"

She was grateful for his willingness to approach the problem with humor. She knew he was frustrated by her refusal to follow through on the kiss they'd just shared. She was frustrated, too. At that moment she wanted nothing more than to race up the stairs with him, dive onto his bed, demand that he skip his shower and make love to her at once.

But she knew, however subliminally, that what was blossoming between her and Griffin was much too important to risk on the fleeting satisfaction they could enjoy that morning. She didn't want to take the chance of screwing up again.

"Maybe if we established some ground rules..." she proposed vaguely.

"Ground rules," he echoed, tucking a loosened strand of her hair behind her ear. "All right—here's my ground rule. If you don't want me to make love to you, you aren't allowed to look at me that way."

"What way?" Jill asked, instantly lowering her eyes.

He chuckled, a soft warm sound rising from deep in his throat. "*Any* way. You've got gorgeous eyes, Jill. And gorgeous hair—" he ran his fingers down along the weave of her braid "—and beautiful lips and great legs and—I'm only guessing, but I think it's a safe guess—a fantastic body."

"Is there any part of me you don't like?" she challenged him, smiling at his extravagant compliments.

He gave her a comprehensive inspection. "Your nose is too long."

Unreasonably hurt, she glared at him and discovered him laughing.

"Do you really want to know what I don't like about you?" he said. "You're being too damned sensible right now, and you're analyzing too much."

"I'm sorry, Griffin. But I think we should establish some rules here."

"Okay," he conceded. He crossed to the corner of the counter where a stack of books and magazines rested and lifted a lined pad from the pile. Then he took a pen from a drawer below the counter. He carried the pen and pad to the table and pulled out a chair for Jill. "Write some rules," he offered grandly. "I'm going upstairs to wash up. When I come down, we'll put these rules of yours to a vote." He gestured for her to sit, then sauntered to the doorway, heading for the stairs.

"One aye vote and they're automatically enacted," Jill called after him.

"Oh, yeah?" his disembodied voice floated down the stairs to her. His tone held laughter but also a clear challenge.

Jill stared at the pad for a minute. She ran her fingers over the plastic surface of the pen, as if she could erase from her fingertips the tactile pleasure she'd experienced in embracing Griffin.

She didn't have to write down any rules. There was only one rule, anyway: that they keep their work on the Wynan-Van Deen story separate, that they never discuss it, never share it, never even think about it when they were together.

Just one single rule—a tough one admittedly, but obeying it would prevent them from retreating into competitiveness and distrust. If they had to be rivals, so be it—but not when they were away from their work, not when they were with each other, not when she was falling in love with him.

One single rule, she decided—and it wouldn't be open to a vote.

Chapter Five

"I'd like to shadow Alvin Wynan today," Jill told Doug.

He leaned back in his massive leather chair and studied her quizzically. "What's with the dimples?" he asked.

She blinked in bewilderment. "What dimples?"

"You're grinning like a jack-o'-lantern."

"Great," she snorted. "Three years of orthodontics and my mouth looks like it was carved out of a pumpkin."

Doug eyed the doughnut box on his desk. It was empty except for a few stale crumbs left over from the previous Friday. "Why do you want to shadow Wynan?" he asked. "You've got to buy the doughnuts today. It's your turn."

"I'll buy them tomorrow," she promised.

"And what about the report you're supposed to be working on concerning the water table problems in Scituate?"

"Doug, what's wrong with you? I thought Wynan was the big story, the story that's going to put the *Record* on the map. Why should I kill a day looking at a reservoir in Scituate?"

"Why? Do you want to know why?" He impaled her with his sharp eyes. "Because I spent the entire weekend listening to Karen blather on and on about diamond solitaires and the odds of our getting our wedding announcement published in the *New York Times*. That's why."

Jill scowled, unsure of what Doug was getting at. "I think your odds are pretty good, given that you're both well pedigreed," she opined. "What does that have to do with the Scituate reservoir?"

"It has to do," Doug explained with forced patience, "with the fact that I spent the past two days being harangued on the topic of women and their emotional needs. Now you come waltzing in here after, I assume, spending at least part of the weekend with Griffin Parker—who just happens to be working on the Wynan story, too, shadowing Wynan and all the rest—and for the first time since I've known you, Jill, you've got dimples. I want to know what gives."

"If you think I'm planning to pair up with Griffin to shadow Wynan, you're wrong," Jill insisted. "Griffin and I made a pact not to talk about our work on the story."

"Swell," Doug grunted. "Meanwhile you've got those damned dimples. What are you, in love or something?"

"Of course not," Jill declared. "Griffin and I have only just met."

"Ever hear of love at first sight?"

"I'm a reporter," she reminded her boss. "I'm much too jaded to believe in that stuff. Now, be a pal, Doug, and ask Miriam to get the doughnuts today. I'll take my turn tomorrow. And send Hank to the Scituate reservoir—he'll have the time of his life there. I want to spend the day finding out what Alvin Wynan does with his life when he's not meeting mayors in rundown motels."

"Jill—" Doug halted her in the doorway. She spun around to face him, and he gave her a stern look. "You'd better not let Parker get wind of what you're doing."

"Don't patronize me," she retorted. "If you want me to write this story, then give me some room to maneuver." With that, she left Doug's glass-enclosed cubicle, stopped at her desk to grab her purse and notepad and stalked out of the office.

She honestly didn't believe in love at first sight. But she was well past "first sight" with Griffin, and she wouldn't put up a strenuous argument if someone labeled what she was feeling for him love. A very embryonic love, perhaps. An early-stages, grounds-for-optimism, giddy sort of love.

But no one had the right to accuse her of letting her emotions interfere with her professionalism.

Griffin had been surprisingly amenable to her "rule" yesterday. "It's okay with me," he agreed once he returned to the kitchen, freshly shaved and smelling of shampoo. "We won't talk about our work. Now can I get you upstairs?"

Jill suspected from his playful leer that he was teasing. "Patience is a virtue," she admonished him.

"I've never thought too highly of virtue," he shot back, grinning. "I tell you what. It's a nice day—let's go out."

They drove downtown, accompanied by a tape of Bruce Springsteen's *Born to Run* album in the Chevy's cassette deck. Griffin parked his car in the employee lot outside the *Journal* building so he wouldn't have to worry about stuffing coins into a meter on the street, and then he and Jill took a leisurely stroll along the bricked-in pedestrian arcade running through the center of the shopping district. They window-shopped and bought ice-cream cones and talked. And talked.

Griffin told Jill all about his scholastic basketball career at UMass. "I got my nose broken once on the freshman team and once on varsity," he informed her. "It became a joke. One of my teammates got me a hockey goalie mask to wear during the games." He'd been a point guard of modest talents, he told Jill, but he'd played for the joy of it, not because he expected to become a professional. "I'm only six foot two," he pointed out. "A runt by NBA standards. Anyway, I always knew I was going to be a journalist when I graduated."

He told Jill about the night he'd scored thirty points during a home game—"shooting from the outside, and this was in the olden days, before they had three-point field goals." His father had driven from Worcester to Amherst for the game, and he'd noticed a woman just a few seats away, attending the game with her two young daughters. The woman had commented loudly and enthusiastically upon Griffin's inspired play, and Griffin's father had felt it incumbent upon himself to introduce himself as the proud father...and a year later, he and Angie were married.

Jill confessed that she'd never had more than a passing interest in basketball. "I had three brothers, and they were always running at the mouth about sports," she told Griffin. "I guess I just learned to tune them out."

"It must have been nice, a big family like that," Griffin reflected. "Even with the shortage of bathrooms."

Jill had never considered her noisy, disorderly family either nice or not nice. It simply *was*. But Griffin offered her a new perspective. His own family was so tragically small when he was a child—no wonder he envied her her numerous siblings.

The afternoon passed much too quickly. Jill was surprised by how relaxed she felt with Griffin, how easy it was to talk to him. When they finally returned to his car, she was strongly tempted to accept his invitation to stay for dinner.

But she didn't. She knew that if she said yes to dinner, he would ask her to stay after dinner—and she would be just as tempted to say yes to that. No matter what they'd talked about during their stroll, she had never lost her awareness of what had occurred between her and Griffin when he'd kissed her, what she'd felt, what his lips and arms and his body had revealed to her about his own feelings.

It was much too soon to think about spending the night with him. "I'll take a rain check on the dinner," she said wistfully when they finally arrived back at his house.

Griffin escorted her to her car and watched as she unlocked the door. Before she could open it, he pressed his hand against it, holding it shut. "Tomorrow night?" he asked.

"I don't know." It was a truthful reply. She might be able to leave work by dinnertime the following evening, and she might not. "Call me at my office tomorrow," she suggested. "I'll have a better idea then of what the day is going to be like."

He nodded. He knew how unpredictable things could be in their line of work. "I'll do that," he vowed. He moved his hand to the back of her head, ran his fingers around her braid to the nape of her neck and leaned forward as if to kiss her. When his lips were only a whisper away, he abruptly changed his mind. Giving his head a slight shake, he smiled and straightened up.

His refusal to kiss her now was as disconcerting as his earlier kiss had been. Jill gazed up at him, wondering whether he was aware of how much she would have welcomed a kiss from him now, wondering whether he was depriving her of the pleasure as some sort of revenge for her refusal to stay with him through the evening.

No, it wasn't revenge. Griffin was depriving himself, as well. His sweetly rueful smile informed her that he had sensed her yielding and heard the slight catch in her breath as his fingers had glided over the sensitive skin of her neck. He let his hand drop and took a step backward as if to prevent them both from caving in to their mutual desire. "I'll call you tomorrow," he promised.

Jill recalled his parting words as she left the office Monday morning. She wondered why she had asked him to phone her at work and then deliberately arranged to have her work keep her away from her telephone. She wanted to find out how Wynan went about earning his daily keep—but was it possible that she also wanted to avoid Griffin's phone call?

The thought troubled her, and as she climbed into her car and started the engine, she tried to refute it. She had no good reason to avoid Griffin. Even if she didn't want to have dinner with him tonight, she had nothing to fear from his call. And she did want to have dinner with him—if not tonight, then soon.

She was willing to admit, to herself if not to Doug, that what she felt for that tall hazel-eyed man with the lush hair and the hypnotic smile was something akin to love. She wanted to be with Griffin, to spend time with him, to give their love a chance to blossom.

But she couldn't think about romance now. She was on an assignment that required her full concentration: tailing Alvin Wynan, Jr. He was the big story, the story that was going to make the Granby *Record* a contender and Jill a star—but only if she got it into print before anybody else did.

She still didn't trust Griffin. Yes, she trusted him not to pressure her, she trusted him not to have a wife hidden away somewhere. She trusted his affection, his warmth, his humor. But when it came to the big story, her big break, Wynan and the mayor of Granby, her trust evaporated. She didn't need Doug to lecture her on the risks of falling in love with Griffin. Her own instincts warned her that, no matter how badly he desired her, nothing would stop Griffin from getting the story he was after—the story they both were after.

Nothing was going to stop Jill, either.

She left the highway as it skirted the downtown Providence area, and her car crept through the congested city streets in the direction of the apartment complex where Alvin Wynan lived. She tried not to think about the downtown stroll she and Griffin had taken yesterday, the way he'd held her hand and helped himself to a taste of her ice-cream cone. She thought only of following Wynan.

She had dressed for the occasion in a blouse, a sweater, tailored trousers of a gray wool flannel and comfortable walking shoes. It was the sort of outfit that would allow her to blend into her surroundings yet would be easy to move in if she had to stalk Wynan on foot. She had no real experience in this sort of stakeout work, but she knew how to be unobtrusive. Growing up in such a large family, she'd had plenty of experience in going unnoticed.

She was familiar with Wynan's apartment complex, having driven there a week ago to interview his neighbors for that phony security clearance. Braking to a stop near his building, she scanned the residents' parking lot. The silver Nissan Maxima with the license plate reading Buck was parked in one of the numbered spaces; Jill hoped that meant Wynan was home. Counting windows and floors, she calculated which terrace belonged to his apartment. No lights were on, but then, the south-facing apartments wouldn't need any artificial light on such a bright morning.

Jill lifted her large leather purse from the seat beside her and groped inside it for the portable opera glasses she'd brought with her. She snapped them open, lifted them to her eyes and counted the terraces up to Wynan's again. The sun reflected off the glass panes of his windows and terrace door in such a way that, even if he was moving around inside, she would be unable to spot him.

Sighing, she folded the opera glasses shut and tucked them back into her bag. Then she searched the parking lot again. The presence of Wynan's car didn't mean a thing, she conceded. He could have gone somewhere on foot or ridden somewhere in someone else's car. She'd wait awhile, maybe a half hour...

Maybe fifteen minutes, she amended after the longest, dreariest minute of her life elapsed. Did police detectives actually have to do these stakeouts often? They couldn't possibly be paid enough to compensate for having to endure such boredom. She should have brought the magazine from yesterday's *New York Times* with her. At least then she could have amused herself with the crossword puzzle.

Another minute crawled by. Jill glanced at her watch, yawned, stared at the opaquely glaring windows of Wynan's apartment, checked her watch again and cursed when she discovered that the minute digit hadn't changed since she'd last checked it. Ten minutes, tops, she decided, and then she'd...what? What would she do if Wynan didn't appear in ten minutes? Go interview his blabbermouth neighbor again, she decided.

The building's lobby door opened, and Jill bolted upright. She wouldn't have to interview the blabbermouth neighbor, after all. Wynan had just made an appearance.

As usual, he looked gorgeous in a polished fashion-model way, his blond hair slicked back from his face, his attire well suited to his trim physique. He carried a small zippered case in his hand, about the size of an old-fashioned transistor radio or a fat calculator. Glancing both ways, he tucked the object into the hip pocket of his trousers and strode nimbly across the parking lot.

Jill grabbed the ignition key and cranked the engine of her car. As soon as it caught, she realized that Wynan was heading not for his own car but for an exit gate. "Damn," she muttered, glancing out her side window and discovering that she was parked by a fire hydrant.

She twisted around and skimmed the block with her gaze. There wasn't a single legal parking space open along either side. How the hell was she going to tail Wynan if he was walking and she was stuck with her car?

By driving very slowly, that was how. As soon as he left the parking lot for the street, she pulled away from the curb. Wynan, she quickly learned from her speedometer, was walking slower than three miles per hour—

a speed the driver of the delivery van behind her found intolerable, judging by the way he was riding her bumper.

Wynan turned down a side street, moving toward the Trinity Square Theater. Jill prayed that there would be a parking lot in the vicinity of the theater, and her prayers were answered as a municipal lot loomed into view. She veered into it, screeched to a halt and thrust her entire key chain at the attendant.

"Hey, lady—just the car key!" he ordered her.

She fidgeted with the key ring, anxiously following Wynan with her eyes. He bypassed the theater, continuing east.

"Here," she said, pressing the car key into the attendant's palm.

"Let me get you a ticket," he said, lumbering to his enclosed booth on the other side of the entrance.

Wynan strode out of Jill's line of vision. Gritting her teeth, she dashed to the booth and grabbed the ticket from the attendant, not bothering to acknowledge his question about when she'd be back to pick up her car.

She ran out of the lot and down the sidewalk, searching the swarming pedestrians for Wynan. She reached the corner just as the traffic light changed to red, but she darted across the street anyway. To her relief, she spotted Wynan two blocks ahead. He walked at a brisk pace—it felt faster than three miles an hour to her now that she was no longer driving—but she was able to keep him in sight. Smiling, she relaxed slightly.

On the next block, Wynan ducked into a drugstore. Jill loitered in the awninged entrance of a shoe store a few doors away, watching for his reemergence. After a few minutes he stepped outside carrying a bright yellow box of film.

A camera. That was what the object in his back pocket was—one of those pocket-size 35 millimeter cameras. He dropped the film into his shirt pocket and continued down the street.

When he passed through the sliding glass doors into the Biltmore Hotel, an imposing brick structure overlooking Kennedy Plaza, Jill knew she couldn't wait in a neighboring doorway until he happened to come out again. What Wynan did in hotels was precisely what she wanted to learn. Inhaling deeply, she followed him inside.

The Biltmore was an elegant establishment, not at all like the Granby Motor Lodge. Jill's feet sank into the plush burgundy carpet covering the lobby's floor as her gaze took in the marble stairway, the matching marble check-in desk, the stately wine-colored walls and the multitude of flora. There were potted plants, potted trees and flower arrangements scattered throughout the spacious lobby.

She was so entranced by her sumptuous surroundings she lost track of Wynan. Trying not to seem too obvious, she paced the huge room, hunting for him. She smiled nervously at the bell captain, pretended to be fascinated by the restaurant's decor, read the blaring headlines of the tabloids for sale at the newsstand...

There was Wynan, inside the newsstand, buying a candy bar.

A candy bar! How did he manage to keep his slim male-model figure if he snacked on candy bars? Jill wondered, fingering a racked copy of the *Enquirer* and watching him out the corner of her eye. The issue, she sternly reminded herself, wasn't how he fed his body but, rather, how he used it. She still hadn't completely discounted the possibility that he was a homosexual gigo-

lo. Perhaps he was at the Biltmore for another
assignation with Mayor Van Deen. Perhaps they'd decided to splurge on a nicer room this time....

"You buying that or just sweating on it?" the clerk
asked, glowering at Jill from his post at the cash register.

Jumping, she lifted the copy of the *Enquirer* she'd
been toying with and offered the clerk an ameliorating
smile. "Buying," she said, pulling her wallet from her
bag in time to see Wynan leave the newsstand, unwrapping his candy bar as he went.

She tossed a five-dollar bill at the clerk, grabbed her
change and hurried out into the lobby. Wynan was
standing at the glass door that opened onto Kennedy
Plaza, consuming the last of his candy bar and talking
to a young woman in a leather skirt, black patterned
stockings and an expensive-looking cashmere sweater.
Jill edged closer to them, but it was impossible to hear
what they were saying over the dull buzz of voices, the
muted ringing of a courtesy telephone and the Muzak
wafting through the restaurant's open door.

She stole closer to Wynan and his companion. Lacking an alternative, she ducked behind a tall, shrubby
potted plant. She leaned against the wall, held up her
newspaper, peeked through the foliage and eaves-
dropped.

"Look, I'm not going to give you ABC's here, Nina,"
Wynan was saying. "You do what you've got to do, and
I'll do what I've got to do."

"I've got a right to be prepared," the woman argued.
"I don't want any surprises, you know? I wanna know
what to expect."

"I already told you what to expect," Wynan said patiently. "He wants you to look like a lady—which you

do, Nina, that's a great skirt, by the way—and then he likes it kind of rough. Not painful, just rough.''

"That's a fine line," the woman remarked.

"You're a professional," said Wynan. "You can handle it."

If the woman with Wynan was a professional, Jill reasoned, that made Wynan . . . a *pimp*? Maybe she was making an imaginative leap, but the dialogue she'd overheard certainly sounded a lot like an exchange one might hear between a pimp and his prostitute arranging for an upcoming appointment.

"Yeah," the woman said, "I can handle my end of this trick. But I wanna know, are you going to be there? Are you gonna do one of your jack-in-the-box numbers?"

Jack-in-the-box numbers? Jill bemoaned her lack of worldliness. She knew the facts of life, but she'd never heard of that before. Then again, she didn't have much personal knowledge of prostitutes—or ménages à trois.

Jill made a mental note to ask Doug and turned her attention back to Wynan. He was ushering the woman to the elevator bank. The woman stepped inside an elevator, Wynan waved her off, and the doors slid shut, leaving him in the lobby. He glanced at his wristwatch—an expensive-looking gold one, Jill noticed—and glided across the thick carpet back to the door. Waiting for the customer, she surmised.

People came and went—a trio of matronly looking women, a pair of pin-striped businessmen, a uniformed chauffeur juggling several Louis Vuitton suitcases, a starchy woman scolding a weepy-eyed little girl in a middy blouse and skirt, a few more blandly attired businessmen. Wynan checked his watch again. The doors slid open and in walked Griffin.

Griffin? He was Wynan's customer? Jill flattened her hand against her mouth to stifle her cry of shock, and her newspaper rattled noisily against the leaves of the plant before drifting to the floor.

Griffin walked directly past Wynan, receiving not even a glance from the handsome blond man. Instead, Wynan permitted himself a reserved smile as he greeted a portly gentleman in a dark blue suit who entered the hotel just ahead of Griffin. The two men shook hands and walked together to the elevator bank.

Jill watched until they vanished into one of the elevators. Then she bent to gather up her newspaper. She peered around the rubber plant looking for Griffin. He was gone.

HE'D SEEN HER almost at once. How could he have missed her? People didn't stand behind potted trees gawking and spilling the pages of the *Enquirer* all over their shoes.

At first he'd suffered a blend of anger and amusement at finding her there—anger that she was being so flagrant, quite possibly alerting Wynan and that clown from the public works department that they were under surveillance, and amusement at the absurdity of her location.

But he wasn't going to stop and exchange pleasantries with her. He was going to follow Wynan and his client as far as the elevator, then wait to see if Wynan came back downstairs alone or stayed upstairs to photograph his prey for blackmailing purposes, as Ivy's client had suggested he might.

He did his best to disregard her. He permitted himself one brief glimpse of her—she was still on her knees, collecting the scattered pages of her newspaper—and then adamantly refused to look in her direction again. Instead, he settled himself into an easy chair from which he could spy on both the elevators and the stairs. He shook open the morning edition of the *Journal*, which he'd brought with him, flipped to the crossword puzzle and started solving it.

"Abet," Jill murmured into his ear.

He winced, then turned and glared at her.

"Fourteen down," she said. "Aid a criminal. Abet."

He took a deep breath and caught a whiff of her light cologne. She'd been wearing the same scent yesterday, and it had haunted him long after she'd left his house, long after he'd gone inside and eaten a sandwich, watched some television and gotten into bed...especially there. He'd had a damned uncomfortable night.

"What are you doing here?" he muttered without looking up.

"Following Wynan. What are you doing here?"

"None of your business," Griffin grumbled. He doubted that Jill knew Wynan's client was a low-level functionary in the city government. For that matter, she probably didn't care. Her goal was to link Wynan to Van Deen.

"You're mad at me," she accused Griffin, dropping onto the chair next to his and straightening out the wrinkled pages of her newspaper. "You're mad at me because I've got enough initiative to crack this story without any help from you, and because I'm obviously getting close to cracking it."

He issued a short, caustic laugh. "I'm mad at you, Jill, because of your gorilla impersonation. If you want to keep an eye on someone without being noticed, don't go hiding in a tree like some third-rate Inspector Clousseau. Sit down and read a newspaper. Be normal."

"I am normal!" she said hotly.

"Normal people don't stand in trees in hotel lobbies."

"I wasn't *in* the tree," she protested. "I was behind it. And I *was* reading."

He eyed her newspaper disdainfully. "The *Enquirer*? You ought to be ashamed. Why don't you read the Providence *Journal*? Much better reporting."

"Yeah, if you're dying to know everything there is to know about the city's budget audit," she scoffed.

He knew she was baiting him, and he baited her back by ignoring her. Shifting slightly in his seat, he presented her with his back and penciled in "A-B-E-T" into the spaces of fourteen down.

He felt her eyes on him, and he heard the rhythm of her breathing. By sitting so close to him, Jill was making them both dangerously conspicuous. When Wynan returned, he would undoubtedly spot them. Their faces would register on him subconsciously if not consciously, and the next time Griffin tailed Wynan, he might be spotted again and remembered.

Jill was jeopardizing his story. "Maybe you ought to go back to your tree," he suggested gruffly.

"Maybe you ought to jump in a lake," she retorted. "I can't believe you could be so—so cold to me today, Griff."

The plaintive quality of her voice when she said his nickname touched him. The last thing he wanted was to be cold to Jill. Even with his back to her he could picture her eyes, dark and beseeching, and her full lower lip curved in an unintentionally sensual pout. Smothering a groan, he lowered his pencil. "You established the rule, lady," he reminded her without looking directly at her.

"You said we're not supposed to share our work. Well, I'm working now, Jill. And I'm not sharing."

"I have as much right to sit here and watch the elevator bank as you do," she reminded him.

"Sure. You also have the right to march up to Wynan and point me out to him and tell him who I am. Is that what you want to do?"

"Of course not. I want to scoop you on this story fair and square."

"Fine." He wouldn't risk invoking her wrath further by making any jibes about how many light-years ahead of her he was on the story. Regardless of whether he was ahead of her, the fact that they were sitting side by side, surreptitiously watching the elevators for Wynan's reappearance, could wind up ruining the story for both of them.

"Twenty-two across, Acer," she whispered. "Maple genus."

"Thanks," Griffin muttered emotionlessly.

"Are we having dinner together tonight?"

"Now isn't the time to discuss it."

Jill subsided for a minute. Then: "Who was the guy he was with?"

"You're breaking your own rule, Jill," Griffin said through gritted teeth. He wondered whether Jill was deliberately trying to rile him, to goad him into leaving the hotel so she could get an exclusive. "You want to know? Ask Wynan."

"What's a jack-in-the-box number?" she inquired, her tone surprisingly earnest.

"What?"

"It's something sexual, Griff. Do you know what it is?"

He turned and gaped at her. She looked as earnest as she sounded. Earnest, curiously innocent and perilously seductive, her eyes wide and questioning, her lips parted, her hair braided back from her face to display the delicate line of her throat. "Come to my house tonight and I'll demonstrate it for you," he whispered, forgetting his resolve to think only of his purpose for being here. He had no idea what a jack-in-the-box number was, but he'd be glad to find out for her. Or he'd improvise.

"Will you really?" she asked, her eyes widening. "I thought it took three people to perform."

Griffin let out a low chuckle and shook his head. He wanted to kiss her right then and there, to kiss that deliciously baffled look off her face.

The door to the elevator nearest his chair slid open, and he smothered his laughter and spun around in time to see Wynan emerging alone. The sudden motion attracted Wynan's gaze, which passed briefly over Griffin and Jill before he stalked past them, heading back to the Kennedy Plaza entrance.

Griffin cursed. "Thanks a lot," he snapped at Jill, folding his newspaper shut and rising. "Next time," he added sarcastically, "maybe you can hang a billboard out front announcing our presence."

"Hey, it's not my fault!"

"Go climb back into your tree," he muttered by way of parting. Not a particularly pleasant farewell, but he was too irritated to care. Jill's stupid, poorly timed comments had distracted him—and they'd made Wynan notice him. Thanks to her, he'd come close to botching the story but good.

He wondered if she'd plotted it to happen that way.

No, he didn't think Jill was capable of such nefarious scheming. She was too cocksure to believe she had to undermine Griffin in order to beat him to publication. She'd been acting guilelessly. He could blame her for her ineptitude, nothing more.

Wynan left the hotel, and Griffin followed him out. He'd catch up with Walter Costigan from the public works department later. Plump lustful Walter, who liked it rough but not painful, according to Griffin's source, would have an interesting tale to tell. And Griffin had a sneaking suspicion he'd be able to cajole Walter into telling it, even if only off-the-record.

Since he wouldn't be able to talk to Walter until the bureaucrat returned to his office, Griffin decided to go back to the paper and tidy up another story he was working on. It was a mild day, too cool to qualify as Indian summer but brisk and sunny. In his sneakers, Griffin half walked and half jogged through downtown Providence.

As usual, the newsroom was brightly lit and cacophonous. Griffin's colleagues seemed to operate on the twin mottoes: Never Walk When You Can Run, and Never Talk When You Can Shout. Above the jangling of telephones and the purring of word processors came the roars and bellows of his fellow reporters congratulating themselves or swearing, begging their editors for favors or castigating their underlings for mistakes. Griffin moved through the room to his own desk, tossed down his newspaper and reached for the power switch on his word processor.

"Griffin Parker?" Jeanine's squawking voice rose above the general din. "Move it over here."

He dutifully strode to his editor's desk at the end of the room.

Jeanine was, not surprisingly, lighting a cigarette. Although her voice sounded more like a crow's than a woman's, her appearance reminded Griffin of a canary—feathery yellow hair splayed out from a narrow face with a long jutting nose and a recessive chin. Jeanine was thin and small boned, and her hands fluttered when she spoke—usually strewing ashes from her cigarettes in all directions. To look at her, one would assume she was fragile. To know her was to know better.

"What's up?" he asked.

"You tell me," she returned, flicking her cigarette in the vicinity of an overflowing ashtray.

"I just got back from the Biltmore," Griffin reported. "Wynan was with a yo-yo from public works, but he wasn't taking pictures. I'll do a follow-up this afternoon."

"Did you take any pictures?" Jeanine asked. "Did you get Wynan and the yo-yo together on film?"

"The occasion didn't call for it."

Jeanine stared up at Griffin for a moment, appraising him. Then she drew on her cigarette and expelled a jet in smoke in his direction. "What's with the lady from the Granby *Review*?"

The question caught Griffin off guard; he hadn't discussed Jill with his editor, and he had no intention of discussing her now. He took his time weighing various responses. "It's called the Granby *Record*," he finally said.

"Whatever. I hear you're fooling around with one of their reporters."

"I'm not fooling around with her," Griffin said in a deceptively calm voice. He was tempted to tell Jeanine to keep her nose out of his private affairs, but he was too curious to find out what she was getting at to cut her off right away.

"All right. You're not fooling around, you're serious."

"Maybe," he allowed. "Who told you I was seeing her?"

"You think you're the only one who's got sources?" Jeanine commented with a haughty sniff. She took another drag of her cigarette, then jammed it out in the ashtray. "Is your sweetheart onto the fact that Granby's mayor is about to swim into Wynan's net?"

Griffin once more took his time before answering. "I'm not sure what she knows."

"Well, find out, damn it," Jeanine chided him. "I don't care how serious you are about this lady, Griff—find out what she knows and make sure it's not as much as you know. I don't want that two-bit paper cutting in front of us on this story."

Griffin remembered what Jill had told him of Doug Mallory's concern about her dating a rival reporter. Griffin had assumed that at a big, professionally run newspaper like the *Journal* he'd be immune from such interference. "Don't do this, Jeanine," he said, his tone quiet but firm. "Don't bring my social life into the office, okay?"

"Griff," Jeanine said, trying to sound sympathetic but failing miserably. "All right, you like her, you love her, you want to take her home to meet your pa—but so help me, if you lose this story to her..."

Griffin's impulse was to reassure Jeanine that there was absolutely no chance of that occurring. He checked the impulse, however. "If I lose the story to her, what?" he asked.

"I'll kill you," Jeanine declared bluntly.

"I'll bear that in mind." Griffin straightened up and headed back to his desk.

He turned on the word processor, called up a file and stared at the glowing green monitor without focusing on it. *Damn Jeanine,* he thought, *damn her threats, damn her implications that, thanks to Jill, I'm in danger of losing the Wynan story.*

And when he was done damning his editor, he directed his fury to Jill—because, thanks to her, he *was* in danger of losing the Wynan story.

Chapter Six

At six o'clock, Jill entered the restaurant across the street from the Granby City Hall. The place was a bit more crowded than it had been the last time she'd been there, when she'd had a cup of coffee with Griffin after the press conference. But it hadn't taken her long to spot him sitting by himself in one of the booths, watching the front door for her entrance.

He saw her and stood. Before approaching his table, she took a moment to study him. He'd sounded uncharacteristically curt when he'd phoned her at her office a few hours ago. "About dinner tonight," he'd said. "I'll meet you at that sandwich shop on Main Street in Granby. We'll talk then."

She had spent most of the afternoon wondering what they were going to talk about. In any case, she hoped their dinner would recapture the affection they'd felt for each other on Sunday. But judging from Griffin's brusque manner on the telephone—to say nothing of the unromantic setting he'd chosen for their meal—she doubted it. Studying his shuttered expression as he beckoned her to the table, she felt her doubts increase.

He was dressed in his usual garb; his jaw wasn't quite stubbly, but it wasn't freshly shaved, either, and his dark hair was tousled. He must have driven directly to Granby after work without bothering to stop at his house and freshen up first. Not that Jill could fault him for that; she'd come to the sandwich shop straight from her own office. She had wanted to take a quick detour to her house to change her clothes and touch up her hair, but she'd had to rewrite Hank's turgid piece about the water level problems in Scituate for the Tuesday edition of the *Record*, and she hadn't had time for a trip home.

She waved away the hostess and strode through the restaurant to Griffin's table. He greeted her with a nod and an emotionless smile. Swallowing her dread, she slid into the booth facing him. He resumed his seat and passed her a menu.

She didn't bother to open it. "What's going on, Griff?" she asked in an admirably steady voice.

"What makes you think anything's going on?" His smile became wry, and although Jill sensed no warmth emanating from him, she was relieved by his tacit acknowledgment that something *was* going on and that she had a right to question him about it. "Let's order, and then we'll talk," he recommended.

After giving him another searching look and finding no visible clues to explain his behavior, she opened the laminated menu. No chateaubriand and Bordeau, she mused, scanning the lackluster offerings. She wondered when she and Griffin would have their long-awaited elegant dinner at a real restaurant.

Maybe never. Maybe Griffin was going to tell her tonight that he never wanted to see her again. Maybe he was going to tell her that, while he wasn't married, he was in fact engaged to an heiress in Newport, and since he was also amusing himself with three floozies on the side, he didn't have room for Jill in his hectic schedule...

"What'll it be?" a gum-chewing waitress broke into Jill's dismal thoughts.

"I'll have a turkey club sandwich," she answered listlessly.

"I'll take a steak, medium rare," Griffin requested, "and a beer. What brands have you got?"

"We don't have a liquor license," the waitress informed him.

He eyed Jill contritely. "Sorry—I didn't know," he said, before ordering a Coke.

Jill hadn't planned on having a drink. But Griffin's vague apology led her to the conclusion that this was going to be the sort of meal she'd need a few stiff ones to survive.

With a building sense of foreboding, she confronted Griffin across the table from her. He remained poker-faced, his eyes guarded, his thin lips cutting a straight line, his hands folded loosely on the table in front of him. He returned her stare impassively.

She recalled what had happened that morning when she'd accused him of behaving coldly toward her: he'd yielded, softened, smiled one of his beguiling smiles and let her know, however playfully, that no matter what else was happening between them at that moment, he cared for her. She wondered whether he'd respond the same way if she repeated her accusation now. Somehow she knew he wouldn't.

"Look, Griff," she ventured, figuring someone had to say something, "just because we bumped into each other on a stakeout this morning—"

He cut her off with a short, acerbic laugh. "*I* was on a stakeout, Jill," he corrected her. "I'm still not sure what you were on, but my first guess would be some sort of a controlled substance.''

She scowled. All right, so he was angry with her for having been clumsy in her attempts at spying. Being clumsy wasn't a crime. She honestly didn't think she'd done that much damage to his investigation—or her own. "Okay. Maybe I was a little obvious at the hotel. I haven't had much experience doing that sort of thing, but it doesn't mean—''

"*Much* experience?'' He snorted. "I'll bet you haven't had any. Which isn't surprising, given the kinds of stories the *Record* usually runs, but—''

"Leave the *Record* out of it,'' she snapped, her own anger rising to match his. "It's not as if I've spent my entire life at the *Record*. I've done time with one of those big newspapers, too.''

"Have you?'' He arched his eyebrows in surprise.

"Yes,'' she said, annoyed by the condescension in his tone. "The *Chicago Tribune*. Perhaps you've heard of it.''

"The *Chicago Trib*? Why in the world would you leave a prestige outfit like that to work for the *Record*?''

"So I could pursue stories like this one,'' she answered pointedly. "My work on the *Tribune* didn't give me the opportunity to do stakeouts. Even so, for someone with little experience, I think I did just fine this morning.''

"Jill—''

"And furthermore, I think the only reason you're mad at me is because you know I did well. You know I'm getting close, and it bothers you.''

"Jill." His voice was gentle but firm. "Please cool it. We've got business to discuss, and I think we should discuss it calmly."

"I thought we decided we weren't going to discuss business at all," she reminded him, too late. She felt her already deflated mood sink even lower at the realization that, despite her noble effort to draw an unbreakable line between their professional competition and their personal compatibility, the rule she'd established for them yesterday wasn't going to do them much good today.

The arrival of their dinners spared Griffin the necessity of responding right away. He eyed his undersized overcooked steak with apprehension, then poked his fork dubiously through the watery mound of succotash occupying one end of the plate. Jill silently congratulated herself for having ordered a sandwich.

Griffin opened a foil-wrapped square of butter and placed it on his soggy microwaved potato. Then he leaned back and scrutinized Jill. "What's the deal with Mallory?" he asked.

Jill foundered for a moment. What did Doug have to do with anything? "I've already told you," she said a touch too sharply. "He's my boss, and other than that we're old schoolmates."

Griffin cut into his steak and tasted it. Then he prodded his slab of meat on his plate with the tines of his fork, shook his head and lifted his gaze to Jill. "Is Mallory still upset about our seeing each other?" he asked.

Jill permitted herself a small measure of optimism. If Griffin could phrase the question that way, it implied that they *were* seeing each other, in some fashion or other. "I don't know," she admitted. "He seems suspicious, but he and I haven't really talked much about it."

"What is he suspicious of?"

Jill's patience began to ebb. "Why don't you get to the point, Griff?"

He reached across the table and covered her hand with his. The warmth in his clasp sent a dark thrill of longing up her arm, but it was gradually replaced by something less erotic yet ironically more potent—comfort, reassurance, empathy. No matter what was eating at Griffin, his clasp seemed to say that he was still her friend. "The point," he drawled, "is that Jeanine's giving me a hard time, too."

Jeanine? Who was that? The heiress in Newport? "I don't recall your ever mentioning anyone named Jeanine," Jill said warily, trying to keep her hand from fisting inside his.

"She's my editor. Jeanine Tomaszewski."

"The tough broad," Jill remembered, feeling her fingers unclench within the curve of his palm.

"She's afraid I'm going to lose the story to you," Griffin declared.

"It's her job to worry about things like that."

"It's my job, too," he noted, tightening his hold on Jill. "What happened at the Biltmore today..." He exhaled. "It wasn't just that you may have attracted Wynan's attention, Jill—it's that I lost my concentration. I should have been able to ignore you, to ignore everything except the story I was after. But I couldn't. I let you distract me."

She struggled to interpret his enigmatic expression. Did he think she'd distracted him on purpose? "It wasn't a plot," she swore. "I didn't deliberately set out to keep you from doing your job."

"I know," Griffin said, but he didn't sound positive.

She pulled her hand from his and tucked it in her lap. She didn't like what he was implying. She didn't like his appropriating his editor's suspicions—and her editor's, too—and using them as an excuse to stop trusting her. She didn't like the way the border between professional and personal was growing blurry in spite of her rule.

"It's not like I was breaking any laws being there today," she said in her own defense.

His gaze fell to his now empty hand lying idle at the center of the table. He drummed his fingers against the table for a moment, then withdrew his hand and lifted his eyes to hers again. "Of course you weren't."

"But . . . ?"

"But nothing." A grudging smile tugged at his lips. "But neither of us is going to get the story if we keep bumping into each other on stakeouts."

"Meaning what? I'm supposed to stop working on it?"

"Meaning, maybe we ought to extend your rule a little bit," Griffin said slowly, carefully. "Maybe we're going to have to keep our distance from each other."

"Great," she snapped, giving in to anger so she wouldn't do something embarrassing like burst into tears or throw her knife at him. "We don't have to see each other ever again, Griffin. That would be just fine with me."

"I didn't say we shouldn't see each other ever again," he argued, apparently recognizing the cause of her fury and hastening to neutralize it. "I'm only thinking, maybe we should go our separate ways until this story is behind us."

"In other words, until I get it into print," she taunted him.

"Until one of us gets it into print," he corrected her gently.

"Swell." She was steaming. The nerve of him, deciding unilaterally that they shouldn't see each other anymore just because he found her distracting. She supposed she could take his decision as a compliment, but she was too upset by the thought of being cut off from him to feel flattered. "Swell. Wonderful. I'll be on my way right now," she resolved, pushing herself to her feet.

Griffin extended one long arm across the table and grabbed her wrist. He easily pulled her back down into her seat. "Jill, you were the one who said we needed some rules."

"Yeah, and *you* were the one who said we were both adults and we could handle it."

"That was before you fell out of a tree in the Biltmore lobby."

"I wasn't in a tree!" Jill exploded, attracting a few curious glances from the other diners.

"Jill." Griffin's tone was as low and controlled as hers was enraged. "It's not that I don't want you. I *do*. I want you a lot—too much, maybe. That's the problem."

"Right," she snorted sardonically. "My very nearness interferes with your ability to function."

"Yes," Griffin said bluntly. "It does."

She didn't know what to make of his candor. She allowed herself to revel briefly in the sheer flattery of his statement, then steeled herself. If he was going to break things off with her, she'd be wise not to entertain any kind thoughts about him. "Well," she said frostily, "I'd hate to make you dysfunctional."

He laughed in spite of himself. "Oh, Jill..." His voice drifted off for a moment, and his laughter waned. "Don't make this harder than it has to be. I'm not thrilled about it, either. I'm just trying to be practical."

"Fine," she capitulated. He'd made up his mind; she could think of no way to change his position. "In the meantime, what are our rules concerning the story? I can't offer you any guarantees that you aren't going to run into me on another stakeout."

"If we run into each other," he said resolutely, "you don't know me. And I don't know you."

"If that's the way you want it."

"It's not the way I want it," he murmured. "It's the way it has to be."

She consoled herself with the thought that their separation would last only a few weeks. Maybe less, maybe only a week or so. And maybe, during that week, they wouldn't bump into each other. Maybe it wouldn't be so very difficult.

Sure, she thought with a disconsolate sigh. And Van Deen and Wynan had probably been reading Scripture together at the Granby Motor Lodge.

IT WAS with a renewed sense of purpose that Jill stalked into Jim Valenti's office on the second floor of the City Hall the following afternoon. She didn't want to analyze whether her impatience to crack the story resulted from her eagerness to elevate the *Record* and her own career or from her eagerness to put the story behind her and resume her relationship with Griffin.

Whenever she thought about him, she thought about how much she missed him and how irrational it was for her to miss someone she'd actually kissed only once... and how much more than that one heated kiss existed between her and Griffin. It didn't seem fair that they should have to exercise such restraint just when they were on the verge of discovering something so good, so vital. It didn't seem fair that at long last Jill's career should be taking off at the same time as her love life—and that she should wind up being sensible, allowing her career to take precedence and putting her love life on hold.

It didn't seem fair that she should feel so lonely without Griffin, that knowing him should make her so profoundly aware of the emptiness in her life.

Nothing was to be gained by feeling sorry for herself, however. The only way to get back together with Griffin was to finish the Wynan story. She was infused with energy, willing to chase every lead, willing to chase even nonexistent leads if they'd speed up the process.

She'd spent much of the morning chatting on the telephone with Doug's beloved, Karen, who wanted to enlist Jill as an ally in her battle to wheedle a marriage proposal from him. "You've known Doug longer than I have," Karen had observed. "What's with him? Is he gun-shy or something?"

"I have no way of knowing, Karen. He was never so serious about a woman before," Jill had replied, which cheered Karen considerably.

"Well, I hope he comes around soon. I'm going to be turning twenty-seven a week before Thanksgiving and I feel like an old maid."

Thanks a heap, Jill had muttered silently, feeling ancient. "Be patient," she'd lectured Karen. "He'll come around in time."

"Be patient," she'd grumbled to herself after hanging up. That had to be the most useless advice in the world. If someone had advised Jill to be patient regarding Griffin she would have been tempted to bite his head off.

Deciding her best tactic was to avoid the telephone, she left the office and drove to the Granby Motor Lodge, where she bribed the desk clerk into revealing that, as far as he knew, Mayor Van Deen had visited the motel only once—"With that blond guy, and I don't know nothing about what they did," he swore. An additional ten dollars stimulated his memory a tad. "The bed wasn't used," he recollected, fondling the ten-dollar bill. "The sheets were untouched, so we just left 'em on for the next customer."

Not bothering to conceal her disgust at that unsanitary practice, Jill thanked the clerk and hurried away.

Her next stop was the Foto-Finish shop on Main Street, where the *Record* always took film for developing. There were other film-developing services in town—drugstores, convenience stores and the like—but Foto-Finish was the only one that did the developing on the premises.

Jill didn't know what she was looking for, but she'd seen Wynan with a camera in his pocket and a roll of film. What sort of pimp needed a camera and film for a job?

Clark, the amiable young man who worked behind the counter, knew Jill from the newspaper and was willing to answer her questions for free. She described Wynan and asked him whether he'd developed any film for Wynan or featuring Wynan's picture. Clark insisted he hadn't. Nor had he developed any unseemly pictures of Mayor Van Deen. "Sylvia Van Deen brought in a roll back in September," Clark recalled, "but it was just family vacation pictures."

Skipping lunch, Jill drove to the Van Deens' stately brick Georgian house, which was located on a majestic tree-lined boulevard in the northern end of town, where Granby's elite families lived. Doug's parents owned a house just two blocks from the mayor's residence, and Doug himself had bought a house not far from his parents' home when he'd returned to Granby.

Nothing appeared to be out of the ordinary at the Van Deen house when Jill coasted to a halt across the street. An Oldsmobile station wagon was parked next to a black Lincoln Town Car in the double driveway. The front yard was strewn with a layer of yellow leaves from the shady maples and sycamores that loomed over the acre lot. A basketball hoop had been affixed to the wall above the garage. It was a charming home, the sort of place that put one in mind of God and country and Norman Rockwell—and proper New England mayors and their lovely wives.

Closing her eyes, she tried to come up with an idea of where to head next. The sound of irate voices broke into her thoughts, and she snapped to attention.

The front door to the Van Deen house opened and the mayor stormed out. Jill didn't begrudge him a trip home in the middle of the day; mayors didn't get thrown out of office for sharing an occasional lunch with their families. Jill felt safe in assuming that was what Van Deen had done, since he was dressed for work in one of his well-made suits, with nary a silver strand of his hair out of place.

His usually benign, vote-for-me expression was nowhere in evidence, however. "Another crack like that, Sylvia, and you'll pay!" he shouted through the screen in the storm door.

Sylvia Van Deen appeared in the doorway, her face flushed with rage. "Me? Pay? For your stupidity? You do whatever you've got to do to get this situation out of our lives, George. But so help me, if you so much as touch the children's college money—"

"I earned that money, Sylvia. Don't you dare issue any ultimatums about my touching it!"

"You won't be earning anything if you don't get this situation cleaned up, mister. That money's for the children, and so help me, if you take one cent of it—"

"I won't," Van Deen growled, marching down the walk with his shoulders hunched forward. "The money's been taken care of."

"*I* haven't been," Sylvia muttered. "You've got more than money to worry about, George." She slammed the front door on him. Snarling something unintelligible, he climbed into the Lincoln and backed down the driveway.

Jill waited until several minutes had passed before she started her own car. During the wait, she replayed as much as she could remember of the argument she'd overheard.

Money. *The money's been taken care of.*

With a fresh surge of optimism, Jill headed south through town to City Hall, parked in the lot behind the domed building on Main Street and bounded up the stairs to Jim Valenti's office.

At the press conference the previous week, Mayor Van Deen had sworn that the financial records of the city were open to the public and that the city treasurer, Jim Valenti, would accommodate anyone who wished to look through the books. Jill didn't have an appointment—and she had no illusions about discovering any checks identified as "entertainment expenses" and paid to the order of the Granby Motor Lodge—but if she kept pushing, something might just break her way.

The city treasury department occupied a suite of offices on the top floor of the City Hall. Jill entered and walked up to the counter. One of the three secretaries approached Jill. "Can I help you?" she asked.

"I was wondering if I could speak with Jim Valenti," Jill requested. "My name is Jill Bergland. I write for the Granby *Record*."

"Wait right here," said the secretary. After a few minutes the secretary returned with Jim Valenti. He was a short, stocky man with curly salt-and-pepper hair and a robust grin. He was in his shirtsleeves, with his tie dangling loose from the unbuttoned collar of his shirt. The rumpled condition of his clothing gave the impression that Jill had called him away from some strenuous labor.

"Ms. Bergland?" he boomed, extending his right hand to her over the barrier.

Jill shook his hand and mirrored his high-voltage smile. "How do you do, Mr. Valenti? I was wondering if I could have a peek at some of the records of the city's recent financial transactions. At the press conference last week, Mayor Van Deen said the books were available for inspection."

"They most certainly are," Valenti assured her, opening a gate built into the wooden counter and ushering her through. "Usually we require an appointment, but I'm familiar with your byline, Ms. Bergland, so I'll make an exception for you. Come on in."

"Thank you," she said, trying not to be discouraged. If Valenti was so willing to let her view the city's financial records, they probably didn't contain anything particularly incriminating.

"I'm a big fan of the *Record*," Valenti went on, leading her down the corridor past several doors with frosted-glass windows in them. "And I believe it's the responsibility of the government to accommodate the media whenever possible. I believe in open government, Ms. Bergland."

"So do I," she admitted, suspecting that Valenti had a political campaign in his future. He seemed to be trying out his stump speech on her.

"Here we go," he said, escorting her into a spacious office, this one featuring a window, a cozy sitting room, a wall full of cabinets and a single L-shaped desk. The woman seated behind the desk wasn't much older than Jill, but she was dressed much better, in a becoming wool suit and high-heel pumps. "Glenda?" Valenti greeted her. "This is Jill Bergland from the *Record*. Please help her in any way you can. Jill, my right-hand lady, Glenda Hauser." With a nod at Jill, he swept out of the office.

Glenda rose from her swivel chair and smiled hesitantly. "I'm Jim Valenti's administrative assistant," she identified herself. "What can I do for you?"

"I'd like to see a record of financial transactions dating back to..." Jill did a swift mental calculation. "Nine days ago," she computed, figuring she'd begin with the Sunday she'd seen Mayor Van Deen at the Granby Motor Lodge.

"Deposits or withdrawals?" Glenda asked, gliding from behind her desk and pulling open a file drawer.

"Withdrawals," Jill requested.

Glenda pulled a stack of spread sheets from the drawer and carried them to the upholstered couch in the sitting area. "What we have here," she explained, sitting on the couch and gesturing for Jill to join her, "are the daily logs that Granby Savings and Loan sends us at the end of each business day. These are all codes.'' She pointed to one of the columns. ''This three-digit code indicates the kind of transaction—cash withdrawal, check, wire transfer or simply earmarked funds. And this second column indicates where the money went. For instance, this here—UTL—is a utilities expenditure. That money didn't actually leave the bank, but it's earmarked. This here—PTY—is for our daily petty cash fund. Think you can follow it?''

''I think so,'' Jill said, sliding the broad green-and-white-striped printouts from Glenda's lap to her own and smiling gratefully at the aide. ''If I have trouble, I'll give a holler.''

''I'll be right here,'' Glenda affirmed, moving back to her desk.

The first spread sheet Jill studied covered transactions for the day after she'd seen Van Deen at the motel. Although the codes were confusing, Jill struggled through them. She figured out the listings for personnel expenses, insurance, petty cash, public relations, various working lunches, various working dinners. She interpreted the subdirectory for police services, which had its own bank account and was cross-referenced to another spread sheet in the pile, and the ones for the maintenance department and the department of education. She worked her way down the list with her index finger, squinting at the smudgy numbers and trying not to let the wide paper sag between her legs.

Her finger stopped at a listing code ''000—cash withdrawal, $1000.'' There had already been a separate listing for petty cash—and even if there hadn't been, a thousand dollars seemed like too much money to replenish a petty cash till. Jill made a mental note of the listing, then flipped the page to study the Tuesday transactions.

There, near the bottom of the spread sheet, was another mysterious listing: "000—cash withdrawal, $1500." Even if the Monday cash withdrawal had been for petty cash, City Hall wouldn't require another fifteen hundred dollars the next day.

"Excuse me," she called across the room to Glenda, who was hunched over a sheaf of papers at her desk. Glenda looked up and Jill asked, "What does the code 000 stand for?"

Glenda smiled tolerantly. "That's not a code," she told Jill. "What that means is that the transaction hasn't been properly coded."

"Well, in two days alone there was a grand total of twenty-five hundred dollars in uncoded cash withdrawals," Jill informed her.

Glenda appeared perplexed. "I can't believe that," she said as she stood. "If a transaction goes through without the proper code, the bank is supposed to contact us the next day so we can correct the record. Two uncorrected transactions in a row is very unusual."

"Make it three uncorrected transactions," Jill alerted her, flipping the page and scanning the spread sheet for Wednesday until she found an "000" listing next to another one-thousand-dollar withdrawal.

Glenda lowered herself to the couch beside Jill and scowled at the listings Jill pointed out to her. "This is very unusual," she repeated.

"Let's see if there are any more," Jill suggested brightly. She wasn't sure what she'd uncovered, but it seemed promising.

Thursday's transactions didn't include any uncoded withdrawals, but near the bottom of Friday's list, Jill and Glenda located another "000" cash withdrawal, this one for fifteen hundred dollars. "That's five thousand dollars in one week," Jill summed up.

Glenda lifted the spread sheets onto her own narrow lap. "Here's another one," she announced, her frown creating a delicate crease above the bridge of her nose. "Transacted yesterday. Two thousand dollars. I'm surprised we haven't heard from the bank. This is extremely unusual."

"Who's empowered to withdraw money from the city accounts?" Jill asked.

"Jim Valenti, naturally," Glenda said. "And me—but I always code my transactions properly. The corporation counsel has access to the accounts, and a few other department heads. And Mayor Van Deen, of course."

"Of course."

"It's always possible that someone might have accessed our computer link with the bank," Glenda conjectured. "A hacker somewhere might be bleeding our treasury—on paper, let's hope. The bank wouldn't release actual funds to anyone lacking the proper credentials."

"A hacker. That must be it," Jill concurred, hoping with all her heart that the unexplained withdrawals had nothing to do with some school-age whiz kid who'd plugged into the bank's records. If the explanation turned out to be something that mundane, Jill would get a story out of it—but not the story she wanted.

"I'll have to discuss this with Jim," Glenda declared, stacking the spread sheets into a neat pile and standing. "It's quite unusual."

"So I gather." Jill pulled her notepad from her purse and jotted down the amounts of the questionable transactions and the dates on which they occurred. On a clean sheet of paper she wrote her name and the phone numbers at her house and at the *Record* offices. "Here, Glenda," she said, tearing out the page and handing it to the woman. "I'd appreciate your giving me a call as soon as you and Jim Valenti have had a chance to review this."

"I'll do that," Glenda promised, placing the notepaper under a crystal paperweight on her desk. "I can't say precisely when it will be, though. Jim is really snowed under today."

"Then call me tomorrow—or I'll call you," Jill said as she headed toward the door. "As you say, it's probably just a hacker or some computer error."

"Probably," Glenda muttered, frowning at the spread sheets cradled in her arms.

Jill made her way out of the treasury department's offices and was halfway down the wide marble stairs to the lobby when she sank onto a step, closed her eyes and thought.

Seven thousand dollars. Even if Van Deen had withdrawn the cash to pay Wynan for the services of a hooker, seven thousand dollars seemed like much too steep a price. Jill simply couldn't imagine that any prostitute, no matter how many jack-in-the-box numbers she performed, could be worth that much.

Then again, if Van Deen had taken the money out of the city's coffers, he was probably planning to withdraw a good deal more than seven thousand dollars. He wouldn't run the risk of committing grand larceny for what could be considered a relatively small amount. Given the altercation she'd heard between Van Deen and his wife, Jill felt safe in assuming that he was facing severe money problems. The argument had seemed much too heated to be about a seven-thousand-dollar debt.

Furthermore, if he was indeed the person withdrawing the money, he was removing it a little at a time. If the entire sum he needed were seven thousand dollars, he'd probably have withdrawn it all at once and been done with it. For that matter, he'd have found a way to bury the seven-thousand-dollar withdrawal within a properly coded account. There had to be a discretionary fund of some sort within which he could hide a withdrawal, even one as large as that.

If Van Deen *had* taken the money, it was undoubtedly for some illicit reason. But still…that much money for a prostitute? Had the lady been worth it?

Glenda was probably right. It was probably just a hacker somewhere, gleefully fouling up the computer's records for a cheap thrill.

But on the chance that it wasn't, on the chance that Jill's admittedly flimsy hypothesis was true… Griffin didn't have this part of the story. Griffin didn't know that, whatever Wynan and Van Deen were up to, it was costing Granby's mayor a hell of a lot of money—city money—and it might well end up costing him his office and some jail time, if Jill managed to break the story.

For a brief, malicious moment, Jill realized that her motivation wasn't to finish up and race back to Griffin's arms. Her motivation was to beat Griffin to the punch, to get into print with this blockbuster before he did.

She hated herself for thinking like that. If her competitive streak was truly stronger than her affection for Griffin, their relationship was dead in the water. And she wouldn't be able to blame it on Doug or Jeanine or Griffin or even circumstances beyond anyone's control.

The fault would be hers alone.

Chapter Seven

"I had enough to go to a grand jury with," Maureen Krieger was saying. "We could have gotten indictments on at least four counts of pandering—I'm convinced of it. But all of a sudden, word came down that we should drop all the charges and give the guy a one-way ticket out of town."

Griffin scribbled in his notepad, then lifted his gaze back to Maureen. She was an attorney in the Erie County D.A.'s office, working as a prosecutor in downtown Buffalo. Griffin had found her through a colleague of his at the *Journal* who used to live in Buffalo. One of the colleague's old contacts had supplied Griffin with the names of three prosecutors who might have some pertinent information concerning a former local pimp named Alvin Wynan, Jr. Griffin had telephoned all three, hit the jackpot with Maureen Krieger and flown out to Buffalo to talk to her in person, as well as to poke around the police department searching for any possible arrest records with Wynan's name on them.

Maureen Krieger was a looker. She had lush red hair and carefully made-up green eyes, a tiny nose and a tall, slim physique. Her legs weren't as shapely as Jill's, but then, she didn't seem like the sort of woman who would ride a bicycle on weekends.

Griffin sighed. Only three days had elapsed since he'd last seen Jill, yet he was becoming progressively more obsessed with her. Considered objectively, Maureen Krieger's legs were just as attractive as Jill's—for that matter, her nose was vastly superior—but Griffin had lost all objectivity.

Damn, but he missed her. He missed her spirit, her spunk, her stubbornness, her luminous brown eyes and her tawny braid and her disproportionately long nose. He missed her buoyant laughter and her doggedness and her innocently quizzical expression when she'd asked Griffin if he happened to know what a jack-in-the-box number was.

He tried to remain confident about the odds that he and Jill would get together eventually. In the meantime, he was attempting to sublimate his yearnings through basketball. Last night, during his regular weekly game at the Y, he'd played frenetically—and poorly. After he'd missed the fourth easy lay-up in a row, one of his teammates had asked him if he was getting enough sleep. The truth was, he hadn't slept well in days. Three days, to be precise.

Frustrated and restless, he'd gone home after the game, noticed that Ivy's kitchen light was on and banged on her back door, sorely in need of sympathy and reassurance that he'd done the right thing in putting his relationship with Jill on hold. Ivy had been home and awake but not alone. She'd introduced her guest as Bob Calabria, the assistant professor from Brown University. Bob was a short dark-haired man who, not surprisingly, bore an uncanny resemblance to Al Pacino.

"Come on in," Ivy insisted when Griffin, reluctant to interrupt what was apparently a romantic get-together, had excused himself and started to leave. "Really. You look like hell, Griff. Please come in."

Bob Calabria eyed Griffin dubiously through the open doorway. "Excuse me, Ivy," he said imperiously, "but if you and this gentleman wish to spend the remainder of the evening together, perhaps I ought to leave."

"You don't have to leave," Ivy assured Bob.

"That's not your decision to make." He lifted his jacket from the back of a kitchen chair, slipped it on and started toward the door.

"*I'll* leave," Griffin whispered to Ivy.

She clamped her hand around Griffin's arm to stop him. "You will not. Bob, you're acting like a baby," she scolded her date.

"I'm acting with courtesy," he countered. "If you wish to visit with this other gentleman—" he craned his neck and glowered up at Griffin "—I will do you the favor of making myself scarce. You know where to reach me."

Griffin and Ivy watched Bob stalk out the door, off the porch and across the yard to his BMW, which was parked in Ivy's driveway. He started the engine, shot Ivy a farewell scowl and then backed out of sight around the side of the house.

"You didn't have to do that," Griffin said as he followed Ivy back into the kitchen. Belatedly he straightened out his sweatshirt and shoved his sweaty hair back from his forehead.

Ivy handed him a beer. "Forget it. He wasn't going to spend the night anyway."

"How come?"

"Don't be so nosy," she snapped, then took a beer for herself and wrenched off the cap. "Because Jamie doesn't like him, that's why," she answered, slumping at the table and issuing a groan.

"Why doesn't Jamie like him?" Griffin asked, more than willing to forget his own problems and concentrate on Ivy's.

"Jamie says Bob is too moody—which he is," she acknowledged. "That's part of his appeal, if you ask me. He keeps me on my toes. I never know what to expect. He isn't boring."

"Did you explain that to Jamie?" Griffin asked.

Ivy groaned again. "More or less. Jamie said he also doesn't like Bob because he talks like a professor."

"He *is* a professor," Griffin noted.

"Yeah, but sometimes he talks like one. He uses words like *antithetical* and *repute*. Jamie thinks he's a snob."

First impressions could be misleading, but Griffin sensed something snobbish about Bob Calabria, too. The guy drove a BMW, after all.

Ivy looked so glum, though, that Griffin couldn't very well give voice to that observation. "Look, Ivy," he said gently. "I'm not a dad, so maybe I'm way out of line here, but you can't let Jamie dominate you. If you want to date the man, date him. If Jamie doesn't like it, tell him to keep his opinions to himself. Or send him over to me."

"Right," Ivy grunted. "You're never around to send Jamie to. Tonight you were playing basketball."

"Give me advance warning and I'll let you know what my schedule is."

Ivy glanced up hopefully. "You free tomorrow night?"

Griffin shook his head. "I'm flying to Buffalo tomorrow. That's where Wynan lived before he came to Providence. I've got some investigating to do there."

Ivy nodded and took a sip of her beer. "How's that story coming, anyway?"

"All right," Griffin said. Thinking about the story brought his attention back to his own difficulties, and he sighed.

"So what's bothering you?"

"Jill."

"Figure it out," she muttered. "Jamie thought she was a fox."

"He did?" Griffin smiled slightly. "The kid's got taste."

"The kid is much too young to be noticing women that way," Ivy argued. "So what's going on with Jill?"

"We've agreed to stay away from each other for a while," he explained. "It was my idea. The way we're competing on this story, it seemed like a reasonable thing to do."

"That doesn't seem like such a big problem," Ivy remarked. "It's not as if she hates you or anything. All you've got to do is finish up the story quickly and you'll be back on track with her."

"I'm trying to finish it up," Griffin claimed. "I'm hoping this trip to Buffalo will open up some leads. Maybe everything'll fall into place and I'll be able to write the thing up." He took a long drink of beer, set the bottle down with a thud and swore. "The catch is, if I get the story into print before Jill does, she might never forgive me."

"I thought one of the things you liked about her was that she understood what it meant to be a reporter," Ivy reminded him. "Part of what it means is trying to get a story into print before anybody else does. Won't she understand that?''

"Sure, she'll understand," Griffin conceded. "She won't forgive me, though."

"Have a little faith in her. I'll bet she misses you as much as you miss her."

"You really think so?" Griffin eyed Ivy hopefully.

"Yeah, I really think so. Now quit moping and drink your beer."

Griffin dragged his thoughts back to the present and focused on Maureen Krieger, who was tapping her manicured fingertips together and awaiting further questions. "You say word came down not to prosecute Wynan," he noted. "Came down from where?"

"That's still a mystery," Maureen admitted. "Somewhere high up, I believe. Wynan was a petty bust, you know? Pimps are no big deal around here. I'd like to see them off the street, but it wasn't a significant case one way or the other. If someone had given me a valid reason to drop the charges, I wouldn't have balked about it. Nobody ever gave me a reason, though. They just said, 'Do it.'''

"What's your theory?"

She shrugged. "The obvious one—Wynan had the goods on somebody."

"What kind of goods?" Griffin pressed her.

She leaned forward, affording him a whiff of her perfume and an improved view of her dainty chin and the slender gold chain circling her throat. "According to one of his call girls, he had photographs of a heavy hitter from the mayor's inner circle in what is euphemistically called a compromising position."

"Do you know who the heavy hitter is?"

Maureen gave her head a small shake. "The woman mentioned a name, but I never saw the evidence and we never brought charges. I really can't give you that information."

"I understand," Griffin said.

"According to the woman, Wynan would hide in a closet with his camera and then jump out and start taking photos at the crucial moment. He'd just spring out into the hotel room like a jack-in-the-box."

"Right." Griffin grinned, suddenly enlightened. Now, at last, he knew what a jack-in-the-box number was. He could confirm for Jill that, yes, it entailed three people, although not in the way she envisioned.

No, he couldn't tell Jill that. He couldn't tell her anything. To tell her would be to reveal important facts about the story, facts she would never be able to get on her own.

He forced all thoughts of Jill back into deep storage. "What about his girls?" he asked Maureen. "Are they still doing business with heavy hitters from the mayor's inner circle?"

"If they are, I don't know about it. I kind of doubt it, though. Wynan went out of his way to cultivate an elite clientele. As far as I know, none of the other pimps around town specialize in that sort of business."

"It seems to me," Griffin hazarded, "that Wynan might have done much better for himself if he'd kept a low profile and dealt only as a pimp instead of trying to blackmail his customers. A satisfied customer would come back again and again, and Wynan would make more money in the long run."

"You're thinking smart, Mr. Parker," Maureen remarked. "Wynan was a jerk. He didn't care about the long run. He just wanted a lot of money, fast."

"Well." Griffin closed his notepad and tucked it into an inner pocket of his jacket. "I appreciate your taking the time to talk to me."

"Have you got to run off? It's—" she twisted her slender wrist to read her watch "—four-fifteen, and I'm ready to call it a day. Maybe we could go out for a drink or something before you return to Providence."

"Thanks, but I'll have to pass," Griffin said, suffering only the tiniest measure of regret. What he regretted, he realized, wasn't having to turn down Maureen's invitation but the fact that he'd lost interest in having a drink with a strikingly pretty woman like her. It was ghastly being so taken with a woman you were avoiding that you didn't even want to distract yourself with someone else. Ghastly, and possibly insane.

"Plane to catch?" Maureen asked.

"I'm afraid so." Griffin stood, and she did, too. They shook hands across her desk and she walked him as far as the door leading out of her office. "I'll be in touch if I've got any more questions," he told her.

"Good luck with your story, Mr. Parker."

It was sleeting when he reaching the street. Griffin knew that Buffalo was right in the heart of the snow-belt, but he hadn't expected to encounter sleet in mid-October. Buffalo clearly hadn't expected it, either; the trees still held most of their brightly colored leaves, and late-blooming flowers wilted beneath the frozen deluge. Turning up his collar, Griffin hurried through the parking lot to his rental car.

The trip had been worth it, he decided once the heater kicked in and he thawed out enough to think. He wished he could have learned the name of the mayor's crony who'd been captured on film by Wynan, not because he wanted to destroy that man's career but because he would have liked to talk to him, to find out what Wynan's modus operandi had been. It would have added power and credibility to Griffin's story if he could have written, "Not only has Wynan been approaching city and state officials in Providence, but previously, in Buffalo, he approached so-and-so and blackmailed him."

Soon, he promised himself. He no longer wanted to wait until Wynan reeled in a fish bigger than Walter Costigan or George Van Deen. Griffin just wanted to publish what he had and get on with his life—especially his love life.

Despite the sleet, the roads weren't slick. He made it to the airport without much trouble, turned in his rental car and hurried into the terminal, figuring he'd grab a sandwich while he waited to board.

What he hadn't counted on when he arrived at the gate for his flight fifteen minutes later with a cellophane-wrapped ham and cheese on a hard roll was to find Jill waiting to board the same plane.

She was standing by the wall of broad floor-to-ceiling windows that looked out onto the tarmac; her back was to Griffin as he handed an airline attendant his ticket and confirmed the information on his boarding pass. Jill was wearing her pretty peach-colored suit again, the suit she'd had on at the press conference, the first time Griffin had seen her legs. Not one to waste an opportunity, he checked them out again, admiring the firm curves of her calves and the delicate bones of her ankles and visualizing her thighs beneath the A-line flare of her skirt. The image made him groan softly.

The airline attendant returned his boarding pass, and he took a couple of deep breaths to clear from his mind all speculation regarding Jill's anatomy. He knew there could be only one explanation for her presence at the airport: she'd followed the Wynan story to Buffalo, too. For all Griffin knew, she might have spoken to Maureen Krieger earlier that day. Or she might have spoken to Captain Albrecht at the precinct house, as Griffin had. Or she might have spoken to the member of the mayor's inner circle who had been eternally preserved on film fooling around with one of Wynan's hookers.

Jill might be ahead of Griffin on the story, damn her.

He walked across the enclosed sitting area to her. She didn't turn until he was only a few feet away, and when she saw him she let out a little shriek.

"We can't go on meeting like this," Griffin commented wryly.

She gave him a bashful smile, which quickly faded as she glanced toward the window again. Griffin noticed that her complexion appeared unnaturally pale and that she'd bitten off most of her lipstick.

"Rough day?" he asked.

"Griffin, I—" She spun back to him, blinking back tears and struggling to shape a feeble smile. "No. It's been a productive day, actually."

"Then why do you look like you're ready to pass out?"

She closed her eyes and shook her head. "You'll laugh at me."

"Never."

"I'm scared," she confessed, opening her eyes and grimacing at the scene beyond the window. Her fingers flexed at her sides. "It's so icy out there, Griff. I hate flying in bad weather. The plane's wings are going to get ice on them, and the runway's going to be slippery, and..." A strange sound that could have passed for a sob fell from her lips, and she turned away, obviously embarrassed.

He was astonished. Feisty Jill Bergland, who could unleash a barrage of potentially humiliating questions at the Granby mayor's press conference and who had no hesitation about doing a stakeout even though she lacked the experience, was afraid to fly. In his wildest dreams, Griffin would never have pictured Jill dissolving into tears or admitting fear. She was so tough, so competitive, he could scarcely believe that she was actually allowing him to glimpse her weakness.

The realization that she had blew him away.

He touched her. When she didn't flinch or shrug him off, he cupped his hand over her shoulder and eased her around to face him. Then he closed his arms around her and hugged her. "Nothing's going to happen to the plane."

"It's sleeting out there, Griffin," she whispered, her words muffled by the soft corduroy of his jacket as he cushioned her head against his shoulder. "We could skid off the runway—"

"We're not going to skid off the runway," he promised, even though he had no basis for issuing such a guarantee.

"I can just barely tolerate flying in good weather," she went on, her nervousness causing her to babble. "But this—it's so gloomy out. All those dark clouds—and it's October, for crying out loud. It's practically a blizzard out there, and it's only October!"

"It's not a blizzard," he murmured, kissing the crown of her head. "Don't be scared. If you want, I'll see if I can switch my seat and sit next to you, and you can clutch my hand for the whole flight."

"Even when we change planes in La Guardia?" she asked, leaning back and lifting her face to him.

A few tears had escaped her eyes and skittered down her cheeks. Griffin wasn't the sort of man who needed to play the role of savior with a woman, but he secretly enjoyed thinking of Jill as a damsel in distress and himself as her rescuer. "Let me go see if I can switch my seat," he said, dropping another light kiss onto her brow. "You wait here—and for God's sake, don't look out the window if it's going to make you so miserable."

Not surprisingly, she was looking out the window when he returned to her ten minutes later, after successfully trading his seat with the passenger assigned to sit next to Jill. "The rain's letting up," he fibbed, steering her away from the window and leading her to a chair.

"It's not rain, it's sleet," she said, "and it's coming down harder."

"Here." Griffin ignored her agitation. "Split this sandwich with me." He unwrapped it and did his best to tear it in half.

Jill eyed the sandwich doubtfully, then shook her head. "I had a big lunch," she said. "I'm really not hungry."

"A big lunch, huh." Griffin took a bite and sized her up. Whom had she had lunch with? Someone from the mayor's inner circle? Someone from the police department?

No, he wouldn't ask. Bad enough he and Jill were together. He wasn't going to make matters worse by talking shop.

"I've missed you," he said instead.

She lowered her eyes to her hands, which remained balled into fists in her lap. "I've missed you, too."

The roll was stale and the ham rubbery. Griffin tossed the remains into the nearest trash can and returned to Jill's side. He gathered her hands in his and tried to rub the clamminess out of them. "You wanna make out for a while?" he asked, grinning lecherously.

Jill laughed in spite of herself. "I'd love to," she said. "It could be the last desperate act of a doomed woman."

"The plane isn't going to crash," Griffin declared firmly—and a bit too loudly. A woman seated not far from him gave him a look of sheer terror.

"On the slim chance that you're right," Jill murmured, allowing her fingers to relax within the warm enclosure of his hands, "maybe we ought to hold off on making out until we've finished our Wynan stories."

Griffin swore under his breath. "Yeah," he said, all playfulness gone. "It was my stupid rule. I guess I've got to live by it."

"It wasn't a stupid rule," Jill assured him. "It was a very smart rule. It's thanks to that rule that I've really busted my butt on this story."

"Wonderful. Glad I could be of assistance," Griffin muttered sarcastically.

Jill linked her fingers through his. "How long have you been in Buffalo?"

"Since this morning," he told her. "Do you think I'd give up my weekly Wednesday-night basketball game just to chase some crummy two-bit story to Buffalo?"

"I got here this morning, too," said Jill. "I flew out of Providence on the 6:40 Business Express. I wanted to come last night so I could get an earlier start this morning, but Doug wouldn't let me."

"Why?"

Jill made a face. "The *Record* budget is too tight to cover hotel bills. I'm supposed to be grateful that they'll reimburse me for my plane ticket."

"What an outfit," Griffin said with a disdainful sniff. "You ought to work for someone bigger, someone who can finance investigative trips."

"Like who? The *Journal*?"

"For example."

"No, thanks," Jill snorted. "By the time I publish my story, the *Record*'s going to be more famous than the *Journal*."

"And Mallory'll still be nickel and diming you over expenses." Griffin felt both irked and thrilled that her combative spirit had returned. He was glad she was no longer weeping over her imminent demise on the airplane, but he didn't want to start bickering with her over which one of them worked for the better newspaper.

The airline attendant who'd checked them in announced that their flight was ready for boarding. Jill instantly became edgy, the color draining from her cheeks and her fingers trembling against his. "Relax," he whispered, helping her to her feet and walking with her to the connector.

"If I die," she whispered back, "contact my parents for me, okay?"

"Ellington, Indiana. I'll get in touch with them." He humored her.

"I haven't got much of an estate."

"Don't sweat it."

"You can have my bicycle," she offered, tossing him a nervous smile.

He laughed. "Forget it, Jill. What would I do with a girl's bike?"

She shot him an intense look, one part dread and two parts gratitude. "I'm really glad you're here, Griff."

"I'm glad you're here, too." He squeezed her hand.

Shaping a heartbreaking smile, she preceded him onto the plane.

WHEN SHE'D FIRST turned around to discover him behind her in the waiting area by the gate, Jill's immediate reaction had been that the coincidence of their having traveled to Buffalo on the same day was too huge to swallow. But the more she thought about it, the more sense it made. She'd had to come on a Thursday on the chance that she would gather enough material to be able to write something up for the Friday edition of the *Record*. And apparently Griffin had had to come to Buffalo on a Thursday so he wouldn't miss his weekly basketball game.

Besides, they had both probably reached pretty much the same point in their investigations. Of course, Jill was in possession of data Griffin couldn't possibly have regarding the unauthorized withdrawals of money from the Granby city coffers—but he was undoubtedly in possession of information she didn't have. They were both close, but not close enough. It made sense that two equally intelligent reporters would fly to Buffalo at the same time on the trail of their elusive quarry.

She refused to take Griffin's presence as an omen that her investigation was losing ground. She'd started out way behind Griffin, after all, and if she was close to having caught up with him, she was doing well.

Anyway, she didn't want to think about work. If she thought about it, she would feel guilty for sitting beside Griffin, for being so elated by his unexpected company. They hadn't deliberately broken their rule. Powers beyond their control had brought them together, and Jill wasn't foolish enough to resist fate.

As the plane began to taxi away from the terminal, a flight attendant moved up the aisle, inspecting the passengers to make sure their seat belts were fastened. When she arrived at Jill's row, Jill asked, "Excuse me—are the wings going to be deiced before takeoff?"

The flight attendant grinned. "It's forty degrees out."

"But it's sleeting!"

"It's colder in the clouds than down here," the flight attendant explained. "The ice is melting as soon as it hits the ground. Now, don't you worry about a thing."

Unpersuaded, Jill waited for the flight attendant to move on and then grumbled, "She's paid to say that. What's she going to say, 'Start worrying—we may not make it'?"

Griffin laughed and gathered her hands in his again. "She's paid to keep passengers like you from freaking out."

The flight attendant began a monotonous recitation of the plane's emergency procedures. Jill closed her eyes and mouthed a silent prayer. If she could take solace in anything, it was that she was going to spend her last moments alive with Griffin.

Somehow, that was an amazingly comforting thought.

"We're about to take off now," Griffin warned her, his lips close to her ear. She opened her eyes and found him leaning toward her, watching her. "Do you want to be distracted?"

She gazed into his eyes. They radiated life and warmth and hope. "If it's a pleasant distraction."

He lifted one of his hands to her cheek and held her face still. Then he bowed to kiss her. His lips were firm, moving with confidence over hers, brooking no resistance.

As if Jill would want to resist. Her mouth eagerly accepted him, opened to him, absorbed him. Her hand covered his, molding it to her cheek. In the distance she heard the roar of the engines being throttled to their maximum speed, and then she felt the abrupt lurch of the plane beginning its sprint down the runway. Griffin's response to the impending takeoff was to intensify his kiss, running his thumb to the tip of her chin and tilting her head so he could slide his tongue deeper.

Closing her eyes, she let the kiss overtake her. Her lips nibbled his, her tongue danced with his, her breath mingled with his. Her head sank into the cloth upholstery of the seat back, and Griffin drew her toward him, lifting his hand to the nape of her neck and caressing the skin beneath her braid. His other hand remained folded around her icy fingers in her lap, and she relished the light pressure across her knees. There was nothing overtly sexual about it. Yet she was keenly aware of the weight of his forearm, the bones of his wrist and the ridge of his knuckles on her thigh, separated from her skin by only a few layers of fabric. Without thinking, she crossed one leg over the other and came close to trapping his hand between her thighs.

Griffin sighed unevenly and shifted his lips a fraction of an inch from hers. "I think we're flying," he whispered.

"Definitely," she agreed in a throaty voice.

His hand moved in her lap, edging upward along her leg. Realizing where he was headed, she moaned softly and gripped his wrist, entertaining the vague thought of stopping him. "We're on an airplane," she reminded him, her tone still rasping.

"That's our excuse for breaking the rules, anyway,"
he said, though he reluctantly let his hand drift back
down to her knees. "I saw a movie once," he continued, "where the heroine dragged a guy into an airplane
lavatory and made love to him there."

"What movie was that?"

"I don't remember. It was a lousy movie. The lavatory scene was the only interesting thing about it."

"I imagine it would be interesting," Jill granted.
"Those rooms are so tiny."

"The actors remained more or less vertical throughout."

"They'd have to."

Griffin smiled. He kept his head close to hers, resting
in the narrow space between the two seat backs, his face
only a couple of inches from hers. She gazed into his
eyes. They were bright with amusement—and desire.

"I don't want to go into the lavatory with you," Jill
declared, as much to herself as to Griffin.

"I don't blame you. I'm no acrobat. Oh, by the
way—" He cut himself off. "Never mind."

"What?"

He settled back in his own seat and lifted his hand
from her knee. Her lap experienced a precipitous drop
in temperature, and while Jill knew that was for the best,
she couldn't shake the disappointment she felt at Griffin's decision to behave himself.

He considered his words, then said, "I think I've figured out what the jack-in-the-box number is."

"Really?" Making love on an airplane would be an
affront to decorum, Jill reasoned, but talking dirty
might serve as an acceptable substitute. "Tell me! I'm all
ears."

Griffin gazed past her out the window and she turned to see that the plane was climbing through a puffy gray mass of clouds. Soon they would be above the storm, and she'd feel completely safe, no longer in need of distraction.

Until landing time, she remembered optimistically. Lots of planes crashed during landings. She'd surely need some of Griffin's unique brand of distraction when the plane approached La Guardia. And again when the plane from La Guardia to Providence took off, and again when it landed. She'd need lots and lots of distraction.

"It has to do with the story," Griffin warned her.

"The story? Oh, you mean the Wynan story." She shoved her fantasies to a remote corner of her mind and sat up straighter in her seat. "The Wynan story," she repeated. "We're not going to discuss that, are we?"

"I'm not sure," Griffin said cautiously.

She studied him for several long minutes. He appeared hesitant, a bit on edge. Perhaps he was aware that he was running the risk of breaking the rule, and he was trying to decide whether he should. Jill's instinct was to encourage him—but if he told her what he knew, she'd have to reciprocate. She'd have to tell him about her meeting that morning with Wynan's former landlady, who had put her in touch with a woman she had thought was his old sweetheart but who, in fact, turned out to be a prostitute who'd worked for him. Jill would have to tell Griffin about the hours she'd spent interviewing this fascinating woman, learning about Wynan's talent for securing the business of powerful men and his taking pictures of said men in flagrante delicto. It was all very kinky and bizarre—but it had the makings of a great story, if she could find a way to link Mayor Van Deen and Wynan to the thousands of dollars missing from the Granby treasury.

Did Jill really want to tell Griffin all that?

"What I'm thinking," Griffin continued, reflecting on each word he uttered and then assessing Jill's reaction to it, "is that if we pooled our knowledge, we could both finish this story a hell of a lot faster—and then we could get back to *us*."

Us. Never had such a little word had such an enormous impact on Jill. She wanted to think of herself and Griffin as *us*. And he wanted to be part of an *us* with her. If only she would tell him what she knew.

"Wouldn't that be unethical?" she posed.

Griffin inhaled and turned away. "Probably. Forget I mentioned it."

"I'm not going to forget you mentioned it. You *did* mention it."

"Not because I want to be unethical," he snapped, suddenly short-tempered. "I suggested it only because I'm going nuts keeping my distance from you. I want you, Jill. I want us to be together, and I don't see us working it out unless we can get Wynan off our backs."

Jill was flattered that Griffin desired her enough to toss aside his professional integrity. More than flattered, she was tempted by his suggestion. She agreed with him that as long as the story stood between them they'd never be able to forge a relationship.

"Griffin..." She sighed and took his hand. She ran her fingers the length of his, stroking his thumb, the bones shaping the back of his hand, the few dark hairs visible below the cuff of his sweater. "I wish I could say yes. I wish we could put together everything we've got and come up with two matching stories. But I can't. I've worked too hard for this one. It's the first time I've gotten to do my own story from beginning to end, with the promise of my name printed above it. I can't give it away—not even to you."

"Okay." He permitted himself a reluctant smile. "You're right, Jill—I know you're right. You're just making me a little crazy, that's all."

Not wishing to drive him further into dementia, she stopped caressing his hand. He twisted it around to hold hers, lacing his fingers through hers and this time opting for safety by letting their intertwined hands lie on the armrest.

"Of course, you *could* tell me what a jack-in-the-box number is," she said playfully.

Griffin's smile expanded. "What's it worth to you?"

Refusing to rise to his goading, she said, "I've already figured out that the jack-in-the-box number isn't what I originally thought. Wynan doesn't participate in the sex itself, so it can't be what I thought it was."

"What did you think it was?"

He was teasing her; she could tell by the smoky glow in his eyes and by his roguish grin. "You can imagine," she mumbled. "Something involving three unclothed people. I think Wynan kept his pants on at all times. As a matter of fact, from what I gather, he's kind of asexual." This Jill had deduced from comments made by the prostitute she'd spent the day with. Although Jill had derived most of her knowledge of pimps from sensational cop shows on television, she had assumed that they frequently engaged in sex with their prostitutes.

Not Wynan, according to the woman Jill had met in Buffalo. "He never touched any of us," she'd informed Jill. "The only thing that turned Alvin on was money."

Griffin appeared astonished by Jill's willingness to share that scrap of information with him. It wasn't worth much, but Griffin was impressed enough by it to say, "This is just a guess, but jack-in-the-box has something to do with Wynan's jumping out of a closet."

"And surprising the client," Jill concluded, nodding at the reasonability of Griffin's theory. "Of course. His lady at the Biltmore on Monday wanted to know beforehand whether he was going to jump out of the closet."

"You know that, then," Griffin concluded, eyeing her thoughtfully.

"I know what?" she asked, equally wary.

"That he takes pictures?"

"Yes."

They both subsided in their seats. Jill reminded herself that she and Griffin hadn't really shared any new information. All they'd done was to discover that they both already knew certain things.

But she still felt exhausted by the exchange, drained yet nervous. She had never talked this openly with a competitor before. She had never taken such a chance with a story.

The flight attendant stopped at their row and asked if either of them wanted a drink. They both declined. Once they were alone again, Jill glanced at Griffin. "Now what?" she said. "Now that we've pushed each other over the line, what do we do?"

"I guess we retreat to the right side of the line before we can do any serious damage."

"Are you going to tell your editor you saw me today?"

Griffin turned in his seat to face Jill. "Not unless she applies thumbscrews. How about you? Are you going to tell Mallory?"

"I don't think so."

"You and he are closer friends than I am with Jeanine," Griffin noted.

"If I told Doug that I saw you, he'd ask one of two things: whether I was able to squeeze anything from you or whether you were able to squeeze anything from me."

"You'd be able to answer no to both questions."

"Maybe. And then he'd ask me whether we were seeing each other, and I'd answer that we weren't, and he'd ask why not, and that would be one too many questions." Jill sighed disconsolately. "Doug and I *are* close friends. Unfortunately, that means we wind up asking each other too much too often. I don't know how to explain to Doug what you and I are doing, Griff. I don't even know how to explain it to myself."

"Neither do I. And that bothers me, Jill. It bothers me a lot."

They fell silent, their hands clasped on the armrest, their gazes darting here and there, out through the window at the darkening sky, down the aisle of the cabin, straight ahead to the patterned weave of the seat upholstery and the textured plastic of their tray tables. Occasionally their eyes accidentally met, and when they did, Griffin's hand would tighten on hers.

His expression was so pensive, so deeply troubled. Would it really be such a terrible breach of ethics for them to reveal the contents of their notepads to each other? Would it really make such a huge difference if the *Journal* and the *Record* ran the story the same day?

Yes, it would, she answered herself sternly. This was what newspaper work was all about—being first, getting an exclusive, beating the competition. Her career was at stake, her byline and her reputation. That she could even consider risking so much for Griffin indicated how much he meant to her.

And there was always the possibility—not that she gave it one ounce of credence, of course—but there was always the possibility that she would divulge more than he would, that he'd get what he was after and give her little of value in return. There was always the chance—God help her for even considering it—that Griffin's sole motivation in laying all that sweet talk on Jill was to scoop her.

"I do trust you," she said out loud. She hadn't meant to verbalize her thoughts, but she needed to hear those words, to make sure in her heart that they were true. "I do trust you, Griffin."

And yet if she trusted him completely and unconditionally, she wouldn't have to say so.

The flicker of anguish in Griffin's eyes at the sound of her declaration told her he knew that as well as she did. He knew she didn't trust him enough.

Chapter Eight

"There's a call for you on line one," Miriam said as Jill entered the office Friday morning, carrying a box of doughnuts. It hadn't been Jill's turn to buy doughnuts, but she'd volunteered. Within minutes of arriving at work, she had wanted to escape. She was hoping a brisk walk in the crisp October morning would soothe her frazzled nerves.

She and Griffin had remained together for the duration of the flight Thursday evening, speaking only about inconsequential things if they spoke at all. When the plane finally touched down at the municipal airport serving Providence, Griffin had walked Jill to her car and kissed her goodbye. As on the airplane, his kiss had been almost unbearably sensual, easily emptying her mind of fear, misgivings, skepticism. She had wrapped her arms around him and returned his kiss with a hunger that bordered on desperation.

Then, just as she'd been about to beg him to come home with her, he had pulled away, taken a step backward and wished her luck with her story. He'd walked away, moving in purposeful strides to his own car, climbing in and driving off, leaving her trembling and desolate.

When she had arrived at the office Friday morning, Doug had practically catapulted out of his office to intercept her. "How'd it go?" he asked, hounding her to her desk. "How was Buffalo? What happened? Are you going to write something for today's edition?"

"The trip went well," she reported dully. "I don't want to write it up, though—not until I can prove that the mayor's being blackmailed."

"Blackmailed!"

"And using city funds to pay off the blackmailer," Jill added in a dreary monotone.

Disregarding her gloomy mood, Doug gathered her into an exuberant bear hug. "Is that really what we're dealing with here? If it is..." His eyes glowed with undisguised glee. "Blackmail, Jill! We're going to sell newspapers from here to Bangor. We're going to quadruple our subscriptions, make tons of money, increase our publication schedule..."

"Let me come up with incontrovertible proof." Her rational words silenced him. "When I've got proof, Doug, we'll run the story."

"When are you going to have proof?" he demanded. Jill could almost hear the wheels spinning in his head as he calculated the increase in profits he expected a juicy story like Jill's to garner.

"Soon, I hope," she said as a small sigh escaped her. She used to think she wanted to finish the story quickly so she could race back to Griffin's arms as soon as possible, but now she almost dreaded that eventuality. She didn't trust Griffin, and he knew she didn't trust him. If she raced back to him, his arms might not be open to her.

Wishing to avoid further interrogation, she bolted from the office on the pretext of buying doughnuts. She walked down the street to the doughnut shop at a sluggish pace, invited two customers to cut ahead of her in line at the counter and requested an extra honey-dipped doughnut for herself once the clerk had boxed a dozen assorted.

Jill ate her doughnut slowly, thoughtlessly. Eating it didn't cheer her up as she'd hoped it would, but it served its purpose by delaying her return to the office.

She could stall only so long, however. She had a job to do—to keep unwinding the thread of the Wynan story until she reached its end. Hiding in a doughnut shop wasn't going to do her any good.

She was still in the second-floor hallway outside the *Record*'s headquarters when she heard the telephone jangling through the thin walls. Fighting off the urge to turn and flee, she pushed open the door and set the box on Miriam's desk. Miriam told her the call was for her.

For an instant Jill prayed it was Griffin, calling to convince her that no matter what she thought, deep down in her heart she did trust him, and he knew she did. Then she came to her senses and prayed that the caller *wasn't* Griffin. She honestly wasn't ready to deal with him or with her ambivalence about him.

"Who is it?" she asked Miriam, hoping her agitation wasn't obvious.

"She said her name was Glenda Hauser." Miriam opened the box and surveyed its sugary contents with a gluttonous smile.

Experiencing a mixture of disappointment and relief, Jill strode around the partitions to her own desk, sank into her chair and eyed the blinking button on her telephone console. She'd spoken to Jim Valenti's aide the day after they'd met, when Glenda had phoned Jill to inform her that she'd brought the mysterious withdrawals from the city treasury to her boss's attention and that he was looking into the matter. But then Jill had gotten caught up in making plans for her trip to Buffalo, and she hadn't been in touch with Glenda since then.

She pressed the button and lifted the receiver. "Jill Bergland here."

"Jill? It's Glenda Hauser." She spoke in a near whisper. "Jill...something's going on here. I'm quite distressed."

Jill sat up straighter. "What is it? Can you talk?"

"Not now," Glenda mumbled. "I'm scared. There's something very strange going on, and if I tell you about it I'm going to lose my job. I just know I am. But if I don't tell you, then I'll feel as if I'm partly to blame. Someone has to hear about this—it's terrible!"

"You won't lose your job if nobody finds out you're my source," Jill vowed, wondering if it was a promise she'd be able to keep. "Let me meet you, Glenda— someplace where nobody will see us together. All right?"

"I can't leave City Hall now," Glenda said. "I can't just walk out of here. It would be too noticeable."

"How about lunchtime? Nobody would ask questions if you left for lunch."

"All right. But I can't have lunch with you. We can't be seen together. Jim knows you're a reporter, and..." Her voice faded to an anguished moan.

Jim? Jim Valenti, the city treasurer and hand-shaking politico, was involved, too? Jill's spirits rose. The thrill of uncovering a city-wide scandal was almost enough to make her forget, at least temporarily, all her confusion regarding Griffin. "Meet me for lunch at the Granby Motor Lodge."

Glenda made a gagging sound. "That disgusting place? I'd rather be dead."

Jill suppressed a wry laugh. Closing her eyes, she pictured the chic woman she'd met at the treasurer's office on Monday. The Granby Motor Lodge wasn't too disgusting for a grubby, impoverished reporter like Jill, but Glenda Hauser was obviously accustomed to swankier surroundings.

They couldn't go anywhere too swanky, though. If they did, they might run into Mayor Van Deen or Jim Valenti or someone else who knew Glenda. Jill had to propose a place that was secluded that Glenda wouldn't object to. "It's a sunny day out," she remarked. "How about the park by the river?"

"The park is full of downtown workers at lunchtime," Glenda pointed out.

"Sure," Jill explained. "Workers like you. None of your colleagues would find it strange that you'd head there for lunch. Then, when nobody's looking, you can sneak around the mill building on the north end of the park. There's a secluded expanse of grass behind the building, above the riverbank. I'll meet you there at twelve."

"All right," Glenda said. "I'm frightened, Jill. I hope I'm doing the right thing."

"You are," Jill assured her. "I'll see you in a couple of hours."

At eleven forty-five, Jill left her office and walked down Main Street to where it ended in a T-intersection with Riverside Boulevard, the broad road that paralleled the Seekonk River along its shore. She crossed the street, entered the park—which was populated by a few brown baggers enjoying an early lunch—and sauntered along one of the winding paths that led down to the riverbank, beyond the edge of the chain-link fence that separated the park grounds from the mill's property. She crept around the fence and then continued along the grassy embankment, which was sheltered by the eastern wall of the mill.

About a hundred yards from the fenced boundary of the park, she stopped to wait. Below her, the river churned in a frothy pattern, battering the rocks that broke the water's surface near the shore. The mill cast a long shadow over the grass and into the river, and Jill turned up the collar of her blazer to shield her neck from the cool autumn air. She checked her watch: twelve o'clock sharp. Then she glanced south toward the park. No sign of Glenda.

The woman had sounded awfully spooked. Jill wondered what Glenda might have learned that alarmed her so much. She wondered whether Glenda viewed her boss as a mentor, a friend, a coattail to ride to power...or something more. She wondered how seriously Jim Valenti would be implicated by what Glenda had uncovered.

She wondered where the hell Glenda was.

The minutes ticked by. What if Glenda didn't show up at all? What if she'd been caught by Jim Valenti, if she was right at this very moment being given the third degree by Valenti and Mayor Van Deen or being asked to type up a resignation letter for herself?

And then Jill spotted her, picking her way carefully around the fence and across the grass in her high-heel shoes. A stiff breeze gusted up from the river and tore at Glenda's coiffure, mussing it. She hugged her arms around herself as if trying to keep the wind from ripping the patterned wool jacket of her suit off her shoulders.

Jill smiled and waved. Refusing to return her smile, Glenda glanced behind her and darted along the embankment. "I'm sorry I'm late," she whispered, so softly Jill had to strain to hear her over the pulsing rush of the current below. "Jim stopped me to ask a question on my way out, and it would have seemed suspicious if I didn't take the time to answer him."

"That's all right," said Jill.

Glenda peeked past Jill, then glanced behind herself again to ascertain that no one was spying on them. She let out a nervous breath and relaxed her hold on her suit jacket. Unbuttoning it, she pulled out a manila envelope. "I photocopied a few things—not all of it, but I got as much as I could. I thought you might want this."

Jill accepted the envelope and shook out its contents: blurry photocopies of account sheets, the printouts she'd examined at Glenda's office on Tuesday.

"They didn't come out too clearly," Glenda said. "I had to do them on the sly. You'll notice there's another of those uncoded withdrawals on Tuesday's account sheet. All told, the uncoded withdrawals total ten thousand dollars."

Jill scanned the top few pages, then returned them to the envelope. "This is fantastic, Glenda. I'm so glad you were able to do this. What did Jim Valenti have to say about the withdrawals?"

"He told me he was going to meet with the mayor to discuss them," Glenda related, nervously moistening her lips and continuing to glance around; she seemed the epitome of paranoia. "When he got through talking to the mayor, he came into my office and told me that the mayor personally swore that these expenditures were necessary and that I was not to mention them to anybody. He said that if I spoke to you again, I should tell you they were simply a computer error."

"*Are* they a computer error?" She already knew the answer, but as a reporter she felt obliged to ask.

Glenda shook her head. "No. Not a chance. All I know is, I'm not supposed to know about them, but since it's too late for that, I'm not supposed to talk about them."

"But your boss knows what they are," Jill surmised.

"You mustn't go to him about this!" Glenda gasped. "If you do, he'll know I've been talking to you."

Jill nodded. "Would he have a valid reason to cover up the mayor's misdeeds?"

"Oh, yes," Glenda said. "He's got dreams of running for office once the mayor moves on to other things. George Van Deen is a force to be reckoned with in this town. You need him in your corner if you want to run for office. I'm sure that's why Jim is covering for him."

Jill nodded again. She had hoped for something more, something concrete, but she was grateful to Glenda for having risked her job to bring her the photocopies. "I appreciate your insights," she said. "I'm not sure what I can do with these records, but—"

"Wait, there's more," Glenda interrupted, gripping Jill's wrist. She leaned closer, bit her lip and shot another fearful glance behind herself before speaking. "Yesterday afternoon at work, Jim withdrew forty thousand dollars in cash from the city's maintenance budget. I wasn't supposed to know anything about it, of course, but I entered his office by accident and saw the money on his desk, four ten-thousand-dollar stacks. Well, of course I questioned him about it, and he told me the mayor had asked him to withdraw it in order to settle a suit a fired city employee had brought against Granby. The former employee was charging discrimination, and the city didn't want to suffer through a protracted trial, so they were going to settle out of court. He explained to me that one of the terms of the settlement was that the case was not to be discussed publicly.''

Jill's heartbeat quickened. ''Jim didn't happen to tell you who the employee was, did he?''

''There isn't any employee,'' Glenda answered indignantly. ''If there were, number one, the city wouldn't be so secretive about it, and number two, the man wouldn't be paid off in cash. He would be paid, probably over the course of several months or years, in regular bank checks. Jill, this whole series of events is so bizarre. The city is out fifty thousand dollars, and not a single dollar of it has been properly accounted for.''

''I think I'm going to be able to account for it.'' Jill smothered the urge to grin, to shout out loud, to kick her feet in exhilaration. ''Have you got any record of the forty-thousand-dollar withdrawal in here?'' she asked, poking inside the envelope.

Glenda bit her lip and averted her eyes. ''I went back to the office last night, after Jim left, and I sneaked into his office. I found some of the paperwork—not all of it—and I copied whatever I could. Then I put everything back so Jim wouldn't know I'd been through it.''

As Jill gave Glenda her abundant thanks and reassured her that nobody would ever suspect Glenda of being Jill's source, her brain raced ahead, analyzing the information. Fifty thousand dollars was a lot of money to be carrying in cash. Even if Van Deen had already paid Wynan the ten thousand dollars, the forty thousand dollars he'd gotten his hands on that morning was still a hefty sum. No sane person would want to sit on that much cash for long.

Van Deen was going to pay Wynan off soon. Maybe tonight.

"I've got to go," Glenda whispered. "If I'm late getting back from lunch—"

"Yes, you'd better go." Jill surveyed the embankment in the direction of the park. "The coast's clear, Glenda. When you arrive back at your office, keep your cool. Don't act nervous, okay?"

"I'll try not to," Glenda said with an anxious nod.

"And remember—you did the right thing in coming to me," Jill said. "You're a true hero."

"I just hope I don't wind up an unemployed hero."

"If, God forbid, someone fires you, you'll blow the treasurer's office sky-high—and I'll supply the dynamite," Jill promised. "No out-of-court settlements for you. Don't forget—you've got the goods on them. They can't afford to treat you badly."

"I hope you're right." Glenda cast Jill one final frantic look and then trotted on her precariously high heels back over the stretch of scraggly grass to the chain-link fence.

Jill waited two full minutes before following Glenda back into the sunshine of the park. When she arrived, Glenda was nowhere to be seen. As Glenda had done, Jill tucked the envelope inside her blazer and then strolled nonchalantly through the park, back to the *Record*'s headquarters.

Having neglected to eat lunch, Jill helped herself to one of the two remaining doughnuts in the box on Miriam's abandoned desk once she stepped inside the office. She glanced at Doug's office on her way to her desk. He was out.

She pulled the sheets from the envelope and perused their blurry numbers. *Griffin doesn't have this,* she thought, vexed that that was the first thought to enter her mind as she inspected her evidence.

Griffin might not know about the unauthorized withdrawals—but he might know other things Jill didn't know. On the airplane last night, he'd revealed that he knew Wynan was a blackmailer as well as a pimp. He must have been able to figure out that Wynan was prepared to blackmail Mayor Van Deen.

Did he know the blackmail money was in all likelihood going to be paid tonight? If he didn't, Jill would shadow Mayor Van Deen, witness the payoff and get her exclusive. If Griffin did know, they'd both shadow Mayor Van Deen—and probably drive their cars head-on into each other in the process.

She considered telephoning Griffin. She got as far as lifting the receiver, then dropped it back into place. How could she discreetly find out whether he knew? How could she keep herself from melting at the seductive sound of his voice and telling him too much? How could she keep him from laughing at her and admonishing her not to make a fool of herself by attempting another stakeout?

The telephone at her elbow rang. She wheeled her chair backward on its casters far enough to see around the partition. Miriam still hadn't returned from her lunch break.

Drawing in her breath, Jill answered, "Granby *Record*, Jill Bergland speaking."

"Don't tell me they had to fire the receptionist to pay for your airfare to Buffalo," Griffin exclaimed with feigned shock.

"No," Jill said curtly. As troubled as she was by thoughts of Griffin, she didn't need him making fun of her newspaper. "We're so awash in money here at the *Record* that Doug told Miriam to take an extra long lunch break," she parried.

"Why her and not you?" Griffin needled her.

"Did you call me just to give me a hard time?"

Griffin didn't answer. His extended silence caused Jill's tension to build. Should she hint at what she knew about the imminent payoff? Should she come right out and tell him? Should she—

"Do you have any plans for tonight?" he broke into her chaotic thoughts.

She fidgeted with the corkscrew-coiled telephone wire. Could he actually have called to ask her out on a date? After the way they'd kissed last night, a date wouldn't be such a preposterous idea.

Except that they had a deal. Except that they were both operating under certain rules—and those rules precluded the possibility of a date.

Except for the fact that he knew she didn't trust him.

"What did you have in mind?" she asked, hedging.

"What I had in mind," Griffin replied dryly, "was a simple answer. Do you have any plans for tonight? Yes or no?"

"Yes."

He paused before continuing. "Dinner and dancing with a lucky guy?"

"None of your business."

He fell silent again. She listened to him breathing on the other end, calmly and evenly. She resented him for being so composed when she felt ready to fly apart. "I want to know whether it's my business or not," he said.

"I just told you—"

"Jill." He obviously wasn't going to let her take control of the discussion—as if there were a chance in hell that she could. "Are you going to be home tonight? Yes or no?"

"Do you conduct your interviews this way?" she retorted. "Because if you do—"

"Yes or no, Jill?"

It suddenly dawned on her that he was sounding her out. He was trying to find out if she was aware the payoff was going to occur tonight. "No," she said, abruptly calming down, too. It was easy to stop panicking once she knew what he was doing, once she understood that she couldn't tell him anything about Wynan and Van Deen that he hadn't already figured out on his own.

"You're going out?"

"Yes."

"Alone?"

"Yes."

There was another lengthy pause, the sound of more even breathing. Finally he said, "Two cars is one too many."

"I agree," Jill said brightly. "You stay home."

"I'm not trying to cut you out of anything, Jill," he chided her. "I'm simply saying neither of us can afford to botch this thing up. And if we go in two cars, we're going to wind up looking like the Keystone Kops."

"Especially if we blow whistles and wear funny hats."

"Jill—don't make me regret having called you," he pleaded.

She absorbed his hesitancy, his anxious tone, his inability to laugh at her lighthearted remark. She was chastened by the understanding of how much it had cost him to make this call. It was a call she might have made to him, except that she'd lacked the nerve to do it. Griffin hadn't. He deserved her respect, and her thanks.

"What's your idea?" she asked gently.

"We'll ride together in my car. We won't talk about what we know, what we see or what we're planning to write. I'll bring my camera, you bring yours. All we'll share is transportation.''

Jill considered his proposition. From a practical point of view, it probably made more sense than chasing Van Deen in two cars. And from a selfish point of view, Griffin's company would keep Jill from growing bored during slow moments.

She swiveled in her chair and spotted Doug about to enter his office. His gaze collided with hers and he raised his eyebrows questioningly. Jill turned away. ''What does your editor have to say about this?'' she asked Griffin, cupping her hand around the mouthpiece and lowering her voice so Doug wouldn't be able to eavesdrop.

''I don't have to clear the details with Jeanine,'' Griffin replied. ''She wants photos of the thing going down. All I'm doing is figuring out the best way to guarantee I'll get them. I think the odds are better if we're in one car than if we're in two.''

''And that's acceptable to her?''

''She cares about the punch line, Jill, not the joke that leads up to it.''

Jill wondered whether she could keep the plan a secret from Doug—and, if she couldn't, whether he'd object to it. She wished she had as much autonomy as Griffin. But then, maybe his editor trusted him because he himself was so full of trust, so willing to trust others. He wouldn't have contacted Jill with this scheme if he didn't trust her.

''Griff,'' she murmured, overwhelmed by his faith in her. ''What would you have said if I told you I didn't have plans for tonight?''

He mediated for a moment before admitting, ''I was sure you would say you did.''

"Why? Why were you so sure I would know what was going to happen tonight?"

"You're a good reporter, Jill."

A sweet warmth filled her. How could she not adore this man when he held her in such high esteem? How could she not trust him? How could she hold back when he had given her the ultimate compliment one journalist could give another?

She wanted to tell him that she loved him, right then, on the phone, in the midst of their negotiations. But that would be playing fast and loose with the rules. So instead she said, "How should we work this? Do you want to pick me up at my house, or should I meet you somewhere?"

"I'll pick you up at your house at five-thirty," said Griffin. "Nothing's going to happen before then—according to my source, Wynan's got other plans for the afternoon."

"Five-thirty, then," Jill confirmed, stifling her reflexive curiosity about who Griffin's source was and what Wynan's other plans might be. "I'll be waiting."

Hanging up the phone, she swiveled her chair a hundred and eighty degrees to confront Doug, who was lurking in the open doorway of his office, watching her. "Do fill me in," he said, raking his fingers through his hair and fixing her with one of his pointed stares.

"Next time, why don't you just listen in on your extension?" Jill stormed to his office. Angry though she was by his prying, she knew she'd have to provide him with at least some information concerning her evening's plans, if for no other reason than that she was going to need to get hold of a suitable camera.

Doug stepped aside to let her precede him into his office, then shut the door and circled his desk. He settled himself in his throne, tapped his fingertips together and cued her with a nod that she should begin explaining.

"Van Deen's going to pay Wynan off tonight," she said.

"Fact or hunch?"

"Hunch," she conceded. "But a damned good one. I plan to be there to see it—and take pictures of it."

"That sounds like an enterprising plan."

"One problem—my camera is a Polaroid. Will Polaroid prints be acceptable?"

"For running in the paper? No," Doug answered. "If you really think tonight's the night, Jill, I'll lend you my Nikon."

"A Nikon," Jill repeated, awed. She was not particularly adept at photography, and she tended to be intimidated by expensive cameras with zillions of dials and buttons on them. "Will I be able to figure out how to use it?"

"It's a self-winding automatic-focus model," Doug informed her. "If you can't use it, you belong in kindergarten. The camera happens to be at Karen's house at the moment—she wanted me to take some black and whites of her, just in case we ever need them to run with an engagement announcement in the society pages. It should be loaded with black-and-white film, so you'll be all set."

"What about a flash?" Jill asked. "It's going to be dark out."

"You'll be using high-speed film," Doug explained. "You won't need the flash. The camera's idiot-proof, Jill. Just swing by Karen's house and pick it up on your way home today. I'll call ahead and tell her to expect you."

"Okay." If she could be tough enough to stake out a brazen blackmailer and a corrupt mayor, she could certainly be tough enough to master a Nikon camera.

"Have you got a strategy mapped out?" Doug inquired.

Jill scrutinized him cautiously. How much of her phone conversation had he heard? "Yes," she replied, opting not to say anything more unless Doug asked.

He, too, seemed to be sizing her up. After a minute's deliberation, he angled his head toward the door. "Well, go for it. Try not to be distracted by the thought that the financial future of the *Record* is resting on your shoulders." He winked to let her know he was kidding.

She dutifully laughed, then returned to her desk. Dropping onto the chair, she folded her arms across the keyboard of her word processor and cushioned her head with them. Closing her eyes, she envisioned a front page of the *Record* emblazoned with a double-height headline reading "Mayor Caught in Extortion Plot." Below it would appear a subheadline: "Van Deen Bribed by Providence Pimp." Followed by a crisp photograph of the two.

Followed by: "Story and Photo by Jill Bergland."

Followed, after a few months, by a Pulitzer Prize.

Chapter Nine

She must have been watching for him, because she bounded out the front door of her house before he could turn off the engine. Her blond-streaked hair was braided back, her face was bright with anticipation, and she was clothed all in black—turtleneck, corduroy jeans, a belt, sneakers.

Griffin chuckled. Did she think they were going to be skulking through the shadows, prancing across roof-tops, breaking and entering? Add a face mask to her outfit and she could pass for a Ninja.

Of course, Griffin couldn't deny that her attire did wonders for her body—and his body experienced some wonderful, if totally inappropriate, sensations in response. The soft cotton of her sweater clung to her full firm breasts and then nipped in at her slender waist. Her slacks gave her legs the illusion of being even longer than they were. Griffin imagined the contours of her calves and thighs beneath the cloth—and then put his imagination on hold. He hadn't arranged this collaboration as a prelude to romance.

He'd arranged it because it seemed like the safest way to get the photographs he needed. If he hadn't offered to bring Jill along with him, she might have gone off on her own, half-cocked—and she might have wound up doing something clumsy and alerting Wynan that he was under surveillance.

She was carrying a soft-sided tote bag, and as soon as she climbed into the car beside Griffin she pulled from its depth a camera and a box of film. "I've got to ask a humongous favor of you, Griff," she said without preamble. "Can you load this film for me?"

Griffin gave her a thoughtful perusal. He liked her no-nonsense attitude—and he hoped it would keep him from dwelling on the way her sweater hugged her body. "Can't you load it?" he asked, taking the camera from her and examining it. It was a nearly new, fully accessorized Nikon.

"It isn't mine," she confessed. "It's Doug's. He told me it was already loaded, but when I picked it up at his girlfriend's house, she said she'd used up the roll of film that was in it and she wasn't sure how to load a new roll. If you can't do it, we'll have to go to Doug's house…and I'd rather not do that," she added pointedly.

He easily deduced that Jill hadn't told her editor of her decision to pair up with him on the stakeout. For some reason that pleased him. He wasn't really jealous of her friendship with Doug, but he'd always admired independence—especially in reporters.

Popping open the back of the camera, he nodded. "It looks pretty straightforward," he said, examining the automatic wind mechanism. "Pass me the film."

She opened the box for him, removed the black plastic canister and shook out the film cartridge. Griffin skimmed the print, curious to know how many exposures she'd have, and then slipped the roll in place, hooking the leader onto the sprocketed edge of the spool. Then he snapped the camera shut, pressed the automatic wind to get the film started and handed her the camera.

"As easy as that," Jill said with a sheepish grin.

Griffin returned her grin and reignited the car's engine. He definitely liked her attitude: cheerful, friendly, possibly a bit too enthusiastic—he eyed her black outfit one more time and swallowed a laugh—but too enthusiastic was preferable to not enthusiastic enough. It was going to be a pleasant evening as well as a productive one.

"I think our best bet," he said as he backed out into the street, "is to head for Van Deen's house and tail him."

"Fine," Jill said, fastening her seat belt and balancing her tote bag between her legs on the floor.

She and Griffin didn't talk during the short drive north through the elite neighborhood of Granby to the imposing brick mansion where the Van Deens lived. Griffin cruised past the house once, taking note of the illuminated dining room window and the shadows of family members moving about inside, and then drove around the block and parked at the corner. "I expect he'll leave after dinner," Griffin predicted.

Jill nodded.

Griffin shoved a tape into the cassette deck—an old Rolling Stones album. "Is that all right with you?"

"It's fine." She tossed him a genuine-looking smile.

He unclipped his seat belt and twisted to lift his Minolta and a paper bag from the back seat. "Are you hungry?" he asked. "I brought some munchies."

Jill glanced toward the paper bag. Griffin pulled a jar of dry-roasted peanuts from it, and two chilled cans of soda. "You still owe me a decent dinner," she reminded him.

He gave her a quick, searching glance. What happened to her friendly businesslike attitude? he wondered. If she intended to raise the issue of their relationship tonight, she'd be just as much of a distraction for him as she would have been if she'd been lurking in the bushes armed with the latest edition of the *Enquirer*.

Her smile was enigmatic as she helped herself to one of the sodas. She popped it open and took a sip. "Rock and roll and junk food," she said. "So this is how you keep from getting bored during a stakeout."

"Not always." Griffin shook out a handful of peanuts and tossed them into his mouth. He chewed and swallowed. "In a hotel lobby, you can't. In the privacy of your car, you can."

"Don't you find it boring sometimes?" Jill asked, accepting the jar of peanuts and taking a few. She ate them one at a time, her gaze on the brick house halfway down the block.

"Now, yeah. I didn't use to."

"You've done a lot of this kind of work?"

He nodded and took a swig of soda. "Back when I first started at the *Journal*, I specialized in crime stories. I followed criminals, hung out at crime scenes...the whole routine."

Jill wrinkled her nose. "Ugh. How morbid."

Griffin shot her a swift look. Yes, it had been morbid. That was precisely why he'd done it—*he'd* been morbid in those days.

Jill seemed aware that her comment had struck a nerve. "Did I say something wrong?" she asked.

"No," he told her. "You said something right. It was morbid."

"Why did you do it, then?"

He considered his response. The one time he'd confided in a woman about his need to immerse himself in the grotesque world of crime—when he'd been married to Wendy—she hadn't even come close to understanding. He didn't want to have to learn that Jill couldn't understand him, either.

"I felt I had no choice," he finally answered, pleased that it wasn't a lie.

Jill grimaced. "Rookie reporters have it lousy everywhere," she concluded, misconstruing his remark. "When I was at the *Chicago Tribune*, I volunteered for anything and everything. I'd have even covered gruesome crimes, if only they'd let me. But they wouldn't. They kept saying I had to earn the right to a byline—and sure, I was willing to earn it. After four years I thought I had earned it a hundred times over, but they still wouldn't give me my own stories. Not even sordid ones."

"You wanted the byline, huh."

"I craved it," she said dramatically, then softened her statement with a sour laugh.

"How come? You like to thrive in the limelight?"

"Not really. Not like my brother Nicky."

"He's the Slug?"

"The rock musician," she confirmed. "He'd do just about anything to get attention."

"Like dye his hair blue," Griffin recalled. He tried to picture a male version of Jill with blue hair...and somehow it wasn't as hard to imagine as he might have expected.

"And pierce his ear," Jill added. She ruminated for a minute, her eyes on the Van Deen house and her finger tracing an abstract line through the condensation on the side of her soda can. "Nicky's outrageous," she murmured. "He can pull it off—it fits his personality. I'm not that outrageous, Griff. All I wanted was my name at the top of a well-written article every once in a while. Some small token of proof that I existed."

"Has your existence come under question?" Griffin probed, intrigued.

She looked briefly his way, then smiled sadly. "I was the middle child in a huge family. It's easy to get over-looked when you aren't brilliant like my sister, Cindy, or flamboyant like Nicky, or rugged like Eli—or the old-est, like Craig. I was just there, always just there. I was kind of taken for granted. I was the Bergland kid who delivered the newspapers." She turned to him again. "I didn't want fame or fortune, Griff. All I wanted was that every now and then my name would appear in print so people would say, 'Oh, that's Jill Bergland's story.'"

"By 'people,' I assume we're referring to your fam-ily?"

"But of course, Dr. Freud," Jill said with a snort. "My family, my teachers in school . . . anyone, really."

"Well, that's okay. I mean, whatever motivated you, it pushed you in a good direction. Look at you now."

"Yeah. Having peanuts and Coke for supper. Is the garage opening?"

Griffin focused on the house and saw one of the ga-rage doors sliding upward. He handed Jill his can of soda, turned on the engine and checked his watch. "He didn't spend much time eating dinner," he observed.

"Maybe he's too nervous to eat," said Jill. She groped in her tote bag and pulled out a flat rectangular object sided in artificial mother-of-pearl. It looked a little like a powder compact. Griffin couldn't believe Jill was going to put on makeup at a time like this—and he was right. She pressed a button on the box, and it popped open into miniature binoculars.

"What is that?" Griffin asked as she squinted through the lenses.

"Opera glasses," she told him, handing the object to him.

He peeked through the lenses. They didn't magnify as well as real binoculars, but they enabled him to see that Van Deen was dressed in a suit and that his silver hair was neatly groomed. Griffin took Van Deen's natty appearance as a sign that he didn't plan to go traipsing through the woods with Wynan. That was a relief.

He handed the opera glasses back to Jill. "I don't go to the opera much," he admitted.

"Neither do I. I bought these in Chicago hoping to prove to my editor how committed I was to investigative work. A lot of good it did, too. The only thing I used these for in Chicago was to watch a guy who lived across a courtyard from me while he worked out with weights."

"You were a Peeping Tom!" Griffin erupted into laughter.

"It wasn't as if he were naked," she defended herself. "He used to wear a tank top and shorts. But he was more interesting than what was on television most of the time."

"Jill, there are dimensions to you I've never dreamed of." Still laughing, Griffin shifted into gear and followed Van Deen's Lincoln Town Car down the street, maintaining what he hoped was a safe distance.

"Is that a compliment?" she asked cagily.

"You don't want to know," he replied, just to rib her.

Pursuing Van Deen's car into downtown Granby, he let the conversation lapse. He hadn't expected Van Deen to execute his transaction in the heart of town, not only because it seemed too public but also because Griffin's source, one of the "girls" Ivy worked with, had told him that Wynan preferred to do his blackmailing business—what he called "making collections"—in out-of-the-way places.

Van Deen, however, was heading for Main Street. Specifically, he was heading for City Hall, for the parking space outside the domed building marked Reserved for Mayor. When Van Deen climbed out of his car and unlocked one of the ground-floor side doors leading into the building, Griffin coasted past City Hall, made a U-turn and pulled into a parking space on the street.

"Do you think Wynan's waiting for him in there?" Jill asked.

"No."

"You sound awfully sure of yourself."

Griffin pondered how much he should reveal to her of what his source had told him. Opting for caution, he explained, "Wynan's car isn't here. Besides, the building is locked. Wynan couldn't get in unless Van Deen let him in. I doubt the night janitor would be in on this."

Jill acknowledged the rationality of Griffin's analysis with a slight nod. Indeed, after a few minutes, Van Deen exited the building, crossed the street and entered a liquor store.

"Do you think—"

"No, Jill," Griffin stifled her. "People don't make payoffs in bustling well-lit stores."

"I guess he's just buying some booze to help him get through the night."

"Maybe. Or a peace offering for Wynan."

"Maybe they're going to drink a toast to their profitable association," Jill commented sarcastically.

A few minutes later Van Deen once again emerged, carrying a bottle-shaped paper bag. As soon as his car merged with the flow of traffic, Griffin pulled out of his parking space and followed the Lincoln down Main Street.

"You're good at this," Jill commented.

It wasn't exactly a glowing commendation, but Griffin was nonetheless flattered. He tossed her a smile, then glanced forward in time to see the mayor turning onto Riverside Boulevard, heading south along the river. Van Deen pulled into the gravel lot adjacent to one of the old mill buildings, stopped his car and sat.

"He's going to get drunk," Jill said as Griffin drove past the lot and turned onto a side street.

"Do you blame him?"

"Liquor's no solution," she muttered. "I hope he wakes up with a whopping headache."

"Cruel, cruel," Griffin whispered, loud enough for her to hear.

The neighborhood abutting the mills south of downtown was run-down, with dilapidated old row houses crowded along the sidewalks, their porches lopsided and their minuscule front yards devoid of grass or trees. Griffin turned his car around in a vacant driveway and pointed it back toward Riverside Boulevard and the dirt lot where the mayor had parked his car.

Jill adjusted her opera glasses in order to spy on Van Deen. Griffin used his camera, focusing the zoom lens until he could decipher the mayor's face behind the wheel of his car. Sure enough, he was taking a swig of whatever was in the paper bag.

"Booze and women'll do it to you every time," Jill declared with all the phony fervor of a grade-B country and western ballad.

Griffin grinned and lowered his camera. "Give the guy a break. He's going to sell a bunch of newspapers for you. Show a little compassion."

"Compassion? For a creep like that?" Jill exclaimed, closing her opera glasses.

Griffin thought she was judging the sap a bit too severely. "Hey, where's your professional objectivity?" he teased, causing her to subside.

The evening sky had faded to a deep blue color. A fat harvest moon rode the horizon, resembling a perfectly round peach. Under other circumstances, Griffin would consider this an ideal night for seducing Jill—dark and quiet and laden with the sounds and scents of autumn.

He harbored a vague hope that she was thinking the same thing, that she was as frustrated as he was by the rules they had established. His thoughts were shattered by the appearance of a couple of teenagers swaggering down the street, clad in leather jackets and torn jeans. They looked menacing.

Jill winced at the sight of them. "Oh, God," she moaned, sliding down in her seat. "Are we about to get mugged?"

Griffin discreetly placed his camera and Jill's on the floor by her feet. "In case you haven't noticed, I don't drive a BMW," he pointed out, reminding himself of the car he'd seen parked outside Ivy's house when he'd left to pick Jill up that evening. "We look broke. I think they'll pass us by."

They did, but not before one of the teenagers met Griffin's glowering gaze. The kid returned Griffin's scowl and exaggerated his strutting walk. There was something brutal in the boy's eyes, something mean and vicious, but Griffin fought off the surge of rage that gripped him. After an immeasurable moment, the boys walked on and Griffin felt his heartbeat slow.

"Are you okay?" Jill asked.

He hadn't realized how tightly clenched his fists were until he tried to unfurl them. His fingers were cramped, his knuckles bloodless. He took a deep breath and willed himself to relax. "Yeah," he said in a tired voice. "Couldn't be better."

"You were right," she murmured. "They were nasty looking but harmless."

Griffin nodded and concentrated for a minute on the Lincoln still parked in the unpaved lot across the boulevard. He took another deep breath and forced a smile. "Yes," he said. "They were harmless."

"I would think," Jill said carefully, "that after having done crime stories for so long, you'd be unaffected by that kind of ugliness."

"You're never unaffected by it," he said, as much to himself as to her. "You just learn to control your reaction."

"Tell me about it," Jill said, sliding closer to him on the seat. "Tell me why you did those stories."

The Rolling Stones tape had finished. Griffin considered putting on another tape, then decided not to. He didn't want the distraction the music offered—he needed to think.

His former wife had never asked him to explain. Jill was practically begging him to. Maybe she *would* understand. Maybe she would understand this as well as she understood so much else about Griffin.

He glanced at her. She was gazing at him, her expression earnest and imploring, her chin tilted inquisitively, a pale contrast to the striking black of her sweater's high collar. "You really want to know?" he tested her.

"Yes."

He directed his gaze back to the Lincoln by the mill. "I told you my mother died when I was seven," he began. His peripheral vision captured the motion of Jill's head as she nodded. "Well..." He ran his fingers along the plastic hoop of the steering wheel. "What really happened was, she was murdered."

"Oh, Griff." Jill placed her hand on his, pulling his fingers from the steering wheel and pressing them gently between her palms.

He knew she must be filled with questions—she was a reporter, and reporters always had questions. Yet she waited patiently until he was able to tell her more.

"From what I gather, it was pretty painless," he said. "Some thug tried to rob her while she was shopping, and she refused to hand over her purse. She was stubborn that way, a real fighter. So the thug hit her on the head with something—the police were never quite sure what, but whatever it was, it killed her. Instantly, according to the autopsy."

Jill ran her index finger along the back of his hand, consoling him with her light caress.

"The thing of it was, I was a little kid," he explained. "Everybody wanted to protect me. For years, nobody would tell me the truth about how she'd died. They told me it was an accident. It didn't occur to me to read the newspaper reports, and I was too shocked about losing my mother to ask a lot of questions. But when I got older, I knew I'd been left in the dark, and I finally made my father tell me what had happened."

He was amazed at how easily the words came to him, how receptive Jill was to what he was saying. He looked at her and found her studying him, absorbing everything he said.

"I appreciate the reason why my father hadn't told me the whole truth when it happened," he went on. "But . . . something was missing. I couldn't—I couldn't figure it out. I couldn't figure out why someone would do that to my mother, or how she must have felt while it was happening, or how the survivors were supposed to cope with it. So when I started working as a reporter, I immersed myself in that universe. I just kept asking questions and writing, and asking more and writing more, until I was able to come to terms with it."

"Have you?" she asked in a hushed voice. "Have you come to terms with it?"

He offered her a pensive smile. "Sort of. I guess." He sighed. "I've done the best that I could. The truth is, you *can't* come to terms with it. No matter how much you study it, it's never going to make sense, and it's never going to stop hurting completely."

"Maybe it shouldn't," Jill observed quietly. "A crime like that will never make sense, Griff. And as long as you remember your mother, it will always hurt. But you don't want to stop remembering her."

She understood. Bless her, she did. He slid his hand from between hers, lifted it to her face and bent to kiss her. It wasn't a heated kiss. Yet there was more passion in it, more emotion, more of his heart than any kiss he'd ever given her before.

He'd known, from the moment he'd seen her solving a crossword puzzle over a cup of coffee at the Granby Motor Lodge, that Jill Bergland was special. Now he was beginning to recognize just how special she was.

Astonished, he settled back in his seat and smiled at her. "I used to be obsessed with crime," he allowed. "It was almost perverse. But now . . . I'm becoming obsessed with you."

"And your perversions center on such things as the jack-in-the-box number," she teased. He comprehended that, after everything he'd just shared with her, she needed to make a joke, to lighten the mood. He didn't blame her.

"Speaking of which," he said, noticing that the headlights of the Lincoln were glowing, "we're on the road again." He started his car and steered back onto Riverside Boulevard, heading south, following the two ruby taillights of the mayor's car as he drove off to keep his date with Wynan.

JILL RUMINATED on Griffin's words, sorting through them a few at a time, digesting as much as she could. What he'd told her had been horrifying—and yet the fact that he'd shared his grief and confusion with her moved her as nothing else could have. She knew from the way he'd spoken, from the way he'd avoided her with his gaze, that he wasn't sure he ought to confide in her. And she knew from the way he'd kissed her when he was done unburdening himself that he was glad he had.

How could she not have trusted him? He trusted her not only in their professional dealings—he wouldn't have offered to hook up with her for tonight's venture if he hadn't—but also in the most intimate personal matters. He trusted her implicitly. She felt humbled by his faith in her and ashamed of herself for having ever questioned his motives. She had to return his trust. No other choice existed for her.

She wanted to tell him, to bare her innermost feelings as he'd bared his, but now wasn't the time. Mayor Van Deen's car was traveling across the southern end of town, navigating along the road that eventually narrowed into a country lane near Lincoln State Park. "Where do you think Wynan is?" she asked.

"The Granby Motor Lodge."

She turned sharply to him. He was obviously privy to some specific information. "What if they do their business inside a room there?" she posed, trying to keep her anxiety out of her voice. "We'll never be able to get them on film then."

"It's not going to take place indoors," he said with the same certainty.

She scrutinized him curiously, wondering how he'd found out such details. He must have a damned good source, she thought.

He seemed able to sense the unspoken questions lurking within her. His gaze fixed on the Lincoln's taillights, he said, "Wynan doesn't want to meet Van Deen indoors. He's savvy enough to worry that a public figure might have the room bugged."

Jill waited for more, but Griffin fell silent, as if aware that he shouldn't have revealed even that much. She clamped her mouth shut against the urge to thank him for that juicy bit of information. If she vocalized her thanks, he'd undoubtedly regret having said anything at all.

The garish neon light reading Granby Motor Lodge— Vacancy loomed into view around a bend in the road, and Van Deen steered into the lot. Jill glanced at Griffin. His face remained impassive, not a trace of concern flickering across his features as he turned up the service driveway that led around the rear of the motel's office and restaurant. He braked to a halt at the juncture of the service driveway and the main parking lot.

Van Deen was still in his car, with the engine running. Another car in the lot roared to life—a compact silver sedan. As soon as the driver turned on the lights, Jill was able to read the license plate: Buck.

"Rendezvous point," Griffin mumbled, half to himself.

Jill nodded, impressed by his skill at following a culprit, reading the scene, knowing the score and maintaining his equilibrium. Until this evening, she hadn't realized what an amateur she was at surveillance. Clearly, all those years of obsessive crime coverage had taught Griffin some valuable lessons in how to go about this sort of activity.

Again she stifled the urge to thank him. She didn't want him to know how grateful she was, or how indebted; she didn't want him to know how poorly she would have handled this situation without him.

As if he didn't already know. The reason he'd invited her to join him was not to help her but to help himself. He'd known that if she'd attempted this on her own she would have blown it—for both of them.

Wynan's car preceded Van Deen's car out of the lot. They turned left, driving into the state forest. Griffin counted to ten before driving out after them.

Jill tried not to panic when they lost sight of the two cars beyond twists and turns in the rural road. She simply folded her hands around Doug's camera in her lap, familiarizing herself with its buttons and dials and exerting herself to remain as collected as Griffin. To keep her tension at bay, she focused on her memory of the placid domestic scene at the Van Deen's house earlier that evening, the dining room windows filled with warm amber light and the silhouettes of family members thrown against the drapes.

It was a far different scene from the one she'd witnessed the last time she'd spied on the Van Deen house, a few days ago. Then she'd seen the usually placid mayor raging at his lovely wife, Sylvia. Had they been fighting tonight? Jill wondered. Did they think that once Van Deen paid off his blackmailer his troubles would be over? Would Jill's article exposing the mayor destroy his family, or would they be relieved to see him suffer for his sins?

She was awed by the power reporters like her wielded. With one clear, accurate newspaper article, she could devastate not just a man but his innocent family. Van Deen was the guilty party in this episode, yet Jill couldn't help feeling a little bit guilty herself.

Eventually Wynan's silver car veered onto a spread of asphalt to the right, a parking lot adjacent to one of the park's picnic areas. Van Deen drove in behind him, and slowing to a crawl, Griffin also entered the turnoff. In the tree-shrouded dark, Jill could barely make out the shapes of the picnic tables and grills and the rectangular rest room that stood at the far end of the parking area.

What she could make out quite clearly were parked cars, lots of them, at least a dozen. Nobody was barbecuing at the moment. In fact, no people were visible. She wondered if someone was hosting a reception in the rest room.

Once more, Griffin provided an answer for her unvoiced question: "It's a popular spot for necking."

"Oh." Jill skimmed the numerous parked cars with her gaze and her imagination supplied all sorts of fascinating pictures of what was occurring inside them. "Do you suppose Van Deen and Wynan are going to neck?" she joked.

Chuckling, Griffin cruised slowly along the row of cars, finally settling on a parking space near the rest room building, not too far from Van Deen's car. He rolled down his window, and the Chevy filled with the sounds of crickets chirping and the muffled grunts and groans of a couple apparently having the time of their lives in the battered old Volvo station wagon parked a few feet away.

"Why don't you open your window, too?" Griffin suggested.

Jill wondered why he would want to listen to such impassioned moaning in stereo, but she did as she was told without question.

Griffin lifted his camera to his eye and focused. Jill followed the line of his lens and noticed Wynan climbing out of his car and striding toward the Lincoln Town Car. He held a large white envelope in his hand. Van Deen got out of his car to meet him. He straightened the knot of his necktie as he stood, as if he were preening for a public appearance.

"Little does he know," Jill muttered to herself, raising Doug's camera to her right eye and tapping at the shutter button to get the autofocus sharp. Little did the mayor know but this *was* going to be a public appearance—once Jill's photos were published on the front page of the *Record*.

As soon as the two men began to speak, she recognized why Griffin had asked her to open her window. Their voices cut through the night air, clear and distinct. Wynan asked Van Deen if he'd brought the money, and Van Deen assured him he had. Van Deen produced a bulging yellow envelope from an inner pocket of his jacket, and he and Wynan exchanged envelopes. Van Deen glanced at the contents of the white envelope and asked Wynan if all the negatives were there. Wynan confirmed that they were, and as he examined the contents of the yellow envelope he asked Van Deen if all the money was there. Van Deen told him it was.

Through it all, Jill snapped photos, one after another. She waited only long enough for the little green light to appear within the viewfinder, indicating that the focus was correct, the light adequate, and then she snapped again.

She became oblivious to Griffin, who was busy shooting beside her, and to the torrid sounds of lovemaking emerging from the Volvo. She tuned out the crickets, the shadows, her feelings about what Griffin had told her about his childhood sorrow and what she had told him about her childhood insecurities. Her mind zeroed in on one thing only: the payoff.

She was certain she got a couple of shots of the actual exchange and at least one fantastic shot of Van Deen inspecting the contact sheets inside the white envelope. She would ask Clark at Foto-Finish to enlarge that photograph; maybe she would be able to discern what was depicted in the fifty-thousand-dollar pictures on the contact sheet.

The transaction complete, the handsome blond blackmailer extended his right hand to Van Deen and expressed his pleasure at doing business with the mayor. Refusing to offer his own hand, Van Deen made an obscene remark and climbed back into his car.

Unruffled, Wynan tipped an imaginary hat toward the mayor. He leaned against the bumper of his own car, watching the Lincoln drive away, and then lifted the flap of his envelope to survey its contents again. He shook out a bank-wrapped wad of paper money and fingered it with reverence. Jill snapped a picture.

Eventually Wynan returned the money to the envelope and jammed it into a pocket of his jacket. But instead of getting back into his car, he gazed carefully around him. His eyes seemed to lock on Griffin's car, and his expression changed subtly, his smile fading. He started toward them.

"He's seen us," Jill gasped.

Griffin grabbed her camera and tossed it, along with his own, onto the floor. Then he gripped Jill by the shoulders and shoved her down beneath him on the seat. His chest bore down on her, and his legs and hers became entangled in the tight space below the steering wheel. He arched one arm around her head and hid her face in the hollow where his neck and shoulder met.

"Griff—" Her lips accidentally brushed the warm skin of his throat, and she silenced herself.

"Shh. Pretend we're making out," he whispered, twining his fingers absently through the loosened hair behind her ear.

For a brief, insane moment she wished they *were*—not so much because she wanted to but because that seemed like a much safer activity than spying on a criminal. Strangely enough, even if Wynan had noticed them, Jill did feel safe. Griffin's hold on her was protective, the weight of his body on hers both erotic and comforting, the motion of his fingers in her hair both soothing and arousing. She felt inundated by conflicting emotions— gratitude and totally misplaced desire, fear and confidence.

Closing her eyes, she labored to keep her breath as slow and rhythmic as Griffin's. It was hard for her to inhale deeply with his bulk pressing into her ribs, but she did the best she could, absorbing his familiar tart scent and taking courage from it. To make more room on the seat, she wrapped her arms gently around his waist, and he sighed almost inaudibly.

"What do you think Wynan's doing?" she asked after a minute.

Griffin shifted slightly, bumping her cheek with his chin. At her muted "Ouch!" he touched his lips to the site of the collision, then settled against her again. "He probably just went to the bathroom, but you never know."

"What do you think he'll do if he catches us?"

Griffin touched his lips to her temple once more, this time not to heal a bruise but to reassure her. "Don't worry about it."

"I'm not worried," she insisted, keeping her voice low. "I just want to know."

"He'll probably ask us to turn over our cameras."

Jill closed her eyes and tightened her arms around Griffin. She doubted a creep like Wynan would let them off so lightly. He'd be apt to smash their cameras—for starters. Then, perhaps, he'd smash their faces.

Griffin evidently felt her stiffen with fear. "Don't be scared," he murmured, kissing her temple once more. "If you ask me, lying here like this has been one of the evening's highlights."

She knew he was joking—except that there was more than a grain of truth to his assertion. Lying underneath Griffin's tall, strong body felt much too good. If only the circumstances were different, if only she and he hadn't established their rules....

Slowly, cautiously, Griffin lifted himself off Jill, raising his head just high enough to peek past the dashboard. "Wynan's leaving the bathroom," he reported beneath his breath.

"Then he isn't on to us."

"Probably not." Griffin rose higher and helped her to sit up. Together they watched Wynan slide behind the wheel of his Maxima and drive away from the picnic area.

"Are we going to follow him?" Jill asked, making a half-hearted attempt to straighten her clothing.

"No. Check the cameras and make sure they're all right."

His ability to recover so quickly from the sensuality of their position bothered Jill. She was still a frenzied mass of nerves, trembling with a heady combination of fear and yearning, and she resented Griffin for being able to maintain such an iron grip on his emotions. He was being sensible, however, and she did her best to emulate him. She obediently lifted the two cameras from the floor, inspected them for damage and found none.

Griffin started the engine and eased out of the parking space. They drove through the dark forest, lost in their own thoughts. As the glaring neon of the Granby Motor Lodge sign tinted the night air beyond the bend in the road, Griffin tossed Jill a quick look.

"Are you okay?"

"Of course I'm okay," she said with false bravery. If Griffin was going to be so stoical about things, she'd be damned if she'd let him know how rattled she was. "Why shouldn't I be okay?"

He gave her another quick look before returning his attention to the road. "I'm not so sure I'm okay," he confessed, surprising her.

"Why?"

He grinned sheepishly. "I should be thinking about how I'm going to write this story up. But all I can think about is how good it felt to hold you that way."

She didn't need him to spell out what way. Her cheeks darkening with a blush, she offered him a timid smile.

"Maybe...maybe someday soon we'll be able to..." She drifted off, also preferring not to spell things out.

He gazed affectionately at her. "As soon as we finish our stories," he said, his voice laden with promise.

Jill couldn't suppress a small sigh of frustration. "When do you think you'll be done with yours?" she asked.

"I plan to work on it all day tomorrow. I guess it'll run either Sunday or Monday, depending on how fast I can pull it all together."

Jill nodded, temporarily shelving her romantic fantasies and assessing the grim realities of her rivalry with Griffin. The next edition of the *Record* wouldn't come out until Tuesday. There was no way she could beat him into print.

Unless she convinced Doug to run a special edition.

That was it. They'd run an extra. With the explosive story she would write, accompanied by the equally explosive photographs she'd just taken, no way would they hold the presses until Tuesday. Doug wanted to increase publication to three times a week anyway. Why not start now, with something big, something that certainly couldn't wait?

"How are we going to work this?" she asked Griffin as he drove through Jill's neighborhood. "Will you call me when you're done?"

"Either that, or I'll climb through your window with a dozen long-stemmed roses. Which would you prefer?"

"Skip the roses," she said, adopting his light tone, as eager as he was to keep their competition from destroying the intimacy of the evening they'd shared. "Just climb through the window. I'll be waiting."

He pulled into her driveway and left the engine idling. "Here," he said, tucking her camera into her tote bag and leaning across her lap to open her door for her.

Her eyes met his for a timeless instant, and then she climbed out and swung the door shut.

"Good luck with your story," he shouted through the open window.

Jill flashed him a bright smile. "Good luck with yours," she returned before racing up the walk and into the house.

SHE SWEPT into Foto-Finish to pick up the developed film shortly after noon the following day. She had dropped off the roll that morning and requested that Clark put a rush on it. "It's hot," she'd warned him. "Please, Clark—keep your lip buttoned."

"Discretion is my middle name," he'd sworn, taking the film from her. "Stop by in a couple of hours. I'll have it developed by then."

She'd spent the intervening time at her word processor, upstairs from the Laundromat. Doug had come into the office to work with her on the story. Jill had written a preliminary draft, revised it once and let Doug call it up on the word processor in his office. Then he'd revised it, and she'd called it up on her word processor again, and she'd returned half of his changes back to their original version. He'd read what she'd done and shouted through his open office door that he thought Jill wasn't sensationalizing the story enough. She'd shouted back that if she wanted to write sensational stories she would be writing for a schlocky tabloid. Then Doug had gotten a call from Karen, and Jill had left the office to pick up the film. If Doug wanted sensational, she thought self-righteously, he'd get sensational. The photos were going to be sensational.

"Bad news," Clark said by way of greeting as she swung into his shop.

"What bad news?" she asked, her step faltering as she approached the counter.

Clark examined her face and cringed. "Well...the pictures didn't come out."

Jill screamed. Then she took a deep breath and gripped the edge of the counter to maintain her balance. "What do you mean, they didn't come out?" she asked, pronouncing each word with the utmost care to prevent herself from screaming again.

Clark pulled out several strips of negatives. Each negative was almost completely opaque. Jill knew that if Clark had bothered to print them, she'd have a proof sheet containing thirty-six white blobs, nothing more.

"How could this happen?" she asked, choking on her fury.

Clark shrugged. "Apparently the film was exposed somehow. It's possible you had a defective film casing."

"No," she moaned, shaking her head frenetically. "I opened the box of film myself. There was nothing wrong with it."

"Then something must have gone wrong with it between your opening it and your taking pictures," Clark conjectured. "The film was exposed. If the casing wasn't defective, then you must have exposed the film accidentally when you were loading it."

"No," Jill argued. "I didn't load it—"

And then she screamed again, a gut-wrenching sound of anguish. Griffin had loaded it. Griffin Parker, who according to Doug was very good at what he did, who was willing to do whatever it took to get a story and get it first . . . Griffin had loaded her film.

He'd sabotaged her. He'd done whatever it would take, all right—ruining her photos so she wouldn't have adequate proof to run a story charging the mayor with stealing city funds and paying them to a pimp. Without photographic proof, the *Record* could never publish such a story. Van Deen would sue the newspaper for libel, and she and Doug would lack the physical evidence to defend themselves.

And in the meantime, Griffin would run his story in the *Journal*, with his clear, magnificent photographs and his famous byline, and he'd win the kudos and the awards and the credit for bringing down a corrupt politician.

Jill had trusted Griffin.

And the bastard had sabotaged her.

Chapter Ten

Doug's face went pale when Jill broke the news to him. His lips tensed and his eyes chilled to the color of ice. "I'm having a little trouble with this," he said, his tone low and bristling. "You're telling me not one single picture came out?"

Unable to meet his gaze, Jill stared past him at the shelf-lined inner wall of his office. "According to Clark, either the film was defective or I loaded it wrong," she explained in a listless voice. She wasn't going to reveal that Griffin had loaded the film. She'd rather have Doug view her as a klutz than a fool.

"You loaded it wrong," he repeated, his rage straining to break free.

"Clark said it might have been a defective film casing." She wished she could believe that was what had spoiled the film, but she couldn't. She doubted Doug would accept that theory, either.

"Well," he fumed, "what do you suppose we ought to do? Sue Kodak?"

Jill figured that the only way she'd survive this disaster was to bank her emotions and remain as dignified as possible. "If you want to take it out on me," she said, "be my guest. It's probably my fault." *And how,* she added silently. Her fault for letting Griffin get Doug's camera into his treacherous hands.

Doug turned away from her and let loose with a spate of invectives. Jill assumed that his controlled release of rage would prevent a full-fledged explosion, and she was right. "Okay, Jill," he said evenly, spinning back to her. "Let's see what we can salvage here. We'll go through the copy word by word and use whatever we can. At least we've got photocopies of the unauthorized cash withdrawals from the city's bank accounts. If we can get into print with something—anything—on Monday, we may beat out your buddy down at the *Journal*. He's probably expecting us to go with our regular Tuesday edition. We'll beat him into print at least, even if we can't run the full story."

Jill felt herself shriveling up inside. Griffin was no buddy of hers. Worse than that, he was not going to let the *Record* beat him into print on this story. He knew exactly what was going on, exactly what setback Jill and Doug had suffered. He'd laid the trap himself, damn him.

"Come on, pull up a chair," said Doug, turning on his computer and flexing his fingers. "Let's see what we can do here."

"I can't work right now," Jill mumbled, watching the green letters swim across Doug's monitor as he loaded her story. "I—I've got to make a telephone call first."

Engrossed in the text before him, Doug shrugged. "Go ahead and make your call. Come on in when you're ready. We're going to milk something out of this, somehow."

Jill left his office, closing the door behind her. She stared at him through the glass and sighed. She ought to be thankful that after his initial eruption he'd taken the situation in stride.

Of course, if she'd told him the whole truth—that she had entrusted Griffin with the camera last night and that he had deliberately ruined the film—Doug wouldn't be sitting so sedately in front of his word processor right now, tinkering with the text and deleting anything that smelled of potential libel. He would be screaming at her, maybe throwing her headfirst through one of the glass walls of his office.

No, Doug wouldn't do that. *She* was the one who wanted to throw somebody through a wall. Unable to vent her anger in such a violent manner, she sat down at her desk and dialed Griffin's number instead. The phone rang twice, and then a woman answered. "Hello!"

Great. The heiress from Newport, Jill thought illogically. "Is Griffin Parker there?" she asked in a muted voice, even though Doug was well out of earshot.

"Who's calling?"

Not only was the imaginary heiress at Griffin's house, Jill thought bitterly, but he had trained her to run interference for him. "Jill Bergland."

"Oh, hi, Jill. This is Ivy," said the woman on the other end of the line. "Griffin isn't home right now. I just stopped by his house to drop off my toaster oven. It keeps getting stuck and burning everything. He said he'd have a look at it."

"How decent of him," Jill muttered through clenched teeth. "Do you know when he'll be home?"

"No idea," Ivy answered. "He's probably down at the *Journal* working. You could try him there."

"Thanks," said Jill, knowing painfully well what he was working on. She bade Ivy goodbye and hung up, then dialed the *Journal* switchboard number.

After a couple of minutes she was connected to Griffin's extension in the newsroom. "Griffin Parker," he said.

His husky voice elicited a visceral reaction from Jill, momentarily making her think not of how he'd hoodwinked her but of how he'd held her to himself, how his mere presence had helped her overcome her fear on the airplane and during the stakeout. A quick glance toward Doug hunched over his keyboard and gnawing stressfully at the inside of his cheek cleared Jill's mind of such kindly thoughts. "I hope you rot in hell," she spat out, her voice doubled in intensity to compensate for its lack of volume.

There was a brief pause, and then, "Jill?"

"Yes, it's Jill."

Another pause. "Is something wrong?" he asked innocently.

Is something wrong? She gripped the telephone receiver so tightly her fingers grew numb. Clinging to the solid object was her only defense against encroaching hysteria. "You know damned well something's wrong. You made it wrong, Griffin. I can't believe—" She bit her lip, aware that her voice was beginning to grow louder and that what little restraint she'd begun with was vanishing fast. She gulped in a deep breath and said as calmly as she could, "You fouled up my film last night."

"What?" He sounded startled.

Oh, he was good. He was very good. She silently offered Griffin her congratulations on his Oscar-caliber performance. Doug had warned her that Griffin Parker was good at what he did—but imbecile that she was, she'd had to learn the hard way. "You exposed my film, Griffin. You destroyed it. You made sure none of my shots would come out. I've got to hand it to you, Griff. You're a real pro. First you set up that we should do the stakeout together, and then you wrecked my film. You really worked it out to the last detail, didn't you."

"Jill." He sounded less startled now than deeply concerned. "What exactly are you saying? None of your photos came out?"

"You know damned well they didn't. I'm just calling to thank you for working me over so nicely."

"Jill. I didn't do anything to your camera," he insisted. "How could you even think I planned such a stunt? You were the one who asked me to load the film for you."

"Sure. I played right into your hands, didn't I," she grumbled, overflowing with self-disgust. "If I hadn't asked you to load the film, you would have asked if you could have a look at the camera, and then you would have secretly popped open the back or scratched the lens or something. I wasn't born yesterday, Griffin. You had me going last night, but I happen to be blessed with twenty-twenty hindsight. Now—too late to do me any good—I've figured out what you were up to."

"Jill—"

"I only wish you'd never kissed me," she said, her voice cracking unexpectedly, her eyes suddenly stinging with unspent tears. "I only wish..." She couldn't burst out crying, not now. Bad enough that Doug might see her; even worse if Griffin realized how critically he'd wounded her. She was mourning not for the loss of her story but for the loss of Griffin, for the loss of the man she'd thought she loved.

"Jill. I didn't do anything to destroy your photos. I swear." Her silence provoked him to reiterate, "None of them came out?"

"Don't be so modest," she snapped, frantically wiping a few stray tears from her cheeks. "You did a damned good job of it, Griffin. I hope you're happy. I hope you can live with yourself." Feeling a huge sob rising in her throat, she slammed the receiver down.

GRIFFIN STARED at the dead receiver in his hand. Two desks to his right in the newsroom, one of his colleagues was hammering away on the keyboard of her word processor, and three desks to his left an unattended telephone was ringing. But for several minutes Griffin was conscious of nothing but the disconnected line between Jill and himself.

How could she accuse him of such a dirty trick? How could she think he was capable of it? He was a professional. He'd go to great lengths to get a story—but he wouldn't destroy a rival's film, for God's sake.

In truth, the accusation didn't bother him so much. What bothered him was that *Jill* had made it. He trusted her so thoroughly, he'd invited her to join him on his stakeout—and she didn't return his trust. He cherished her so deeply that when he'd thought Wynan might have spotted them, he had covered her body with his own to save her life—and she hated him. Griffin had been playing for real in the car last night. He had covered her face, covered her heart, prayed that his body would be enough of a shield to keep Wynan from hurting her. And she thought he was so ruthless he'd ruin her pictures in order to scoop her on a story?

Lowering the receiver to its cradle, he rested his chin in his cupped palms and tried to figure out how he could have misjudged Jill so badly. His initial reaction to her had been physical, of course, but he'd also responded to her intelligence, her guts, her determination and confidence. He'd adored her spunk and her stubbornness, her ability to stand up to him, to her editor and even to the mayor of her town, her willingness to chase a story wherever it took her, without letting her private fears get in her way. Her principles.

The trouble with all those admirable traits was that they could lead a person to be reckless, to swing wildly and endanger the very things that were most worth preserving. For years after he'd learned the truth about his mother's death, Griffin had attempted to picture the murder, the actual series of events that had led to that ultimate tragedy. The only way he could figure it was that his mother had fought back. A mugger had asked her for her purse and she'd said no.

He didn't remember too much about his mother, but he remembered that she was headstrong and confident, spirited and gutsy—and principled. She would never have meekly handed over her purse to a thief. She would have lashed back—even though, as things had turned out, it had wound up costing her her life.

Jill was like that, too. If she got fired up, if she became indignant, she lashed back without considering the costs. In this case, thank God, her life wasn't at stake.

What was at stake was love. She was prepared to throw away Griffin's love because she thought, however mistakenly, that he'd shafted her.

He loved Jill. Until that instant he hadn't acknowledged how strongly he felt about her. He had known only that he could talk to her as he'd never been able to talk to his wife, and that Jill would understand him. He'd known that she could scramble his thought processes, that she could drive him insane with longing, that her strength enthralled him, that she'd become essential to him in ways he'd never imagined.

He loved her.

They hadn't even had a chance to explore that love to its fullest, and he was losing her. Thanks to her stupidity and rashness, he was losing her. He couldn't bear the thought.

Last night he had been prepared to sacrifice his life to protect hers. Was he still willing to make such a huge sacrifice for her? Was regaining her trust and having her love worth that much to him?

The answer came easily to him. He wouldn't have to sacrifice his life to demonstrate his love. All he would have to do was prove to her that he would never interfere in her work. If he could convince her of that, perhaps he would regain her trust.

JILL AROSE early Sunday morning. She dressed in her most comfortably broken-in corduroy jeans and an old sweatshirt, plaited her hair and grimaced at her reflection in the mirror above her dresser. Her face was pale, her eyes ringed with shadows from her restless night, her lips twisted into a scowl.

Disgusted with her appearance, she left the bedroom and went downstairs to the front door. Her subscription copies of the *New York Times* and the Providence *Journal* were lying outside the door on the mat, and she briefly toyed with the masochistic idea of thumbing through the *Journal* in search of Griffin's story—accompanied, no doubt, by a few vivid photos of Van Deen and Wynan committing their criminal act.

Deciding it was too early to torture herself with Griffin's triumph, she donned her boots and her down vest, pulled the magazine section from the *Times* and took off for the Granby Motor Lodge to have breakfast. Driving in the cool mist-shrouded morning, she tried to keep her mind blank. But as soon as she steered into the parking lot she was awash in memories, memories of having been there with Griffin two nights ago, of having thought they were partners, practically a team, colleagues harboring an authentic mutual respect for each other. Memories of the first time she'd met Griffin, when he had horned in on her crossword puzzle and mesmerized her with his stunning eyes, when she'd seen him race out of the restaurant and been dazzled by his long-limbed agility.

She yanked the steering wheel in a sharp turn and barreled out of the lot.

Now what? She couldn't abide the thought of returning home. Not knowing what else to do, she drove to the *Record*'s office. She'd fix a pot of coffee and get a head start on the article before Doug arrived. She might as well wrestle with it herself. It was going to have her byline on it, after all—as if she cared about that anymore.

Climbing the stairs, she spun her key ring in search of her key to the office. The upstairs hall was gloomy, the building echoing in its empty state. A perfect manifestation of her mood, she thought morosely, listening to the spectral *whoosh* of the heating system cranking on.

She unlocked the door, pushed it open and discovered a large rectangular envelope lying on the floor. At first she thought it had slipped off Miriam's cluttered desk, but then she noticed "Jill Bergland" printed on it in bold black letters. Frowning, she lifted it, flipped it over and glanced at the door. The envelope must have just barely fit through the mail slot.

She closed the door behind her and pried up the envelope's flap. Inside were photographs, twelve of them, black-and-white eight-by-ten glossies. The first one was of George Van Deen in his dapper suit, standing beside his car in the parking lot at Lincoln State Park. The second was of Van Deen and Wynan together, Wynan holding a white envelope. The third was of them exchanging envelopes. And on and on, all twelve of them offering blunt, unimpeachable proof of what Jill had witnessed Friday night.

What Jill and Griffin had witnessed together. What they'd both taken pictures of.

Her heart froze. Her breath became lodged in her lungs. For a crazed moment she feared she would pass out. Then a small tremulous cry escaped her, and she snapped out of her trance and took stock of the situation.

Griffin had left the envelope for her. He'd supplied her with his own photos just to win back her trust, just to prove he hadn't been guilty of what she'd accused him of yesterday. In giving her his own pictures, he'd relinquished his chance to beat her to the presses with the story.

It was an enormous sacrifice. And he'd made it, just for her.

Awed by the magnitude of what he'd done, she walked past the partitions to her desk and lifted the receiver of her telephone. She dialed Doug's home number, and when he didn't answer she took the liberty of trying him at Karen's house, where she found him. He was not in the mood to be found, however, and as soon as Karen put him on the phone he began ranting to Jill about how early it was.

"I'm sorry to wake you up," Jill said, cutting off his lecture. "I'm calling you from the office to let you know that we have photos for the story about Van Deen and Wynan."

"What photos?" His tone abruptly transformed from angry to ebullient.

"Photos of the actual payoff. I'd like you to run the original version of the story. I'm leaving the pictures in an envelope in the top left drawer of my desk, along with a hard copy of my original draft of the article. I'd suggest that you keep it pretty much as written—"

"Wait a minute," Doug interrupted. "Sit tight. I'll be right there."

"I won't be," Jill warned him. "You can decide for yourself which pictures to run. I'll see you tomorrow."

"Wait, Jill! How'd you get the photos? Where are you going to be? What happened to—"

She hung up. She couldn't explain anything to Doug right now. As her boss, he had every right to question her on where she'd obtained the photos. But for the time being, she believed that simply having them ought to be enough to satisfy him.

As she'd promised, she placed the envelope of photographs, along with the copy of her original draft of the story, into the top left-hand drawer of her desk. Then she locked up the office and dashed to her car. She intended to track Griffin down and fling herself at his feet.

But before she did that, she'd have to change her clothes. She might not have an overabundance of pride, but she had a reasonable amount of taste, and she suspected that winning his forgiveness might be easier if she was wearing something prettier.

When she steered around the corner onto her street, however, she realized that she wouldn't have a chance to change her clothes. Griffin's car was parked at the curb in front of her house. He was seated behind the wheel.

She slowed her own car, inhaled deeply and sorted her thoughts. He must have driven here after dropping off the photos at the office. Had he been about to give up waiting and drive away? Or had he been planning to stay there all day, all night, as long as it took for her to come home?

And now that she was home, what would he do? What should she do?

Lacking a better idea, she pulled her car into the driveway, set the brake and turned off the engine. She rubbed her hands together briskly, as if she could wipe away their faint trembling, intoned "Courage" beneath her breath and climbed out of her car. After a futile attempt to produce a smile, she walked over to his car, aware that his eyes were on her, measuring her, counting every step she took toward him. When she was within a few feet of his car he rolled down the window.

"Hi," she said, meeting his steady gaze. His eyes glittered with a multitude of colors, a multitude of emotions. She wished she could interpret them: anger, resentment . . . hope, maybe? Yearning? Fear?

"Hi," he said.

A smile tickled her lips, totally unforced. "Um . . . do you want some coffee?"

"Thanks," said Griffin, reaching for the chrome door latch. "I'd love some."

Jill stood quietly by the front bumper of his car while he locked up. They would have to talk once they got upstairs to her apartment, but she couldn't for the life of her think of how she should begin what was bound to be a difficult conversation. Merely thanking him for the photos would be insipid. Pointing out to him that she was aware of the risks entailed in what he'd done might cause him to regret having done it. Begging his forgiveness for yesterday's telephone tantrum would make her come across as groveling. Evading the issue would mark her as a coward.

He didn't say anything as they strolled over the leaf-strewn grass to the door. Nor did he make any move to touch her. He wasn't going to make things easy for her, she understood. Or, more precisely, he wasn't going to make *personal* things easy for her. He'd already rescued her professionally. She didn't have the right to expect more from him.

The only sound in the house was that of two pairs of feet tramping up the stairs. Jill unlocked the inner door, stepped inside and held it open for Griffin. As soon as he'd crossed the threshold, she shut the door and slid off her vest. "Let me have your jacket," she said courteously. Taking care of their outerwear would give her a few extra seconds to think of a way to thank him for his generosity and apologize for her own abominable behavior.

She hung up her vest and his overshirt, then pulled off her boots and set them on the floor of the coat closet. Griffin wandered into the living room, surveying the plain, sturdy furnishings, staring for a moment at the neatly folded sections of the Sunday *Journal* on the coffee table and undoubtedly deducing that Jill hadn't spent her morning plowing through the Providence newspaper in search of his article. She wondered what he thought of that. She wondered what he thought of everything that had happened in the past day and a half, from their exhilarating collaboration Friday night to Jill's contentious phone call yesterday to his decision to forfeit his exclusive...to now. To his standing in her apartment at this moment.

He watched her with a guarded expression as she closed the closet door and padded in her socks across the carpet to where he stood. "Coffee?" she asked.

He shook his head and lifted his hands slowly to her waist. As he rotated her to face him, a shadow seemed to lift from his eyes, and she easily read his hunger for her in their bright depths. She felt an answering hunger stirring awake within her, a spark catching fire and burning along her nerve endings, through her flesh. Her hands reached for his shoulders as he pulled her to himself, and their lips met.

There was no time for tempting, for teasing. Jill opened her mouth at once, luring Griffin in, drawing heat from his lips and tongue, from his arms closing around her and his body moving sensuously against hers. Later they could discuss the photos. Later Jill could explain her thoughtless accusations and apologize for them; she could question his motives and assure herself that his actions hadn't damaged his career.

Not now. Other things took precedence right now.

She pulled back far enough to view his face. As inscrutable as he'd appeared before, his expression was now transparent. Blatant longing lit his eyes, curved his lips in a hesitant smile, energized his hands as they roved her spine. Having him climb through her window, with or without roses, might have been romantic and dramatic. But Jill could frankly think of nothing more romantic or dramatic than what he'd already done— sharing his photographs with her.

Once more she considered raising the subject of the photos. His kiss had given her the confidence to speak; she and Griffin could talk it all out, clear the air, make sure they understood each other.

Yet such a conversation seemed unnecessary to Jill. She already knew from his kiss that they understood each other on the most basic, intimate level. The rest was irrelevant.

She didn't bother to speak at all. Instead, she ran her hands down his arms until her left hand met his right. Lacing her fingers through his, she led him down the hall to her bedroom.

He took a moment to look around. The room offered little in the way of distinctive decor; like her living room, she had furnished it with castoffs and leftovers. The bureau and mirror had been donated by Craig and his wife when they'd bought new furniture, and the night table had been sitting in Jill's parents' cellar collecting dust until she'd confiscated it. She'd sewn the curtains on her mother's sewing machine during a Christmas visit to Ellington—and her ineptitude with a sewing machine was evident in the crooked seams. The double bed was the only item she'd purchased new.

Right now, it was also the most significant piece of furniture in the room. Griffin's gaze lingered on it only long enough for Jill to glean exactly what was on his mind—as if she hadn't already known. She turned as he directed his attention to her.

"I want you," he whispered—as if she hadn't also figured that out.

"I'm yours," she vowed, meaning it on more levels than she could comprehend.

He kissed her brow. Then he reached behind her head and removed her barrette, freeing her hair from its braid. He ran his fingers through the silky locks until they were smooth, then smiled and touched his lips to hers.

She tugged at the ribbed edge of his sweater, drawing it up along his chest. Pulling back from her, he yanked the sweater over his head and tossed it onto her dresser. Then he removed his watch and placed it on the night table. Jill stared at it for a moment, stunned by how right it looked there. If Griffin lived with her, his watch would be on the night table every night when they retired to bed.

She could scarcely believe she was thinking of having him live with her. They couldn't even begin to contemplate such an arrangement until they'd settled more pressing matters...and they weren't going to settle those for a while.

Right now they were going to settle *this*, this passion they'd been trying, with less than total success, to keep under control since the first time they'd kissed. They were going to settle, once and for all, their physical and emotional yearning. After that, Jill hoped, resolving the rest would be a cinch.

She went to work on the buttons of his shirt, slipping them through the buttonholes and spreading back the cloth. Griffin's chest was a smooth bronze sculpture, devoid of hair. As she shoved the shirt off his broad, bony shoulders and down his arms, she marveled at the sleek muscles of his torso, the shadows of his lower ribs, the contours of his abdomen and the tantalizing indentations on either side of his navel that disappeared into the low-slung waistband of his jeans.

Enthralled, she traced the hollows with her thumbs. He groaned, then tugged her sweatshirt over her head. His hands drifted briefly over the lacy beige cups of her bra before circling behind her to undo the clasp. When the bra fell away, he bowed to kiss the warm valley between her breasts. At the searing sensation of his mouth on her skin, she let out a ragged sigh.

Lifting his head, he led her the short distance to the bed, urged her down onto the mattress and lay next to her. His mouth took hers, his tongue probing, surging hungrily, teasing and tantalizing its mate. Jill clung to him, digging her fingers into the muscles of his back, trying not to drown in the fluid sweetness his kiss released within her. She wanted him to finish undressing her and himself, to unite with her, to become a part of her, to love her as profoundly as she loved him. But she couldn't tell him, she couldn't speak. To speak would mean ending the kiss, and she couldn't bring herself to do that.

Apparently, neither could Griffin. Without breaking from her, he lowered his hand to her breasts, gliding his fingers over each pale swell in turn, stroking each nipple until it was taut and aching. When at last he tore his lips from hers, it was only to close them around one swollen nipple.

She felt his tongue on her, his teeth moving gently over her tingling flesh, and an anguished moan escaped her. She curled her fingers through his hair, entertaining the hazy notion of pulling him away before her longing for him drove her over the edge of reason. But her hands disobeyed, holding him closer to her, cradling him as he suckled first one breast and then the other.

At last he pulled back. His breath was shallow, his eyes glazed as he reached for the button of her jeans. With surprising deftness, he stripped them and her panties off. Her socks were neatly plucked from her feet, and then she lay fully naked, utterly vulnerable to his love.

She groped for his belt, and he shifted his attention from her only long enough to shed his slacks and underwear. He kicked the clothes off the bed and rose onto her welcoming body.

Her legs parted invitingly around him. The friction of his aroused flesh against her caused a throbbing heat to radiate from the point of contact inward, burning throughout her body. She closed her eyes and arched to him, no longer able to wait.

He resisted her embrace as best he could, bowing to kiss her throat, her shoulders and collarbone. When she arched again, he wedged his hand between their bodies. Amazed by how ready she was for him, he groaned. He slid his hand to her hip and drew her fully beneath him.

She imprisoned him with her arms and legs. Closing his eyes, he obeyed her unspoken demand, filling her body, taking complete possession of her. His deep, conquering thrusts governed her every thought, every harrowing sensation, every dream that had ever illuminated the hidden recesses of her mind. The only reality in her world was Griffin, his large athletic body, his rhythmic surges, his consuming kisses. His strength, his vitality, his shattering passion.

She heard herself cry out in sudden delirious surrender. Her body exploded around him, then unwound in ecstatic contractions, refusing him any choice but to surrender, as well. She felt him pulsing into her in joyous release, her response heightened by the knowledge that this miracle belonged to both of them, together.

He let out an uneven gasp and sank onto the bed beside Jill, hugging her to him. For several minutes she simply nestled into his firm chest, cushioning her head against the muscle in his upper arm and pressing her lips to his shoulder. He ran his fingers through her hair to the nape of her neck and then down her back, following the delicate ridge of her spine. When he reached the soft flesh of her bottom he began again, lifting his hand to her hair and caressing downward in a hypnotically soothing pattern.

Jill's eyes filled with tears. It wasn't just that Griffin had made such sublime love to her and that in the aftermath he was touching her with such exquisite tenderness. She was reacting to what he'd done before—what he'd done that, even more than their lovemaking, proved how strongly he felt about her.

"Why?" she whispered.

He loosened his hold on her and inched back so he could view her face. His respiration was still labored, but his eyes were clear, his lips curved in an enigmatic smile. "Why what?" he asked, brushing a stray blond tendril back from her cheek.

She almost wished she hadn't spoken. The single word fractured the peace that had settled over them, and now it hung in the air between them, refusing them escape.

She sighed. She couldn't hide her thoughts from Griffin any more than she could hide her love from him. "Why did you give me the photos?"

He wove his fingers through her hair again, then leaned toward her and kissed her brow. "You know the answer to that, Jill."

She could only guess: he did it because he loved her, because he was desperate to win her trust. She felt overwhelmed by what he'd done, grateful and a bit unworthy. She cuddled into his chest again and ringed his waist with her arms, drawing him close. "Does Jeanine know what you did?"

"Not yet." His voice was low and steady, drifting down to her from somewhere above her head.

"You're going to tell her?"

"She's going to figure it out. She's going to check the *Record*'s coverage of the story and see photographs identical to the ones I took, and she's going to figure it out."

"But will she figure out that *you* gave me the pictures?" Jill grazed his chest with her lips. She harbored the irrational hope that if she kissed him enough, none of it would matter.

"She's a smart lady."

"I thought she was a tough broad."

"That, too."

Jill sighed again. She didn't like what Griffin was saying—or not saying. He wasn't saying his decision to give her his pictures was harmless. He was speaking honestly, and while she respected his honesty, she hated to think he was going to have to pay a price for what he'd done.

"Why did you do it?" she questioned him again.

His hands grew still on her back. "Jill..." He exhaled. "Jill, when I was married, my wife always complained that she ran a distant second to my work. She was right, she *did* run a distant second to it—but that was the way it was, that was how I wanted things to be with her." He traced the angle of Jill's shoulder blade, mulling over his words. "With you, Jill... I want you first, ahead of my work. I gave a lot of thought to what I was doing. And then I did it, because you were more important."

"I was horrible," Jill disputed him. "I made all those terrible accusations and called you names—"

"You were wrong," Griffin agreed. "You were upset. All I did was figure out a simple way to show you how wrong you were."

"It wasn't simple," she argued. "And being so good to me when I was so rotten to you—"

"This was your first big story. You couldn't bear the thought that anything could go wrong with it—and when something did go wrong, you went a little nuts. That's all."

"That's not all," she said. "I was a shrew."

"Yes," he finally agreed. "You were." He kissed the crown of her head. "I've lived through a few heartbreaks in my life, and I've learned something about perspective. You size up a situation and figure out what's important. The important thing here is that I love you. The rest is trivial."

The distress she felt at his professional plight dissipated, replaced by a fresh wellspring of love. No one had ever risked so much for her. No one—neither family nor friend—had ever considered her that important.

"I love you, too," she confessed.

He tangled his fingers into her hair and eased her head back for a deep kiss. "Under the circumstances," he murmured when they finally separated, "I guess we couldn't help but break a few rules."

The rules. What were they? As overwhelmed as Jill was by her love for Griffin, she could hardly remember. "Have you finished your story?" she asked.

"Late last night. It won't appear till Monday, though."

"Mine will appear Monday, too."

He nodded. "Maybe we ought to run away before our newspapers hit the stands." He grinned at the idea's appeal. "We ought to tell Mallory and Jeanine to take a long hike, and then we'll run off."

"Okay," Jill agreed, playing along, trying not to be saddened by the fact that their problems couldn't be solved so simply. "Where should we go?"

"I don't care. Wherever you want."

"And what will we do when we get there?"

He curved his hand around her derriere. "This," he whispered, drawing her hips to his.

She moaned in response. "I meant, what will we do for a living?"

"I don't know. We could run a high school newspaper in a hick town."

"I already did that for four years."

"You were just a student then," he reminded her. "We could be faculty advisers. Everyone would call us 'Teach.'"

The sensuous warmth of his voice carried far beyond the import of his playful words. She would gladly go anywhere with Griffin, and let the world call her anything it wanted. "I'll go," she swore. "Whenever you're ready. Just say the word."

"We don't have to run away," he decided, rolling onto his back and lifting her onto him. "We can stay right here forever."

"That sounds good, too." She smiled down at him, feeling his body revive beneath hers.

Mirroring her smile, he guided her legs around him, centering her over him. They joined again, becoming one, and Jill knew she'd never want for anything more if only they could stay exactly where they were. Forever.

Chapter Eleven

"Griffin Parker?" Jeanine's cawing voice sliced through the cacophony in the newsroom. "Get over here. Now."

Griffin hit the key to save the article he'd been working on and then switched off his word processor. He was in high spirits. The world was in grand shape today, the sun bright, the sky clear, the air fresh and cool. When he'd stopped off at his house that morning to change his clothes before work, Jamie had been leaving his own house to catch the school bus. He'd greeted Griffin with the news that "Dr. Bob," as he'd nicknamed the Brown University assistant professor his mother was dating, had taken him to the Roger Williams Zoo yesterday and wasn't really as much of a geek as Jamie had originally thought.

Love was in the air, all around, here to stay—pick a cliché, any cliché, and Griffin would subscribe to it. But he exerted himself to keep his joy under wraps when he arrived at the *Journal* building downtown. He had a strong suspicion that Jeanine was going to drag him over the coals. Her gruff summons confirmed that suspicion.

He took a deep breath, let it out slowly and shoved away from his desk. This wasn't going to be fun, but he had every intention of emerging from the encounter in one piece.

Nearing Jeanine's desk, he wasn't terribly surprised to see that morning's special edition of the Granby *Record* spread open in front of her. A banner headline proclaimed: "Mayor Van Deen in Extortion Scheme: Uses City Funds to Pay Pimp." Below the headline was a large reproduction of the photograph Griffin had taken of Wynan and Van Deen exchanging envelopes. Jill's byline appeared proudly above the story's text.

"I take it you're aware of this," Jeanine said wryly, waving toward the newspaper and then shaking a cigarette from one of the two open packs on her desk.

Griffin noticed the butane lighter beside her ashtray and considered lighting her cigarette for her. Then he discarded the idea—too obsequious. He would survive this session with his boss without resorting to sycophantic behavior.

"I've seen it," he said as she lit her cigarette.

She blew a thick puff of smoke at him. "Well written, don't you think?"

"Very well written." He meant it, too. Jill had done a fantastic job with her story. Apparently she hadn't had an inkling of Wynan's bids for business at the state capitol building, his infiltration of the public works department and his having skipped out of Buffalo under a cloud of suspicion. But she'd gotten something Griffin had missed: Mayor Van Deen's alleged filching of Granby city funds. That would have been hot news in the Providence *Journal*. In the Granby *Record* it was phenomenal.

"Nice artwork, too," Jeanine observed, tapping the photograph with one of her long enameled fingernails.

Here we go, Griffin thought, steeling himself.

"Kind of looks familiar, Griff, don't you think?" she remarked, her scowl a direct contradiction of her benignly phrased question.

"Yes," he agreed noncommittally. "It does, doesn't it."

Jeanine continued to glare at him as she smoked her cigarette down to the filter. She snubbed it out in the ashtray, then motioned toward a vacant chair near her desk. Griffin sat.

"Tell me, Griff," she demanded. "Did you give her the photo?"

Griffin could swear that he didn't, and it wouldn't be a lie. He hadn't personally handed Jill any photos; he'd slipped them through a mail slot. But to equivocate would be childish. He wanted to get this scene over with. "More or less," he said. "Yeah."

Jeanine closed her eyes and digested his confession. She shook her head, then reached for another cigarette and lit it. "This isn't going to be easy, Griff," she conceded. "You're one of the best reporters I've ever worked with. One of the absolute best. You've done some magnificent work, and I've backed you every step of the way. But to give something like this away, to flat out give it away..." She waved at the newspaper photo again and sighed. "What did this Bergland woman do to make you give it to her?"

She existed, Griffin almost replied. *She came into my life. She understood me as no woman's ever understood me before. She stole my heart.* "Nothing," he said.

"You just did it."

"I had my reasons."

"I'm sure you did," Jeanine concurred, her tone totally lacking in irony. "You've always done what you had to do, you've always had reasons. Valid reasons, too." She exhaled, expelling a thin jet of smoke. "Aw, Griff—I don't want to lose you."

"Lose me?" His throat became curiously dry.

"What choice have I got? I can't let this go unpunished."

"Fine. Punish me."

"You're fired," she said.

Griffin went very still as her words sank in. *Fired.* He'd thought it would be bad, but...*fired?* "You're kidding," he finally said.

"I'm afraid not, Griff. I can't believe you'd let another reporter get the goods on you like this."

"I didn't let her get the goods on me," he argued. "What matters here are the stories. She got the local Granby angle; I got the state capital angle. The artwork is secondary."

"Secondary or not, you gave it to her."

"All right," he grunted. "If you're all that ticked off, suspend me for a week. You don't have to fire me, Jeanine."

"It's a tough call, Griff, but I've got to maintain certain standards around here." She shook her head and gazed at the photos. "I just don't get it. This Jill Bergland must be damned clever. You've never been a sucker for a woman before."

"I'm not a sucker," he said defensively.

"Whatever you are," Jeanine countered, "what you did was unprofessional."

He bit back the protest that sprang to his lips. What was to be gained by debating the issue with Jeanine? She was right. He'd committed a journalistic transgression, and she'd passed sentence, and that was that. He saw no point in wasting his time and expending his ego trying to justify himself and the choice he'd made.

And he certainly wasn't going to beg for mercy.

"I'm in the middle of something," he said quietly. "Possible dumping of chemical wastes in the harbor."

"Please finish it," Jeanine requested. "I'd like you to tie up whatever loose ends you've got, and then you can find yourself another job. I can give you a few weeks, Griff."

"Thanks," he said grimly. She'd give him a few weeks, but he doubted she'd arm him with a glowing letter of recommendation.

He stood, gave Jeanine a curt nod and stalked back to his desk. He turned on his word processor and typed every curse word he could think of onto the monitor. Then he deleted them all. Then he typed them again.

He glanced over his shoulder. Jeanine was on the telephone. She still had the *Record* spread open in front of her.

He turned off his computer, propped his chin in his hands and recited the list of expletives in his head. It helped to scorch the rubble from his mind. Once his mind was clear, he might be able to think.

He'd taken a chance, and as things turned out he'd wound up somewhat ahead, somewhat behind. He was ahead because he'd won Jill—and winning her was very nearly enough. To have her love was to have more than he'd ever dreamed of having in his life. She was bright, beautiful, stubborn and funny and so sexy, so very sexy.

Jill was everything to him, everything he needed, everything he could possibly ask for....

Everything except a job.

Aside from a few weeks' grace period, he was essentially unemployed. What was he supposed to do? Find work with another newspaper? Wonderful. He'd land another job someplace, thousands of miles away, and if he was lucky he might get to see Jill two weeks out of the year. He'd won her love, and now he'd never get to enjoy it.

Maybe, since he'd sacrificed his job for her, she'd give hers up for him—hers was a hell of a lot less to give up, too, he pondered—and they could move thousands of miles away together. They could become faculty advisers for a high school newspaper somewhere, just as he'd fantasized yesterday.

Funny that he'd raised that idea. He must have known, even as he plunged headfirst into love with Jill, that he was annihilating his career in the process. He must have known it subconsciously, and he'd been sounding Jill out about their prospects.

She hadn't responded too negatively to the notion of running off with him, he recalled. He hoped she'd come with him, wherever he went. He could bear losing his job, but he didn't think he could bear losing her. And losing both...that would just about demolish him.

Turning his word processor on again, he loaded the article he'd been playing with concerning the chemical dumping in the harbor. He had only a few slivers of information to work with at the moment, but the interview he'd set up for that afternoon ought to open some new leads, and a meeting with a lobsterman working out of Point Judith was scheduled for tomorrow, and . . . God, it was hard for Griffin to think about tomorrow when Jeanine had just slammed the door on his future.

He glanced at his watch. He glanced at his monitor. He closed his eyes and filled the screen of his mind with Jill's image, her sun-streaked hair, her enticing lips and her body, her glorious body . . . Would she still love him if he was unemployed? Would she offer to support him on her measly salary from the *Record*?

Would she risk as much for him as he'd risked for her?

His image of her was so real, he didn't realize right away that he wasn't hallucinating when he opened his eyes and saw her standing at the main entrance to the newsroom. Then he recognized she was actually there, and he gave a classic double take.

She was conferring with one of the uniformed doormen who usually stood guard downstairs at the building's entry. She looked terrific—better than terrific, Griffin amended. She was clad in a beige wool suit, conservatively cut. Under the jacket she wore a prim white blouse with a high collar adorned by a flouncy bow. He stood to greet her.

She wasn't looking at him, though. She was looking in the direction the guard had pointed—to Jeanine's desk. Jill's face brightened, and Griffin could read her lips as she thanked the guard and started into the room.

Her gaze skimmed the entire newsroom. Spotting Griffin, she grinned and waved. Then she gave him a thumbs-up sign, blew him a subtle kiss and waltzed across the room to Jeanine's desk.

Griffin watched as his boss rose and welcomed Jill with a cordial handshake. She gathered up her cigarettes and her copy of the *Record*, led Jill into one of the soundproof glass-walled conference rooms abutting the newsroom and closed the door. Inside, she gestured for Jill to sit, then pointed to the front-page article Jill had written. Griffin saw the animated motions of Jeanine's hands, the vigor in her smile, and he knew. He knew she was praising Jill, complimenting her. Courting her.

Grinding his teeth together so hard his jaw began to cramp, he smacked his fist against the switch of the word processor, shutting off the power.

"Hey, Griff, are you okay?" one of his fellow reporters called to him from the next desk.

He didn't bother to answer. He knew why Jeanine was flapping her hands through the air so exuberantly, why she was beaming and fluttering around Jill. Jeanine was going to offer Jill a job at the *Journal*.

Griffin's job.

And, given her ambition, Jill was going to take it. Griffin knew in his gut that she would. What he'd given up for love, she was going to take without a qualm. He knew it; he understood her as well as she understood him.

He slammed his fist onto his word processor one more time, so hard he almost cracked the plastic frame. Then, ignoring the pain in his hand and the curious stares of his colleagues—his soon-to-be former colleagues—he stormed out of the newsroom.

"I WAS SO IMPRESSED by your work for the *Record*," Jeanine Tomaszewski gushed. "I had to call you first thing and get you down here."

Suppressing a cough as Jeanine blew cigarette smoke through the enclosed room, Jill smiled. At first glance, Griffin's tiny, blond, somewhat frazzled-looking editor wasn't what Jill had expected. But Jeanine's voice was the voice of a tough broad, no question about it. And if she'd asked Jill to come to the Providence *Journal* for the reason she suspected, she was going to love the woman, no matter how much the cigarette smoke irritated her throat.

"You seem like a sharp woman, Jill—may I call you Jill?" Jeanine didn't bother to wait for an answer. "You seem smart, Jill. I'm sure you don't want to spend the rest of your life at the *Record*, like Hank What's-his-name."

Jill's smile expanded. How many dreams could come true in twenty-four hours? she wondered. She loved Griffin, he loved her, and now they were going to get to work together on the same newspaper. They were truly going to be partners, out in the open, able to assist each other, able to collaborate...able to put aside their rivalry forever. They'd be able to get married—well, she might be rushing things a little, but she and Griffin did love each other, so why not?—and they'd be able to commute to work together and come home in the evenings together and turn on some Bruce Springsteen music and eat shredded wheat for supper, and then they'd jump into bed and love each other all night long....

"I beg your pardon?" she mumbled, realizing that Jeanine had been saying something important.

"The photo accompanying your story," Jeanine repeated. "It's uncredited. May I ask where you got it?"

"Uh...that's privileged information, I'm afraid," Jill said discreetly. Jeanine might have figured out the source of the photo, as Griffin had predicted she would, but Jill wasn't going to implicate him if she could help it.

"Having managed to get it shows great enterprise on your part," Jeanine complimented her.

Jill smiled vaguely. It had taken no effort on her part. Griffin had done it for her. He'd done so much....

"All in all, Jill, I'm impressed. Very impressed. Now, it just so happens that we've got an opening we need filled as soon as possible on the metro desk. Are you interested?"

"Am I interested?" Jill exclaimed. She was thrilled by the thought of the power and prestige that would come from working for a major newspaper, the generous expense accounts, the resources...the glory of having a famous byline.... "'Interested' barely scratches the surface," she admitted.

"How much are you currently earning up at that kiddie press?"

Jill refrained from bristling at Jeanine's put-down of the *Record*. "That's also privileged information, I'm afraid," she said coolly.

"Fair enough." Jeanine reached for another cigarette before she noticed the previous butt still smoldering in the ashtray. She extinguished it, then lit the new cigarette. "Let me describe our package, and you tell me if you can live with it," she said, puffing more smoke into Jill's face. She mentioned a salary figure that Jill couldn't prevent herself from coughing over and then elaborated on insurance benefits and vacation policies. "I don't have all the figures—you'd have to go to personnel for that. Just tell me if I'm in the right ballpark."

Jill swallowed to stifle her coughs. What Jeanine was offering her was more than twice what she was earning at the *Record* and substantially more than what she'd earned at the *Chicago Tribune*. "Yes," she managed. "You're in the right ballpark."

"Good. Think about it, and give me an answer as soon as you can."

Jill almost blurted out her acceptance at once, but she was shrewd enough to check the impulse. "It shouldn't be a difficult decision to make," she conceded, turning to gaze out at the buzzing, bustling newsroom. She noticed that Griffin's desk was empty and turned back to Jeanine. "You know that Griffin Parker and I are friends," she said, figuring that she ought to make sure there weren't going to be any hassles about nepotism if she and Griffin did eventually get married. Her plans were blossoming every which way, but the most important way had to do with Griffin, with her love for him. She wasn't going to let anything, not even a potential nepotism policy, stand in the way of that.

Jeanine pursed her lips. "Well, try not to take it personally," she said. "I've got to exercise my editorial prerogatives."

"You mean in story assignments?"

"In giving him the ax."

"Giving him the ax!" Jill spun around and gaped through the glass at the empty desk where she'd last seen Griffin. It looked ordinary, like the desk of a busy reporter out covering a story. Not like the desk of someone who'd just been fired.

"As I said, don't take it personally. I want you on the staff, and I know you'll do a good job."

"Of course I'll do a good job. But—" Her voice faded as she stared at the empty desk. It suddenly seemed like the most depressing sight in the world.

"But what?"

"But Griffin and I are friends," Jill declared. "How could you do that to him?"

It was a reflexive thing to say; not until she'd uttered the words did she acknowledge that by criticizing her future boss she was imperiling the professional opportunity of a lifetime. The job Jeanine had just offered was exactly what she'd dreamed of all those years ago when she'd been bicycling through Ellington delivering newspapers and reading *All the Presidents' Men*. This was a job in which Jill could write for a strong reputable newspaper, truly write and not just proofread copy for the senior reporters. She could write, get credit for her work and receive adequate compensation.

This was it. She had arrived. She'd finally reached her goal. Was she going to throw it all away for Griffin?

Jeanine eyed Jill through a cloud of smoke. "I do what I feel I've got to do," she said. "And you, Jill— you do what you feel you have to do."

Jill lowered her gaze to her hands, which were curled into fists in her lap. "I'm not sure I can work here if Griffin's been fired," she said in a small, bleak voice.

Jeanine studied her for a minute. "Think about it, Jill. I'll give you some time to make up your mind." Gathering her cigarettes and her ashtray, she left the office, closing the door behind her, abandoning Jill to sort through her battered dreams alone.

IT WAS ONLY TEN-THIRTY in the morning, much too early for anybody to be at a bar. But then, someone who'd just been laid off—and who'd seen his lover march gleefully into his workplace at the invitation of the woman who'd laid him off—could very well be drowning his sorrows in a bottle of booze, regardless of the time.

The bar was located half a block from the *Journal*'s headquarters, and following the directions of the reporter who'd been stationed at the desk next to Griffin's, Jill found it without difficulty. She entered to find two dissolute-looking fellows slumped on stools at the bar, staring fixedly at a television on an overhead shelf. A game show was on, and the barroom resounded with the clanging of bells and gongs and the screams and applause of a typically hyperactive television audience. Doing her best to ignore the raucous broadcast and the inebriated barflies, Jill strode through the gloomy front room to the tables in back.

She spotted Griffin seated alone at a table, poking through a plastic bowl of peanuts with his index finger. A bottle of beer stood at his elbow, an unused glass beside it on a cocktail napkin.

He saw her the same instant she saw him, but his expression didn't brighten in welcome. Jill remembered the way his eyes had come alive yesterday during their lovemaking, the way they'd burned with passion and then shimmered with satisfaction. Today his eyes appeared dead to her.

She stormed to Griffin's table and took a seat facing him. He didn't appear terribly surprised by her arrival. In fact, his face registered no emotion at all. His gaze remained blank as he reached for the bottle of beer and took a sip.

"Do you know what time it is?" she chided him.

"Time to get sloshed," Griffin answered. "Getting sloshed isn't easy for me, Jill. I've got a high tolerance for liquor, so I've got to get an early start."

Jill reached to cover his hand with hers, but he pulled it away before she could touch him. Stung by his unspoken rejection, she rapped her fingers on the scarred wooden surface of the table and studied him. How could he recoil from her? Didn't he love her? Didn't he realize she would never do anything to hurt him?

Her thoughts about-faced, and she remonstrated with herself for resenting his attitude. It had taken her so very long to realize that Griffin would never do anything to hurt her. Before she'd realized it, she had thought the worst of him. He had every right to think the worst of her now.

She couldn't blame him. It hurt like hell to think he trusted her so little, but she couldn't blame him. She deserved it.

"I've got good news for you," she told him, trying to keep her distress out of her voice.

"I'll bet," he drawled, eluding her hand as he reached for his bottle and lifted it to his lips.

"I got your job back," she said.

He misunderstood her. "I know you got my job. Enjoy it in good health. Maybe I can go pester Mallory, see if he'll toss a few free-lance stories my way so I can keep up with my mortgage payments."

"No," she said, setting him straight. "I got your job back for *you*. At the *Journal*. Jeanine Tomaszewski is going to rehire you."

Griffin's eyes hardened slightly. He sat up taller and gave her a long, intense stare. "What did you say?"

Jill glanced at his bottle. He hadn't drunk very much. If he needed her to repeat what she'd said, it wasn't because he was plastered. "Jeanine's going to take you back. Same job, same pay. I didn't ask her for a raise for you—I thought that would be pressing my luck.''

"What did you do?'' he asked warily. "How did you get her to rehire me?''

"What do you think I did? I told her that an emu was a large ratite and that Agra was the site of the Taj Mahal. She was so delighted to complete her crossword puzzle, she would have agreed to anything.''

Griffin continued to stare at Jill. He didn't look as pleased as Jill had expected. "Get serious, Jill. It's my career you're talking about.''

"Okay. You want the truth?'' Jill leaned back in her chair. "She offered me a job. Your job, maybe—I don't know. And I told her she couldn't have me unless she took you back, too.''

"Really?''

Jill suspected she looked smug, but she didn't care. "I guess she must want me a lot if she's willing to eat crow and give you back your job.''

"She certainly must. She doesn't like to eat crow.'' Slowly, almost reluctantly, Griffin relented, the tension ebbing from his face, the anger dissipating. "She wanted you *that* much. That's amazing, Jill. That's—that's great!''

His reaction puzzled Jill. He seemed more excited by Jeanine's eagerness to hire her than by his own reemployment. Then her puzzlement vanished, washed away by a huge wave of affection. He was more excited about Jill's success because he cared for her. He took greater pleasure in her professional triumph than in his own—because he loved her.

"She wanted you, too,'' Jill pointed out. "To tell you the truth, she seemed kind of eager to accept my terms.

She pretended to be tough about it, but we went back and forth a few times, and I finally phrased things as an ultimatum—''

"Jill, that was dangerous. It could have backfired on you."

"I took my chances," she said with a jaunty smile. She could be nonchalant about it now, given that her negotiations with Jeanine Tomaszewski had worked out beneficially. "I got the impression that she was just looking for an excuse to rehire you without losing face. I think she really wants you back."

"I don't," Griffin said. "She had a major fit because I gave you the photos."

"So she had a fit, and she blew off some steam," Jill rationalized. "You know how we newspaperwomen are—shoot first, ask questions later."

He weighed her explanation, then shook his head. "I think the only reason she agreed to take me back was because she wanted you so badly."

"Nah," Jill said modestly. "I'm not that special, Griff."

"Oh yes, you are," he murmured, capturing her hand and enveloping it in his. "You're about as special as they come. Working at the *Journal* is a big step up from what you've been doing, and you took the risk of losing the job. You gambled it all for me."

"I didn't do anything you wouldn't have done for me."

"But you did it. That's what counts." He dragged her out of her seat and around the table to him. Then he pulled her into his lap and circled his arms around her. "What are you going to tell Mallory?" he asked.

She kissed Griffin's cheek, inhaled his delicious male scent and sighed contentedly. "I'll tell him that I'd rather work with you than against you." She kissed his cheek again. "I think he'll understand my reasons for leaving. He knows I wouldn't be content to fritter away the rest of my life at the *Record*. I wrote the big story he wanted, and maybe he'll get a bunch of awards for it. He's welcome to them. I've got something better."

To emphasize the point, she gave Griffin a deep, lingering kiss, which he enthusiastically returned. "You've got something better, all right," Griffin whispered hoarsely. "Better wages."

"You guessed," she played along. "You know my only goal in life is to get rich quick. That's why I decided to become a newspaper reporter instead of an investment banker."

"Mmm," he murmured, nuzzling her throat. "If you're such a gold digger, you're going to go crazy when you see my bedroom. I'm so wealthy I've actually got matching furniture."

"I'd love to see your bedroom. Right now. Right this minute. I think this morning calls for celebration."

"What about work?"

"Jeanine'll give you the day off," Jill assured him. "If she doesn't, I'll refuse to accept the job."

"Push that button too many times and it's going to stop working," he warned.

"Nonsense. I'm indispensable."

Laughing, Griffin set Jill onto her feet, stood up and placed a few dollars on the table to cover the cost of his drink. Then he slung his arm around her shoulders and escorted her away from the table. "You're about as indispensable as any reporter who can't do a stakeout and can't load a camera with film.''

"But who, in spite of these shortcomings, knows how to get her story,'' she said, gazing up at Griffin with undisguised joy as they sauntered past the bar, heading outdoors into the bright morning sun.

As if on cue, the audience from the television game show erupted in cheers.

Epilogue

"How did you guys do it?" Doug asked, sotto voce.

The spacious living room of Karen's parents' house in the northern end of Granby was packed with well-dressed guests. A towering Douglas fir stood in one corner of the room, bedecked with Christmas ornaments, but this wasn't a Christmas party. It was an engagement party. A very large, elegant, formal engagement party.

At Griffin's and Jill's laughter, Doug rolled his eyes and ran his finger around the inside of his collar, as if it were strangling him. "I thought giving her a solitaire diamond at Thanksgiving would satisfy her. I didn't know I was going to have to face a mob scene at an engagement party, too. At this point, the wedding is going to be anticlimactic."

"But you love her," Jill reminded him.

"Do you think I'd put up with all this garbage if I didn't?" Doug groaned. "I still think you guys were smart to elope."

"We didn't elope," Griffin argued.

"That's right," Jill said, poking Griffin in the ribs. "You promised me you were going to climb through my bedroom window with a dozen red roses, and you never did.''

''When I made that promise,'' he teased, taking delight in her feisty beauty, in the belligerent tilt of her chin and the challenge blazing in her eyes, ''marriage wasn't what I had in mind.''

Letting loose with a trill of laughter, she took aim at his ribs again. He easily captured her hand and held it safely within his.

It hadn't been an elopement. Eloping implied secrecy, and there hadn't been anything secretive about Griffin's and Jill's marriage. They had driven downtown to City Hall and signed the necessary papers, with Ivy and Bob Calabria serving as their witnesses and Jamie serving the equally important function of providing an excuse to go out for pizza and ice cream afterward. Declaring that pizza and ice cream were essential to proper weddings, Jamie hinted broadly that he thought his mother and Dr. Bob might consider arranging a similar affair for themselves. Bob mentioned something about how the apotheosis of the wedding rite ought to include a good champagne, but everyone was in too good a mood to ride him about his choice of words.

The weekend after they'd tied the knot, Jill and Griffin had traveled up to Worcester to visit with Griffin's father and stepmother. A week later, at Thanksgiving, they'd flown out to Indiana so Griffin could meet Jill's family.

Quite a family it was, too. There were so many of them—not only her sisters and brothers but countless tagalongs. Her brother Craig arrived in Ellington with his wife and three children, her sister, Cindy, brought a fellow graduate student, her youngest brother, Eli, dragged along two fellow Outward Bound instructors who insisted on camping out in the living room when they noticed the shortage of available beds in the house, and Nicky, the blue-haired rock musician, arrived with an extremely flamboyant but devoted groupie dangling from his arm.

No wonder Jill had grown up feeling overlooked. In a family like that, Griffin would have been overlooked, too.

He wasn't overlooked at Thanksgiving, however. Everyone had to meet Jill's new husband, had to corner him and interrogate him and generally check him out. Apparently he passed muster, because by the end of the four-day weekend Jill's mother was hugging him, Jill's nephews and niece were climbing all over him and Jill's father was asking him to take out the garbage.

Jill wasn't overlooked, either. After Thanksgiving dinner her parents ushered her into the den, where, amid assorted trophies and mementos, a framed copy of Jill's story, from the Granby *Record* was hanging on display above the sofa. "It's got your name on it," her father had crowed. "Your first front-page byline. We're so proud of you."

She'd burst into tears at her father's glowing words. Merely seeing her smooth cheeks streaked with tears of happiness had caused Griffin to fall even more deeply in love with her.

Here at Doug's and Karen's engagement party, with Jill all dressed up in a white satin blouse and a narrow black velvet skirt with a deceptively revealing slit rising from the back hem, Griffin was falling deeper and deeper. She'd worn her hair loose, and it flowed past her shoulders in faint ripples, which had been crimped into the locks by her braid. Whenever she tossed her head he glimpsed the pale nape of her neck; whenever she took a step he glimpsed the back of her knees through the skirt's slit. Whenever she caught his eye, he calculated how much longer they'd be obliged to stay at the party.

"So, do you miss the *Record*?" Doug was asking her.

"Sure I miss it. I miss working my rear end off for peanuts." She sipped from the glass of wine she held.

"If you come back I'll let you cover Van Deen's indictment and trial."

"I'm covering it for the *Journal*," she told him. "Much to the annoyance of the suburban-north gang."

"If you come back," Doug persisted, "I'll give you a raise. Thanks to you, the *Record* has doubled its advertising revenues. Your exposé did incredible things for our reputation."

"I'm glad," Jill said earnestly. "Really. You deserve it. But I'm happy where I am."

Doug's eyes shuttled from Jill to Griffin and back again. "That's kind of obvious," he commented, giving her a meaningful wink.

Griffin watched the warm exchange between the two old friends and wondered why he'd ever suffered any jealousy over Doug Mallory. He was a nice enough guy, but he definitely wasn't Jill's type.

One of Karen's numerous aunts broke into Doug's dialogue with Jill, latched a manicured hand onto his shoulder and dragged him away to meet a distant cousin. Griffin once again had Jill all to himself.

There were a lot of things he wanted to do with her, but given their environment, he exercised willpower and opted for the safety of conversation. "Since when have you been assigned to cover Van Deen's indictment?" he asked her.

She sipped her wine and smiled up at him. "Since Jeanine gave me the word this morning. She thought I'd be the best person for the job. Assigning me to the story put a few noses out of joint, but, hey, what can I do? Jeanine's the boss."

He could tell by Jill's radiant smile that she was enormously gratified by the assignment. She deserved it; she'd been the one to uncover Mayor Van Deen's theft of city funds. It was fitting that she should follow the story to its end.

"The trial won't start for some time, though," she went on. "Van Deen's got an army of lawyers tossing out motions left and right. Jim Valenti was granted immunity in exchange for his testimony, and Glenda Hauser's also going to testify, so Van Deen's running scared. My guess is his lawyers are going to stall until the summer at least." Her eyes glittered mischievously. "So while I'm waiting I'll have time to investigate this fascinating little tidbit I've dug up about the health department's restaurant inspections in Providence."

Griffin ought to have gotten nervous. He knew everybody in the city's department of public health, and he had just begun to cultivate some leads concerning payoffs that health inspectors had allegedly been demanding from restaurant owners. Jill's comment indicated that she was sniffing around in Griffin's territory, and his reporter's reflexes warned him to head her off at once.

But he only laughed. "Corruption in the health department, huh?" he said with a careless shrug. "Do you think you're going to scoop me on this one?"

"I think I've got information you haven't got."

"Sure," he said, knowing full well that she couldn't possibly have anything he hadn't obtained ages ago. "Maybe you could take some photographs of your information," he taunted her. "You might get some interesting camera angles if you climb into a tree and—"

"Griff!" She set down her glass and folded her arms sternly across her chest. "If you were a decent, respectable husband, you'd teach me how to load 35-millimeter film."

"I'm a husband," he granted, "but I've never been too good at being decent and respectable. Especially with you." He put one arm around her slender waist and pulled her to him. Then he lowered his lips to hers for a swift, electrifying kiss. "Right now," he whispered, "I'd like to do some very indecent things with you. Can we cut out of here?"

She smiled seductively. "Only if you'll teach me how to load film afterward."

"You drive a hard bargain, lady," he murmured. "But I knew that going in."

"Then we've got a deal?"

"We've got a deal. As usual, you got the better end of it," he complained, releasing her so they could walk to the small front parlor where they'd left their coats. Moving behind her, he helped her on with her coat and lifted her hair out from under the collar. The exposure of her neck was too tempting to resist, and he touched the silky skin with his lips. "I lied," he confessed in a whisper. "I definitely got the better end of the deal."

She turned and kissed his cheek. "Wrong. I did."

"You want to fight about it?" he asked, shrugging into his own coat.

"Let's," she replied enthusiastically. "Let's fight about it for the rest of our lives." Smiling up at him, she tucked her hand into the crook of his elbow and accompanied him out into the starlit winter night.

Harlequin American Romance

COMING NEXT MONTH

#285 HOME IS THE SAILOR by Kathryn Blair

Sarah Mitchell was a strong believer in the power of love to heal. It was behind her every move at Puppy Power. Her dogs had brought a lot of happiness into people's lives, but they were not enough to fill the emptiness of her own—until she placed a puppy with her new neighbor, and the elderly woman's merchant marine officer son came into her life to challenge her convictions and her heart.

#286 TIES THAT BIND by Marisa Carroll

When Kevin Sauder came to Lisa Emery's quiet world on the wooded shores of a Michigan lake, he was looking for a sanctuary. But the young conservation officer and her little family, consisting of a teenage brother and sister, opened their lives to him—and Lisa opened her heart. And soon Kevin realized he may have found more than the courage to face life—he may have found love.

#287 FEATHERS IN THE WIND by Pamela Browning

Her face had been her fortune, but Caro Nicholson couldn't rely on her beauty anymore. She wanted to run, to forget what had happened. Mike Herrick was a man determined to make her feel alive again . . . alive in ways she thought long buried. But was he a man willing to wait for the woman he loved?

#288 PASSAGES OF GOLD by Ginger Chambers

Linda Conway knew there was only one way to save her family legacy . . . and Amador Springs, California, held the key. Gold, shiny and yellow, was there, and Linda had the fever. She would be strong and unafraid. That is, until Tate Winslow entered her heart and made her reveal her deepest fears. . . .

CHRISTMAS IS FOR KIDS

AMERICAN ROMANCE PHOTO CONTEST

At Harlequin American Romance® we believe Christmas is for kids—a special time, a magical time. And we've put together a unique project to celebrate the American Child. Our annual holiday romances will feature children—just like yours—who have their Christmas wishes come true.

A reddish, golden-haired boy. Or a curious, ponytailed girl with glasses. A kid sister. A dark, shy, small boy. A mischievous, freckle-nosed lad. A girl with ash blond braided hair. Or a bright-eyed little girl always head of the class.

Send us a color photo of your child, along with a paragraph describing his or her excitement and anticipation of Christmas morning. If your entry wins, your child will appear on one of the covers of our December 1989 CHRISTMAS IS FOR KIDS special series. Read the Official Rules carefully before you enter.

PROOF OF PURCHASE

AMERICAN ROMANCE

———— OFFICIAL RULES ————

1. **Eligibility:** Male and female children ages 4 through 12 who are residents of the U.S.A., or Canada, except children of employees of Harlequin Enterprises Ltd., its affiliates, retailers, distributors, agencies, professional photographers and Smiley Promotion, Inc.

2. **How to enter:** Mail a color slide or photo, not larger than 8½ × 11″, taken no longer than six months ago along with proof of purchase from facing page to:

> American Romance Photo Contest
> Harlequin Books
> 300 East 42nd Street
> 6th Floor
> New York, NY
> 10017.

Professional photographs are not eligible. Only one entry per child allowed. All photos remain the sole property of Harlequin Enterprises Ltd. and will not be returned. A paragraph of not more than 50 words must accompany the photo expressing your child's joy and anticipation of Christmas morning. All entries must be received by March 31, 1989.

3. **Judging:** Photos will be judged equally on the child's expression, pose, neatness and photo clarity. The written paragraph will be judged on sincerity and relationship to the subject. Judging will be completed within 45 days of contest closing date and winners will be notified in writing and must return an Affidavit of Eligibility and Release within 21 days or an alternate winner will be selected.

4. **Prizes:** Nine Prizes will be awarded, with each winner's likeness appearing on a cover of our December 1989 CHRISTMAS IS FOR KIDS special series. Winners will also receive an artists signed print of the cover. There is no cash substitution for prizes. Harlequin Enterprises Ltd. reserves the right to use the winner's name and likeness for promotional purposes without any compensation. Any Canadian resident winner or their parent or guardian must correctly answer an arithmetical skill-testing question within a specified time.

5. When submitting an entry, entrants must agree to these rules and the decisions of the judges, under the supervision of Smiley Promotion, Inc., an independent judging organization whose decisions are final. Sponsor reserves the right to substitute prizes of like substance. Contest is subject to all federal, provincial, state and local laws. Void where prohibited, restricted or taxed. For a winner's list, send a stamped self-addressed envelope to American Romance Photo Contest Winners, P.O. Box 554, Bowling Green Station, New York, N.Y. 10274 for receipt by March 31, 1989.

Photo-2

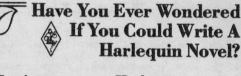

Have You Ever Wondered If You Could Write A Harlequin Novel?

Here's great news—Harlequin is offering a series of cassette tapes to help you do just that. Written by Harlequin editors, these tapes give practical advice on how to make your characters—and your story—come alive. There's a tape for each contemporary romance series Harlequin publishes.

Mail order only

All sales final

TO: **_Harlequin Reader Service_**
Audiocassette Tape Offer
P.O. Box 1396
Buffalo, NY 14269-1396

I enclose a check/money order payable to HARLEQUIN READER SERVICE® for $9.70 ($8.95 plus 75¢ postage and handling) for EACH tape ordered for the total sum of $_____ *
Please send:

☐ Romance and Presents   ☐ Intrigue
☐ American Romance   ☐ Temptation
☐ Superromance   ☐ All five tapes ($38.80 total)

Signature_____
                                                       (please print clearly)
Name:_____
Address:_____
State:_____ Zip:_____

* Iowa and New York residents add appropriate sales tax.

                                                          AUDIO-H

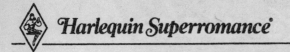

CALLOWAY CORNERS

Created by four outstanding Superromance authors, bonded by lifelong friendship and a love of their home state: Sandra Canfield, Tracy Hughes, Katherine Burton and Penny Richards.

CALLOWAY CORNERS

Home of four sisters as different as the seasons, as elusive as the elements; an undiscovered part of Louisiana where time stands still and passion lasts forever.

CALLOWAY CORNERS

Birthplace of the unforgettable Calloway women: *Mariah*, free as the wind, and untamed until she meets the preacher who claims her, body and soul; *Jo*, the fiery, feisty defender of lost causes who loses her heart to a rock and roll man; *Tess*, gentle as a placid lake but tormented by her longing for the town's bad boy and *Eden*, the earth mother who's been so busy giving love she doesn't know how much she needs it until she's awakened by a drifter's kiss...

CALLOWAY CORNERS

Coming from Superromance, in 1989:
Mariah, by Sandra Canfield, a January release
Jo, by Tracy Hughes, a February release
Tess, by Katherine Burton, a March release
Eden, by Penny Richards, an April release

Keepsake

Harlequin Books

You're never too young to enjoy romance. Harlequin for you . . . and Keepsake, young-adult romances destined to win hearts, for your daughter.

Pick one up today and start your daughter on her journey into the wonderful world of romance.

Two new titles to choose from each month.